Hunter's Revenge

The Edinburgh Crime Mysteries #2

Val Penny

Also available:
Hunter's Chase

CROOKED
CAT

Discover us online:
www.crookedcatbooks.com

Join us on facebook:
www.facebook.com/crookedcat

Tweet a photo of yourself holding
this book to **@crookedcatbooks**
and something nice will happen.

To Dean and Jo
Thank you for all your love and support but most of all thank you for accepting me, and mine into your fabulous family.

About the Author

Val Penny is an American author living in SW Scotland. She has two adult daughters of whom she is justly proud and lives with her husband and two cats. She has a Law degree from Edinburgh University and her MSc from Napier University. She has had many jobs including hairdresser, waitress, lawyer, banker, azalea farmer and lecturer. However she has not yet achieved either of her childhood dreams of being a ballerina or owning a candy store. Until those dreams come true, she has turned her hand to writing poetry, short stories and novels. Her crime novels, 'Hunter's Chase' and Hunter's Revenge are set in Edinburgh, Scotland, published by Crooked Cat Books.

Acknowledgements

Although written by one individual, a novel is not the achievement of just that person. My most sincere thanks go to all the incredible people at Crooked Cat Books, particularly Laurence and Steph who ply me with gin when that is needed and to my fabulous editor, Sue Barnard, whose expertise, patience and valuable suggestions brought this story and the characters in it come to life. A novel without a good editor is just a manuscript: thank you, Sue.

My thanks also to Liz Hurst, Paul Cowan, Ruth Grant, David McLaughlan, Hazel Prior, Allison Symes, Michael Jecks and all those at Swanwick Writers' Summer School for their encouragement and for saying the right thing at the right time.

I remain eternally grateful to Dave, Lizzie, Vicky, Margot, Dave, Lisa and my Mum for their belief in me and unswerving support.

Most of all, thank you to all my readers and to everyone who encouraged me to write. Without you, The Edinburgh Crime Mysteries would not exist.

I also want to acknowledge the following resources:
The Real CSI: A Forensics Handbook for Crime Writers by Kate Bendelow
The Crime Writers Casebook (Straightforward Guides) by Stephen Wade & Stuart Gibbon
Forensics: The Anatomy of Crime by Val McDermid

Any errors, of course, are mine.

Hunter's Chase is now available.

Hunter's Revenge

The Edinburgh Crime Mysteries #2

Prologue

East Germany, January 1968

The last thing Georg did on his eighteenth birthday was kill a man.

He really hadn't meant to kill the Stasi officer in front of him, but it was him or Georg – and Georg did not want to die. It was the first time he'd seen a corpse. The streets were slick with ice. The man lost his balance and cracked his head on the pavement. Georg stared down at the body: there was blood and brains all over the pavement. He looked into the officer's eyes. They stared blindly to heaven, but Georg knew there wasn't a Stasi officer on earth who was going there. He looked away from death and towards his friends in horror, but when they saw what had happened, they scattered. Georg picked up the officer's gun and began to run. More Stasi officers appeared as the boys fled.

Georg was out of breath when he got home.

"What's the rush, son?" his father asked.

"Shit, Dad! It's bad."

"You're drunk! No language in this house, boy," said his grandmother.

"Dad, the boys and me were leaving the bar to come home and we saw a Stasi officer"

"So?"

"We were laughing and having fun."

"And?"

"For a laugh I knocked his hat off."

"Idiot! You know Stasi have no sense of humour. Ever. So what next?"

"He pulled his gun and told us to stand silently against the wall."

"And you apologised and complied, I hope."

"I panicked and punched him. He slipped on the ice and fell over. He hit his head on the ground, and when I checked him, he wasn't breathing. He was dead. I just took his gun and ran."

The silence in the room was deafening.

"You did what? You fucking idiot! Did you really punch a Stasi officer? Are you mad? You know we don't even have to openly engage in resistance to draw the attention of the Stasi and incur its retribution. Just failing to conform with mainstream society can be enough. Shit! I sired a fool." Georg's father's red face reflected his rage.

"And now you are here," his grandmother added. "You ran home, leading them straight to us. We will all die now. Thank you."

"What is all the noise?" Georg's mother came through from the kitchen, drying her hands on her apron. His twin sister Ingrid and younger brother Wilhelm followed her. They looked bewildered. Their father rarely raised his voice, especially not to Georg.

As his father explained the issues, Georg's mother burst into tears.

"They will kill him," she whispered.

"They'll kill him?" his father shrieked "Fuck, the rest of us will be lucky if all they do is kill us too! Have you any idea the danger you have put this whole family in, you young imbecile?"

"God, that's true!" his mother sobbed. "Georg has to leave. He must escape right away. Maybe, when they come and find him gone, they will believe we had no part of it."

"You and I both know that is not going to happen," his father said. "They know everybody in the town, and even if they don't already know it was Georg, one of their informers will turn him in for reward or to save their own skin. They will soon find out where he lives."

His wife nodded.

"Mum, where do I go?" Georg pleaded. "Dad, what will you do? I didn't mean anything by it. I was just fooling

4

around."

"Then you are more of a fool than I ever thought," his father said. "It's a bit fucking late to worry about us. We will cope, but we must deny you and any knowledge of this atrocity. I love you always, but you must leave, son. Now. There is no choice, and you must be quick because they will be here all too soon. Make a start on your escape tonight. It's your only hope, and ours."

"Quick, Wilhelm, fetch him my savings and your grandfather Georg's book," said his grandmother. "Georg will need the money, and he can always sell the book."

"I'll pack a meal," his mother said. She gathered up the family Bible, along with some bread, ham, cheese and apples.

"Don't give him too much, it will slow him down," said Ingrid.

"Pack everything in a rucksack. You can put it on your back, Georg, and still run," said Wilhelm as he handed their grandmother's meagre treasures to George.

"I am so sorry, Father. Where do I go? Where am I running to? What will happen to you?" Georg's voice raised to a scream.

His mother held him and kissed his head, but his father grabbed his arm, pulled him from her and shook him.

"You got yourself into this; we will get you out of it. No point in worrying about us. Get out of this country. Don't look back. Just run. Go west, go to Britain. Stay alive. Get out of this house, get out of my sight and never come back. Do you hear me, Georg?"

***

That was the last time Georg saw his family. They paid for his crime.

His father and Wilhelm were lucky. They were made to watch while the women were raped by each of the Stasi officers in turn; then Georg's father and brother were shot. They did not have to live with the disgrace or the memories.

Georg's grandmother never spoke during the remaining six

5

years of her life, not even when Ingrid's baby, Heinrich, was born.

Each woman hoped that Georg had escaped to safety and that their sacrifices had not been in vain.

Chapter One

Edinburgh, Scotland, March 2013

George was excited. His parcel should arrive today. It was only by chance that he had learned about this treasure. Soon, he could add the signed 1926 first edition copy of *Winnie the Pooh* to his library.

Books had been his passion since he arrived in Edinburgh, with the family Bible from his mother, and his grandfather Georg's precious signed first edition of Leyb Kvitko's children's book *Di Bobe Shlak un ir Kabak (Granny Shlak and her Pumpkin)*, published in Kharkov in 1928. His grandmother had added this to his rucksack as he left home. These were the start of his collection, but every addition had brought its own pleasure over the years. Books written for the children he had never had. Beautiful, precious books. They had been his only love: dearer than friends, closer than enemies. George Reinbold loved his books.

It was a bright spring morning. Sunny, but cold. Summer had always been George's favourite season, because it was most different from winter, and he enjoyed it when the salty tang of the North Sea wafted across the city. But Spring came a close second, where the sweetness of the soil is churned by the worms and buried bulbs break green shoots through the soil. He hated winter with its cold and ice and memories, but today the sky was a pale bleached blue, the sun still low in the sky, but enough future promised by little crocuses breaking through the soil to offer hope.

When the doorbell rang George was aware that his heart missed a beat. He smiled. What a thrill. Another book to add to his collection. The delivery was earlier than he expected, but

7

that was all to the good. George hobbled along the corridor to the door, leaning heavily on his walking stick.

He had lived in the same main-door flat in Gilmerton, Edinburgh, since the house had been allocated to him by the council nearly fifty years ago. He bought the property for less than a year's salary during the Margaret Thatcher era. George knew every nook and cranny of his home and none of his neighbours. Edinburgh people are like that, and their lack of curiosity suited George just fine. Britain had been good to him.

People had told him that he should move, that this modest flat was not suitable for a man of his standing. But George had never planned to move, certainly not now. He was safe here. Safer than he had ever been in the German Democratic Republic, the land of his birth. He was safer than he had ever been when he knew his neighbours and they knew him. Then, they could inform on him, whether the information was true or not. He was safer than he had ever been when he escaped from his family's humble home, without looking back. He had crossed Europe to find refuge in Scotland; nobody would look for him here. But, even here, he was not safe enough.

When George opened the door, his happy smile vanished. Comprehension, consternation and dread crossed his face. He spotted the gun, but couldn't even shout in the time that the shot was fired.

It was a perfect shot. The bullet hit George squarely in the middle of his forehead, its hollow-point cavity filled with blood and tissue forcing it to mushroom as it travelled past the cranium wall and through George's brain, ripping apart everything in its path.

The mushroom of the hollow-point bullet reduces the speed of a bullet considerably, and in many cases, there is no exit wound because the bullet lodges within the target. However, at such close range the power of the gun was more than enough to push the bullet through George's brain, leaving an impressive exit wound about the size of a grapefruit. Part of the left side of his skull disintegrated as if a creature had cracked it when hatching out as if from an egg. Bone, blood, brain matter, hair and skin splattered against the walls and floor of the entrance to his home, covering them in a sticky red mess.

He hit the ground like a half-empty flour sack. A pool of blood quickly began to form around his head as his front gate clicked shut.

His assassin got into a car and drove away.

Chapter Two

Linda's 'Daygo' delivery van pulled up at George Reinbold's door. She liked this new job. It combined her love of driving with working with people. It didn't pay a fortune, but it paid the bills, with a bit left over to save for that holiday in Spain she and Bob had promised themselves. She grabbed the box out of the back of her van. She looked at the house and was surprised that the front door was open.

She walked up the path and pushed it open a little further. Something was stuck behind the door so it wouldn't open. She peeked around the door into the entrance of the house – and vomited all over George's corpse.

It was Linda who called for an ambulance, but there was nothing for the paramedics to do but wait for the police. Linda sat on the front lawn, sobbing and wailing. She shivered on the wet grass. It was a chilly morning, but she had to wait somewhere, and there was no way she was going near that place again. The paramedics said she had to wait for the police to get here.

What an awful horrible job this was. Why had she even taken it? It didn't even pay that much.

***

DI Hunter Wilson and DC Tim Myerscough pulled up just behind the ambulance. Hunter liked spring: he could almost smell the world waking up. The freshness of the air encouraged crocuses and daffodils to decorate flower beds, and buds of leaves to appear on trees. Edinburgh had a beauty in every season, but he found his city especially lovely in springtime. However, today was not one of those fine, balmy spring days. It was bright enough, but sharp and cold. Hunter did not like days like today as much as the warm balmy days he hoped May would bring.

He and Tim got out of the car. The detective constable dwarfed Hunter by an easy five inches, but as Hunter stood and took in the scene with a serious face and intelligent piercing blue eyes, it was clear that he was the man in charge. Hunter quickly identified the girl sitting on the wet grass as the source of a loud and blood-curdling racket that offended his ears. He looked from the girl to Tim and back again.

"You deal with her, young Myerscough. It's far too early for me to be coping with weeping women. Try to get some sense out of her, and get her to be quiet, will you? I can't think with that noise going on."

"Yes, Sir." Tim took two strides and crouched down beside the young woman. "Hello, I'm DC Tim Myerscough. What's your name?"

"Linda."

"Linda?"

"Linda Maguire." She stopped crying but was still sobbing hard.

"So, Linda, it was you who found the body, was it?" Tim asked.

She looked at him as if she thought he was crazy. "Well I don't get this upset just because there's nobody home. I don't get paid enough for this. It's awful. Have you seen it? Don't look. The place is all blood and brains. The back of his head's gone. I can't un-see that, you know." Linda started weeping again as Hunter shouted.

"Tim! Tim! DC Myerscough. Here. Now." Hunter's face was grey. "Tim, you won't believe who the victim is. It's George Reinbold, shot in the head."

"What? Oh No! Not our George Reinbold? Head of the Crime Scene Investigations? No, Boss, it can't be. It must be a mistake, he's just an old man. Who would want to kill him?"

"Don't take my word for it. Feel free to take a look, but hold on to your breakfast." Hunter watched as Tim went over and stuck his head around the door and withdrew it quickly.

Linda was right, you can't un-see that.

"Boss, that's been close range. Tiny hole in the forehead, but they've blown the back of his skull right off."

"Hmm. Bloody awful. It's got to be a professional job. But the murderer would surely be hit by some spray from the blood." Hunter grimaced.

"Definitely. This is surely a case of mistaken identity? Nobody would want to hurt George?" Tim's questions asked for the reassurance that Hunter could not give.

"Well, I don't want our CSIs working on this; it would be too traumatic. I'll call Glasgow and get them to send a team over. PC Angus McKenzie can stay at the door to restrict access while I get DS Jane Renwick to gather a team to organise door-to-door enquiries. One thing is for sure, somebody saw something or heard the gun."

"Yes, Boss." Tim paused "Will Doctor Sharma be able to do the post-mortem?"

"I doubt she would allow anybody else that honour, but it won't be easy for her. She liked George and respected him greatly. You stay here and take the witness statement from that girl. When Meera Sharma and the CSIs are finished, I want you and me into that flat as soon as possible to find out everything we can about George and why he was murdered."

Tim turned back to Linda and walked slowly across the grass. He saw the young delivery woman was now dry-heaving as hard as she was weeping. It must have been a terrible shock for her. He took out his notebook in a vain effort to try to divert her attention. He smiled at her as she lifted her head. His smile seemed to work as a better diversion.

He was aware of her looking up at him. He watched as she swept her hair behind her ear, glanced into his eyes and she allowed her glance to rove from his eyes to his hair, smile and shoulders. For some reason he became self-conscious about his broken nose. This was silly. He blushed, and realised that she had stopped sobbing.

Tim looked at her more closely. Under all the thick layer of make-up and dribbles of snot, she was pretty.

He took down her personal details and then they discussed

how Linda's morning had been going before her shocking discovery.

"What were you delivering to Mr Reinbold?" Tim asked.

"A book. The label just says a book."

"But it also says it's insured for £25,000. That's some book," Tim said, looking at Linda's delivery list.

"I didn't notice that. It's an awful lot."

Tim looked around for help and caught sight of DS Jane Renwick, who had joined Hunter talking to the paramedics. Tim wondered how Jane always looked so elegant, as though she had just walked off a magazine cover.

"Sarge? Sarge, can you help with this?" Tim called to Jane.

"What's up, Tim?"

"Linda here has on her manifest that the parcel Mr Reinbold was expecting was a book, but I've noticed it's insured for £25,000. That seems a great deal for a book."

"It certainly does. Do we know where the parcel is?"

Linda pulled it out from underneath her. "I didn't know what to do. I didn't want to sit on the grass. It's wet," she said by way of explanation.

Jane looked at the girl and sighed. Then she held out her hand and, in the presence of Linda and Tim, opened the parcel.

"It is indeed a book. A signed first edition of A.A.Milne's *Winnie the Pooh*. My goodness. It's amazing! Include this in the statement, Tim, and give Linda a note to say that we now hold the book. I'll take it back to the station. We'll need to get a proper valuation."

"Wow! All that for a kiddies' book." Linda finished her statement and agreed to come down to the station to sign a typed copy whenever Tim phoned her to tell her it was ready. He caught her allowing herself one more gaze into his eyes before they stood up. Tim was over a foot taller than her diminutive five foot two inches.

"Thank you for all your help today, Linda," Tim said.

"It's all right, but I suppose I better get on with my deliveries. I'm ever so late. It would be me who found the bloody body."

"Only if you're not in shock and are fit to drive. Do you

want the paramedics to check you over?"

She looked at the paramedics: a portly man in his fifties and a woman with badly-dyed red hair. "Nah, I'll be alright thanks."

"You know you must not discuss this with anybody, Linda."

"Alright. I won't go selling my life story to the papers."

Chapter Three

"Good morning, folks. Attention please." DCI Allan Mackay called the briefing in the incident room to order.

Mackay's pomposity always made Hunter want to prick him with a pin, just to see if he would deflate.

"We have too much to get through this morning, and too little time to do it," Hunter said.

He looked around at his team and noticed the young woman standing nervously at the back of the room. Hunter decided to get her out of her misery. "First, I can confirm what most of you already suspect, DC John Hamilton has resigned from the force," Hunter said.

"You mean he jumped before he was pushed? Good riddance," DC Colin Reid said. Colin had worked closely with John for years.

Hunter grimaced, but did not seem surprised that Colin sounded bitter.

"He was an idiot to use cocaine, especially supplied by Arjun Mansoor, but he has done the right thing now, DC Reid." Mackay said. Colin was serious and reliable. Mackay valued those qualities.

"At last," Colin said.

Hunter knew that Colin had found John's drug abuse unforgivable.

"As a result of that we had a vacancy, and I am delighted to introduce you all to DC Nadia Chan, who has joined us from Livingston. Welcome, Nadia. We will get to know you over the next few days, I'm sure. Can you take her under your wing, Mel?" Hunter said.

DC Mel Grant's dark curls nodded faster than her head. She smiled at Nadia and her dimples deepened.

"Thank you, it's great to be joining the team." Nadia blushed furiously and moved towards Mel.

"DI Hunter Wilson was the senior officer attending the shocking murder yesterday of George Reinbold at his home in Gilmerton," Mackay said. "Can you kick off the information we have?"

Hunter nodded and moved forward.

"Now as you all know, our colleague from CSI, George Reinbold, was found dead behind the front door of his main door flat in Gilmerton yesterday morning. He was killed by one bullet, and shot at such close range that I have no doubt his blood hit his killer. A young delivery woman reported the body. Tim, you interviewed her?"

"Yes, Boss. Nothing useful, really. Linda Maguire, recently started working for Daygo Deliveries. The company confirms she had good references, and had been reliable in the six weeks she's been working for them." Tim glanced at Jane, who nodded. "The only strange thing was that Linda's delivery stated the item for George Reinbold was a book, but I noticed that it was insured for £25,000. It was sent from Paris, France. DS Renwick came to assist me and we opened the parcel in Linda's presence. It was indeed a book, but it was a signed first edition of *Winnie the Pooh*."

"I took it up to Katz and Roundall auction house," Jane said. "They have a dedicated team that deals with Rare Books, Manuscripts and Maps. Also, their specialists have established an international reputation for their auctions, selling through the auction houses in Edinburgh, London and also through their online auctions. The specialists are experts not only on books and manuscripts, but also on current market conditions. So I thought if anyone could help, they could."

"Of course," said Hunter. "What did they say?"

"The head of that department is a Ms June Dormer. She carried out the valuation personally, and confirmed that allowing for the condition of the book, and fact the book is a first edition signed by both the author A A Milne and the illustrator, E H Shepard, the value of that book is at least £23,000."

"Thank you. Jane, what have you discovered from the door-to-door enquiries of the neighbours?" Hunter asked.

"Well, Sir, it is Edinburgh. You know what they're like: see no evil, hear no evil, speak no evil."

"I can't believe nobody heard anything."

"No, neither do I, Sir," Jane sighed. "But you know how it goes: the two households above George had left for work, school and so on. Some of the properties to one side were the same, except for the students, who had only come home, drunk, about three in the morning and were still out cold. They say none of them woke up before lunchtime, so they heard nothing.

"Over to other side, the neighbour on the ground floor is as deaf as a post, one upstairs flat is empty. It's up for sale, Sir." Jane looked up at Hunter and went on. "In the other upstairs property the owner was making a cup of tea at the back of the house, and thought a car had backfired."

"For goodness sake!" Hunter exploded.

"It's much the same with the rest, Sir. The only person who noticed anything was an elderly lady who sits at her window, a Mrs Florence Roberts. She saw an unfamiliar blue car stop near George's place, and saw a smart man in a grey suit come out of it. Then her carer arrived, so that's all she saw. Nobody else seems to have noticed anything that they could bring to mind, so when we get the approximate time of death confirmed by Dr Sharma, I'll have the CCTV checked from the main road and get back to you."

"Fine. Jane, just go round them all again and press harder when we have a more precise timing, and keep me in the loop. Have we managed to find George's family, Mel?"

"No, I don't think he ever married. No evidence of any family who immigrated with him either, but I'll keep looking."

"Thanks, Mel. Now, I'll need a careful search of George's home. Tim, Bear and Rachael, you join me for that."

DC Rachael Anderson nodded and swept her long, dark-blonde hair back from her shoulders.

"Jane, I want you to investigate all the cases George has been involved in where the perpetrator may have borne a grudge."

"Fine, Sir, how far back do you want me to go?"

"Start with yesterday and go back as far as you need to. Mel, Nadia and Colin are with you."

Jane nodded and the meeting drew to a close.

Jane moved towards Mel and said, "Perhaps you should continue to search for George's family, here?"

"If he has any."

"If not, I suppose the Boss or DCI Mackay will have to do the formal identification."

"I wouldn't fancy having to do that," Mel screwed up her face and went to make a cup of tea before she went back to the computer records.

"Colin, can you and Nadia make a list of the cases George Reinbold has been involved with?" Jane asked.

"The most recent were the end of last year, right? Will we be looking outside Lothian and Borders, Sarge?" Colin asked.

"Yes, if George's expertise was called on. But I think most of what he did was in this area."

Colin nodded and gestured for Nadia to follow him. They had a lot of files to go through. Thank goodness for computers.

Jane went to see what she could find out about George Reinbold the man. Google was as good a place as any to start.

***

After the CSI team had finished their work, Hunter, Tim, Bear and Rachael got suited up in the white overalls and special shoe covers that would minimise their interference with the crime scene. As Hunter entered George's small apartment, he immediately regretted assigning Tim and Bear to work with him. At six feet four inches and six feet two inches respectively, the two rugby-playing DCs made the place feel overcrowded just by standing there. At least the blood and mess had been cleared up, from the entrance, leaving only livid stains as reminders of the horror that had taken place.

Hunter entered the flat first and walked down the hall towards the living room. The place was immaculately clean and obsessively tidy, just as he would expect George's home to be.

"CSIs told me there was no sign of forced entry," Hunter said.

"Well, he probably opened his door willingly, as he would think it was that book being delivered," Tim said.

When Bear entered, he whistled. "Boss, have you noticed this?"

"Goodness! I had no idea George had such a large collection of books."

"These are not just any books, Boss. This one is a first edition. So is this, and this." Bear turned round to face Hunter. "This collection must be worth a fortune!"

"But they're not all in English," Rachael added. "These in this section are in German, but I don't even recognise this language."

"Russian, I think," Bear said. "Tim, have a look at this; is that Russian?"

"It is, wow, and this is a children's book in Yiddish! It is inscribed to Georg Reinbold, by the author, Leyb Kvitko. Look, Boss, this is incredible! Kvitko was a member of the Jewish Anti-Fascist Committee in the USSR in the late 1940s. If I remember rightly, he was shot and killed for his activities.

"The George Reinbold we knew would have spelt his name Georg in his native language, but he wouldn't have been born at the time Kvitko was executed. It must have belonged to a relative. Maybe a father, an uncle or even a grandfather. Was George Jewish, Boss?"

"Not that I know. It doesn't mean the author wasn't a family friend, though." Hunter said. "This is only illustrating how little we knew about George, the man, isn't it? I know he was a private person, but we really seem to be on the back foot." Hunter shook his head. "Right, let's get started. I'll search his desk for any paperwork I can find. Bear, you take the bedrooms. Rachael, kitchen and bathroom to see if there is anything odd or if he was on any medication. Tim, I think you should make a catalogue of those books. We better get them boxed up and securely stored if they are as valuable as we think."

Rachael rooted around in George's kitchen and bathroom cabinets. The bathroom was full of little packets and bottles. When she had finished the search, Rachael gathered them up. She walked back to the living room and looked again at the bookcase.

"It's interesting, they all seem to be children's books," Rachael said. "But I don't remember George talking about having any children."

"That doesn't mean anything," Tim said. "These have been bought as investments. Very valuable investments. Look how the bookcase has a glass front which encloses them and keeps them free from dust. George would never have let a child touch any of these. He would probably have chopped their fingers off if they'd tried."

"Nice," Rachael replied sarcastically.

"Anything of interest in the kitchen or bathroom, Rachael?" Hunter asked.

"Not much. He was on a lot of medication. I've bagged that up so Doctor Sharma can tell us what they are for."

"Good. Well done."

"Boss, George had also changed his back door from his kitchen into his garden so that the original glass panel in the council's design when he bought the place was no longer there," Rachael added. "He had put in a seriously thick, metal-lined, replacement door instead."

"That's certainly not original. It's not even normal," Tim said.

"That's not all," Rachael went on. "There are three mortice locks evenly spaced on the back door, together with bolts top and bottom. He wasn't taking many chances, was he Boss?"

"He certainly was not," Hunter said. He was sitting in George's armchair rummaging through the papers he found in the small chest of drawers next to it. He found instructions on how to work the washing machine, an old copy of the *Yellow Pages*, and the Home and Contents insurance policy.

"I wonder if the additional security was a condition of his insurance because of his books?" Hunter said as he handed

Rachael the home and contents policy he had found. "Call them and check it out, will you, Rachael?"

Bear wandered back from the bedrooms. "Boss, George seems to have kept the spare room as a study or office. There's another bookcase like that one," he nodded at the shelves behind Tim. "But, I also found this in a box under the bed," He held a pistol in his hand. It was unfamiliar to Hunter, but Bear said, "It's a P1001."

"Really?" asked Hunter. "That's a very old gun." He weighed it in his hand. "And heavy."

"Yes," Bear said. "It was issued to the Stasi. The East German equivalent of the Walther PPK that was made in West Germany during the Cold War."

"How do you know so much about it?"

"My A-level project was on the Cold War."

"You failed that, Bear!" Tim joked.

"If a D is good enough for the royal family, it's good enough for me! I suppose my memory must be better than I thought. But I am really surprised to find one of these here. It's ancient, but in very good condition. There's ammunition for it here, too. No idea how old that is, or how safe."

"Get the firearms guys to come and take this away, will you, Bear?" Hunter asked.

"Of course," Bear nodded.

"Have you noticed the flat is triple-glazed, Boss?" Rachael said. "And these net curtains feel funny. They're very heavy."

Bear moved towards her. He pulled a face and studied the curtains carefully.

"Boss, I think these are Bomb Blast Net Curtains. Why would George need those? They are very unusual and would certainly not be dictated by any house insurance."

"True, Bear," said Hunter.

"And the security at the front door is as heavy as at the back. It must have cost him a fortune to put in all these security features," Rachael said.

"When a simple spy-hole might have done the trick," Hunter said sadly.

"Look what I've found, Boss. Another gun, and this weapon

is much more modern, but it is an air rifle. My guess is it was bought after the last gun laws were passed in 1997 banning hand guns" Tim held out an air rifle hidden behind the second shelf of books. "George wouldn't have needed a licence for this."

"Why didn't he hand in the old pistol during the amnesty?" Bear asked.

"No idea. It would have made sense. I wonder what was he worried about?" Tim said.

"I have no idea. I wish he had confided in me. But now that is what we have to find out," Hunter sighed. "Because whatever it was, it killed him."

Chapter Four

For Jamie Thomson, the good things about sharing a house with his cousin Frankie Hope were that Frankie was tidy and not a bad cook. The downside was that Frankie's two baby daughters, Kylie-Ann and Dannii-Ann, who also lived there, sometimes cried in the night. And their nappies often smelt rank. Still, Frankie helped Jamie run his pop's luxury car showroom, Thomson's Top Cars. The least Jamie could do was support Frankie with the babies.

Jamie was taking his new managerial position at Thomson's Top Cars very seriously. With Pop still in jail, and his last manager, Arjun Mansoor, also locked up for dealing cocaine, that left Jamie and Frankie managing the family business.

"I'm glad we're doing this together," Jamie said to his cousin. "I know having to leave us in charge is stressing Pop out!"

"Aye, probably more stress than his time in prison could ever have done. But at least you've passed your driving test now."

Frankie could have been reading his uncle's mind. Ian Thomson had just under two months to go before he was eligible for parole, and in the meantime could only hope that Jamie and Frankie didn't do anything too stupid to ruin his business. At least the wee receptionist, Jenny Kozlowski, seemed to have a bit of common sense.

"I'll be a bit late in today, Frankie, can you hold the fort?"

"Aye. What you up to, then?"

"Nothing much. It's just that it's Jenny's birthday, and I'm going to pick up cakes for all of us for coffee break."

"If it's her birthday, she should buy the cakes. That's what the rest of us all do," Frankie protested. "You fancy her, don't you?"

"Don't be stupid!"

"Aye you do. Well, I won't tell the guys in the workshop, if I can get a chocky doughnut."

"Piss off, Frankie."

"Am I getting a chocky doughnut, then?"

"Aye," Jamie grinned.

***

Jamie was disappointed to see Frankie at the reception desk when he walked in.

"Where's Jenny, cuz?" he called over to Frankie.

"Dunno. Not even a phone call. And she's well late now."

"Well, she must be somewhere, her coat's here. She looks good in red."

"Well she's not anywhere, as far as I can see."

"She's usually early. Wonder what's up." Jamie rubbed his hands together. It might be spring according to the time of year, but with its wide glass front and the open garage at the back, the showroom was cold.

"She maybe went to get cakes," Frankie suggested hopefully.

"Without her coat? I doubt it!" Jamie retorted.

"Well, she was probably out on the lash last night and slept in."

"Could be, but I still can't see her leaving last night without her coat." Jamie shrugged and turned away, trying to hide his disappointment. "It's fucking freezing in here. I'll make us a coffee first to warm us up, then I'll try phoning her."

"Phone her first, Jamie. You know you want to."

When Jamie wandered back to reception from the office he plonked a mug of coffee in front of Frankie.

"Her mam says she never went home last night. Do you know if she was going out with pals or the like?"

"I don't know. You gave that guy a test drive in the Bentley and I went home. A fellow came in just as I was leaving, but Jenny said she would see to him because she would stay on

24

and lock up with you." Frankie smiled. "I thought, aye aye, nudge nudge, say no more. So off I went. I picked up the twins from their child minder on the way home. You know?"

Jamie frowned. "She wasn't here when I got back, and the showroom wasn't locked up. I was pretty pissed off about that. But I couldn't see nothing missing, so when the guy said he wanted to think about the Bentley, I just locked up and came home."

"Nothing was missing except Jenny, you mean."

"I didn't know that. I thought you'd both just buggered off."

"Like we'd ever do that. Your pop would skin us alive when he got hold of us. Do you think I've got a death wish?"

"Funny accent the man had," Jamie said. "European or something."

"Jamie?" The head mechanic, Gary, called across the showroom. "Where's that old blue Volvo that was waiting to go through its service?"

"What old Volvo? I don't know. Don't you keep a log of all the cars you work on?" Jamie asked angrily.

"Aye, but we didn't get to this one yesterday. It was just waiting outside for us to get started this morning. The customer asked us to give it a service, then put it up for sale. Said he had a buyer for it who'd pay eight grand, but he might need a test drive first. I told him he'd need a brain test if he was paying that much for that car. But it seems like he was right; it must have been sold. "

"So what happened to the paperwork?" Jamie shouted. "We've not sold any fucking old Volvo. Where is the damn thing?"

"No idea."

"So what do I do now? Jenny's not in, and a fucking car has gone missing. This is a truly rubbish start to the day. Pop is going to bloody skin me."

Frankie shrugged, "Phone Jenny's mam back? Maybe the man she spoke to took the Volvo."

"I suppose I should. I don't fancy it though. She shouts. I don't think she likes me. Then what do I tell Pop about the car?"

"I think you'll need a chocky doughnut before you do that. I know I will!"

"I'll need more than a fucking chocky doughnut, Frankie, if we've lost one of his customer's cars."

***

Hunter felt his phone vibrate in his pocket. A call from Charlie Middleton (the desk sergeant at the station), when he was in the middle of searching George's home, couldn't be good news.

"Charlie? What is it? A young woman missing? I don't suppose the girl just took off with a boyfriend?" Hunter listened to his desk sergeant for a moment. He could hear a woman screaming in the background. "I take it that's the girl's mother making that racket? Well, put her into an interview room with a cup of tea. We've got about all we can from here just now. I'll come back with young Myerscough and leave Rachael with Bear to finish up. Send a van out for them. There's a lot to come back to the station." Hunter looked at Tim. "Looks like you and I are going to have a loud conversation with an anxious parent in relation to something we know nothing about. Come on, young Myerscough, back to the ranch!"

"Another little slice of Heaven," Tim grinned. He caught the car keys Hunter threw at him and drove them away from the leafy trees in Gilmerton Road and back to the station at Fettes.

Chapter Five

Jane Renwick looked up from her computer to see Mel standing looking awkward.

"Mel?"

"I can't find any family connected with George at all. He certainly never married here, and he's not named as the father on any birth certificates, as far as I can see. He could have been married before he came here, but he arrived when he was still a teenager, so it is unlikely. Makes me think he was on his own, because he never made a claim for a wife to join him."

"Hmm. Do you want to tell the boss he'll have to do the identification, or shall I?" Jane smiled.

"No contest, DS Renwick; you're the sergeant," Mel grinned. "I'm off to make a coffee. You want a camomile tea?"

Jane nodded and turned back to the screen in front of her.

***

Hunter and Tim grabbed hot drinks for themselves and their interviewee from the machine and entered the interview room. The room was small and dark. The only window had bars across it and was almost at the height of the ceiling. Even Tim couldn't see out of it. The smell in interview rooms was never fresh. It didn't matter how much disinfectant the cleaners used or how much air-freshener the officers sprayed around after the rooms were used. They always smelled of dirt, body odour and farts. This room was no different.

The woman, sitting on the plastic chair facing the door, looked up at Hunter and Tim through streaks of mascara.

"Mrs Kozlowski?" Hunter asked.

"Miss. Bastard went off before Jenny was even born, didn't

he?"

"DI Wilson and DC Myerscough," Hunter said, as he and Tim sat down.

"You're tall," she said to Tim. "I seen your name in the paper. Your dad in the nick or something? And you're a cop? That's funny," she said in a flat tone of voice.

Tim had heard this jibe too often to be riled by it. Certainly, Tim knew his father's fall from grace had been nothing short of remarkable: former Chief Constable of Lothian & Borders Police, then Justice Secretary in the Scottish Parliament, now a guest of Her Majesty in HMP Edinburgh. Tim acknowledged the irony, but did not appreciate it. He had joined the police force, originally, to emulate his father. He had stayed to show he was different. He was grateful to DI Hunter Wilson for challenging him to do that. Tim knew that Hunter despised his father, yet he had taken Tim under his wing.

"You need our help because your daughter is missing, I understand?" Hunter went on, apparently ignoring her comments. "How old is she, Miss Kozlowski?"

"Jenny only turned 18 today." The woman started to sniffle. "But she wouldn't just go off."

"So she's an adult. Could she have gone out to celebrate her birthday with friends, last night?"

"Even if she had, she'd tell me. And she'd have come home."

"How long has she been missing?" Hunter asked.

"I don't know! About a day, she hasn't been seen by those numpties she works for since five o'clock yesterday evening. Fancy leaving her alone with that man coming in."

"What man?" Hunter asked.

She stared at Hunter and Tim as if they were idiots. Then the woman glared at Hunter as she raised her voice.

"She phoned yesterday to say that a customer arrived late. He wanted to test-drive a Volvo that was sitting there, and, as she was the only person there, she was going to have to go with him. She works at Thomson's Top Cars, you know. Those idiots who play at running the place just left her alone with a man who'd just come in. Now she's missing. Who would do that?"

Hunter caught Tim's glance and raised his eyebrows.

The woman continued, "Then, she had plans to go out with a pal for a bit of late-night shopping and a bite to eat at Nando's before she came home. She likes Nando's." She dropped her gaze from Hunter's eyes and fiddled with the piece of tissue in her hands.

"Go on, Miss Kozlowski," Tim prompted quietly.

"I was on night-shift so I wasn't going to see her till tonight, but then I gets a call from that wee smart-arse whose dad owns the showroom. His dad's in the nick too, you know." She nodded at Tim. "I gets woken up this morning, just after I'd got to sleep, with the phone ringing. It's that Jamie asking where's Jenny, he's bought cakes for her birthday and she's not in yet and she's late. I ask you, what's cakes got to do with it? Where's my daughter?"

"Did you ask him where she might be?" Hunter asked.

"Have you ever tried to get any sense out of that one? It was bad enough when the foreign guy was there, but now it seems like they're just playing at it." Ishbel Kozlowski looked drained. Tim wondered just how much sleep the woman had had. "He tells me Jenny left without locking up last night and now she's late and she's in trouble." She paused. "She's in trouble my arse. He doesn't know how much trouble he's going to be in if anything's happened to my Jenny. She's all I've got." Her tears began to flow again.

Hunter sighed and glanced at Tim.

"So Jenny went on a test drive with a customer, alone?" Tim asked.

"Yes. It was near closing time."

"Did she leave a note of the customer's name? Or take a copy of their driving licence?"

"No."

"Did Jenny leave a note of the route the test drive would take?" Tim asked, more in hope than expectation.

"No."

"Jenny has not been seen since she left the showroom with the customer?"

29

"No."

Tim tried again. "So she didn't meet up with her friend as planned?"

"No! No! No! Do you understand? No!" Ishbel Kozlowski screamed at Tim.

"Do you know any more about the car that was taken for the test drive?" Hunter asked in an evident attempt to calm the woman down. It worked to the extent that she stopped screaming.

"No, but Jamie does. I stopped listening to his excuses and came to you. You need to find my Jenny," the woman almost whispered in despair.

"Miss Kozlowski," Hunter began, "it is not long since Jenny was last seen, and she is not a child who needs permission to go out—"

He was faced with another wall of noise coming from the furious mother.

"If you would let me finish," he said quietly. "I was going to say that as you are sure this is so out of character, and Jenny was technically still seventeen when she went missing, we will set up a missing person enquiry now. Do you have a clear, recent photo of Jenny?"

The woman pulled out her mobile phone.

"Isn't technology useful?" Hunter smiled.

Chapter Six

It had been a long day for Hunter, and it was not over yet. He returned from the formal identification of George Reinbold and switched on the coffee machine in his office, hoping the smell of the coffee would erase the taste of death in his throat. Not that the cure would last long. He knew Meera had insisted on doing the post-mortem herself. Hunter had to be there too, for George. He gazed out of his office window across the car-park to the trees beyond. The spring sunshine belied the chill in the air and the chill in his heart. Who had so brutally murdered George? Why was he the victim to such a calculated attack?

Hunter would find out. He would get his revenge.

"Nadia?" he shouted brusquely.

"Yes, Sir?" The nervous PC was in front of him before he had drawn breath.

"Nadia, the post-mortem for that murder victim, George Reinbold, is this afternoon. Have you ever witnessed a post-mortem?"

"No. No, Sir I've never had the opportunity."

"Well, today is your lucky day. The rest of the team knew George Reinbold, so it will be too difficult for them. I want you to accompany me to the morgue this afternoon."

"That sounds like the worst date in the world!" Mel caught the last part of the conversation as she stuck her head into Hunter's office. "I was just looking for Nadia. I didn't want to lose her on her first day."

"I'm going to my first post-mortem today with the boss."

"So I gathered," Mel grinned. "What time is Dr Sharma doing George?"

"Meera Sharma and David Murray both insisted on working

31

George's post-mortem. Their way of paying respects."

"Each to their own. Will it not be difficult for you, Boss?" Mel wrinkled her nose.

"It will. I'd welcome a little respect from you, Mel, please."

"Yes, Sir."

"So 2.30 pm at the morgue. Because this death occurred as a result of criminal activity, the post-mortem will be carried out by Dr Meera Sharma. She is a forensic pathologist, Nadia."

"Okay, Sir. Why a forensic pathologist?" Nadia asked.

"Forensic pathologists investigate deaths where there are both medical and legal implications. In this case, George was shot. We know he was murdered."

"I understand," Nadia said.

"Good. We'll meet in the car park after lunch, Nadia."

"Yes, Sir."

"Rather you than me," Mel teased Nadia as the two DCs left Hunter. "Want lunch in the canteen before you go? Or are you going to watch the proceedings on an empty stomach?"

***

Nadia had never been to a mortuary. The approach to the Edinburgh City Mortuary made her shudder. It is situated in the area of Edinburgh known as The Cowgate. Nadia guessed that the area derived its name from the historic practice of herding cattle down the street on market days.

Although the day was bright, the street seemed dark. Nadia looked around at The Cowgate and saw it was a canyon of a place. The street was only one lane wide in each direction and the pavements were narrow. She stared at the steep gradients leading off to either side. Nadia glanced at Hunter and noticed he was frowning. There was nowhere obvious to park, so she gripped on to the handle of the car door as Hunter swung the car into the morgue car park and drew up at the rear beside the anonymous black 'private ambulances' outside the morgue. His silence throughout the journey had done nothing to put Nadia at ease.

32

Hunter marched in without comment as Nadia trotted along behind him.

"Doctor Meera Sharma, may I introduce DC Nadia Chan," Hunter said, unusually formally. Nadia noticed that Hunter was upset and badly affected by this death.

"This is so sad, isn't it?" Meera said.

"Sad doesn't touch it, does it?" Hunter asked. "I need to know all you can possibly find out for me. I need to find the bastard who did this and lock them up for good."

"Come on then," Meera said. "You get togged up and let's see what we can learn."

Hunter and Nadia put on the white tunics, shoe covers, hats and masks that had been left for them.

"Distinctive smell here, Sir."

"Once smelt, never forgotten. Come on. I hope you don't have a weak stomach." Hunter led Nadia through to the post-mortem room.

"Afternoon, Hunter," Dr David Murray called from across the room. "I will be assisting Meera today, it only seemed right for George. And I hear you have a newbie with you?"

"Yes, DC Nadia Chan. She's new to the team. The others had all worked with George. I thought it would be too hard for them, so I volunteered Nadia to witness the post-mortem with me today."

"Your colleagues don't have a great reputation for seeing out the whole autopsy anyway. Didn't the big guy faint last time?"

"Bear? Yes he did. Hopefully Nadia will fare better."

"We shall see." David Murray smiled at Nadia before pulling up his mask.

"Let's see what's here," Meera began. "We have a white male, aged 73, and identified as Professor George Ernst Reinbold, former Professor of Criminology at Napier University in Edinburgh, later Manager of Criminal Scene Investigators in Lothian & Borders." Meera paused for breath, and Nadia noticed she had tears in her eyes.

"This is hard on everybody, Meera," Hunter said softly.

She nodded, and carried on speaking softly into the

microphone attached around her neck.

"There is a single bullet to the forehead yesterday morning. It would appear he was shot at close range. Forensics may be able to tell us the calibre of weapon if the bullet has been found?" She looked at Hunter.

"I honestly don't know yet. I haven't been told," he replied.

"It must have been so hard for the CSI team," Meera said.

"I called on the team from Glasgow. It would have been too much for our CSIs, Meera."

"Of course," she said. "It won't be long until you're all one force, will it?"

"Don't remind me. I'm still not sure that will work well, but nobody asked me."

Meera smiled and then turned back to the corpse in front of her.

"Brain destroyed in the blast, and the rear of the skull shattered. Fragments recovered. David, will you get those weighed for the report?"

"Yes, Meera."

"Would spray from George's blood have hit the gunman, Meera?" Hunter asked.

"It always depends on how close they were. But the powder burns around the entrance suggest this shot was made at close range, so yes, it probably would. You should call in a ballistics expert to help answer as many of your questions as possible. They will report separately."

"Thank you, Meera," Hunter said.

"Shall we proceed with the measuring and weighing of the rest of the organs?" David asked.

"Not yet," Meera said. "Look at this scar on his left leg. What on earth do you think caused that?"

David walked forward. "Good grief. That happened a long time ago, but it's amazing the wound didn't kill him! It looks as if the left leg was chewed by an animal or a pack of animals, and that scar there, as if it was cut with a sharp knife or hit with an axe."

"It does. Maybe he took a swipe to scare away the animals, perhaps? Let's check the muscle change. No wonder George walked with a stick; that leg has a whole chunk of muscle missing from the front of the thigh. It must have caused him a great deal of pain, especially when walking or even standing. But you're right, David, this is a historic injury. There would be records of the attack if it happened here. There is nothing in George's medical records about it, so it must have occurred before he arrived in Scotland." Meera looked at Hunter.

"I never heard him mention an attack. Did he talk about it to you, Meera?"

"Never. I just assumed he used the stick because of arthritis."

"I'll need to check and try to find out more. Although if it happened before he arrived in Scotland, it won't be easy. He must have been just a kid if it happened that long ago." Hunter scowled.

Meera sighed and continued with the post-mortem. As she began to make the "Y" incision, she glanced up at Nadia. The young DC was staring in fascination as the procedure continued.

"Are you always this careful with bodies, or is it because you knew this man?" Nadia asked.

"Good question," Meera said. "As forensic pathologists we always work to the standards set by our professional body, The Royal College of Pathologists. One of our obligations is to treat the body with respect."

"So what are you doing now?" Nadia asked.

"This long incision down the front of the body allows me to remove the internal organs. David will weigh and examine them. We check for things like blood clots and tumours, although I have no reason to think we will find that George suffered from anything like that."

"Well, you know what killed him," Nadia said.

"It may seem obvious, but we cannot make that assumption. We must check everything, anyway. Then we return the organs to the body. Otherwise the post mortem has no value," Meera said. "Normally I would make a single incision across the back of the head so that the top of the skull can be removed and we can examine the brain."

"Not much point doing that today," Hunter commented sourly.

"No," Meera said softly.

***

"You did well, Nadia," Hunter said as they left the morgue. "Most first-timers vomit or faint. You just seemed to devour the details."

"It was really interesting, Sir. I suppose it was easier for me because I didn't know Mr Reinbold, but once I got used to the smell in there, I found that I learned a lot. It was good of Doctor Sharma to take the time to explain things to me. Thank you for the opportunity."

Hunter smiled, "No problem. You can knock off now and I'll see you tomorrow morning at eight o'clock sharp. Do you need a lift?"

"No thanks, Sir, I'll make my own way. I think I'll go and visit my uncle Fred on my way home. I need to relax. This afternoon gave me a lot of food for thought. See you tomorrow."

Hunter made his way to The Persevere Bar, his local pub. He was glad of the warmth, light and familiarity of the surroundings. The Persevere served up a good pint and tasty food. While it might not look fancy, Hunter enjoyed banter with the locals and the company of the folk behind the bar. He knew he was unusually early for the darts match, and so he was able to get a pie and a pint before he took his place at the ocky.

Chapter Seven

DCs Tim Myerscough and Mel Grant pulled up outside
Thomson's Top Cars. They noticed the look of the showroom
was not as appealing as it used to be. The windows did not
sparkle, and there was litter on the ground between the cars.
The detectives took this as signs that the young managers were
not coping as well as Ian Thomson would have liked.

They went in and found Jamie and Frankie sitting at the
reception desk eating cakes. Both of them looked miserable,
but Jamie visibly cheered up when he saw Mel.

"Darlin'," he said to her. "I have missed your smiling face.
Is this a social call with you looking for a date with me, or are
you here in your official capacity?"

"I'm flattered that you remember me, Jamie, but this is
business. Your employee Jenny Kozlowski has been reported
missing. DC Myerscough and I are here to make some
enquiries."

"I take it her mam told you?"

"Loud and clear," Tim said.

"Hmmm, she is loud, and she clearly disnae like me."

"Imagine that," Mel said sarcastically.

She looked around the showroom and saw the high-quality
cars did not gleam the way they should. A Bentley, a Porsche,
a Lamborghini; you didn't see many of these around. The boys
should keep the place clean and tidy: smart, to go with these
smart cars. And it was freezing in here. She noticed the open
door that led to the garage beyond.

"So can you tell us what happened to Jenny, then?" Tim
asked.

"Well, I wasn't here, so it can't be my fault," said Jamie.

"I wasn't here neither, so it's not my fault either!" Frankie whined.

"We're not looking to blame you, we just need information. We are trying to find Jenny. Maybe you can help? Could you give us an idea of the order that things happened, here, before you closed up last night?" Tim leant on the reception desk and looked straight at Jamie. Mel could see that he was trying to be reassuring.

"Well we weren't busy, really," Jamie said, "so we told everybody else to bugger off. They were out of here so fast, fucking Gary even forgot to log the Volvo that was waiting for a service. So there was only Frankie and Jenny and me here."

"Who's Gary?" Mel asked.

"Our head mechanic. He was in the garage with the boys, me and Jenny were here in the showroom, with Jamie," Frankie said.

"You tell them the rest," Frankie said to Jamie.

"Well, not much to say, really, Frankie, is there? Because we were not here," Jamie repeated slowly.

"Please, Jamie," Mel said quietly.

Jamie sighed and leaned on the reception desk next to Tim. He cupped his chin in his hands, gazed at Mel and began to explain.

"A guy comes in, foreign, and asked to test-drive the Bentley. I gets the keys, we jump in and Bob's your Uncle; we're off for a wee tour of the sights in the best car in the shop. Gary leaves sharp, so Frankie and Jenny are left to close up."

"What did the customer look like?" Tim asked.

"Bit taller than me, light brown hair, beard."

"What was he wearing?"

Jamie shrugged. "Don't know. Nothing special. A suit?"

"Aye. It was a grey suit, but quite sharp. I'd like one like that for in here," Frankie added.

"Shut up, Frankie," Jamie whispered.

Mel looked at Jamie and Frankie. They both looked anxious. Jamie stood about five feet eight inches tall, with fashionably styled dark hair, youth and easy looks on his side.

Frankie always seemed to be the more earnest of the two. At five feet ten inches tall, he was slightly larger than his cousin, and his high cheek bones and wide-set eyes would have made him the more conventionally handsome of the two, but for the greasy sheen over his brown hair and the acne that blighted his skin.

"Then what happened, lads?" Tim asked.

"Well, when Gary stuck his head round the door of the garage to say he was off, Jenny told me just to go and get the twins. She'd wait and lock up with Jamie. He fancies her," Frankie said with a smile.

"You fancy her, do you? Have I got competition, then, Jamie?" Mel teased.

Jamie scowled, first at Frankie and then at Mel. Then he glanced over at Frankie who spoke seriously.

"A man came in just as I was about to leave. I asked Jenny if I should stay with her, but she said not to bother. She said I should go and get the babies. She would help the customer."

"When I got back, they had all buggered off and the lights were still on and the door unlocked," Jamie added. "I was really pissed off. Then Jenny didn't turn up this morning. That's all we know."

"Except..." Frankie started.

"Except what?" Tim asked.

"Shut up, Frankie!" Jamie said.

"Except what, Frankie?" Tim repeated.

Frankie blushed. He scratched a pimple on his chin, looked nervously at the pus collected in his fingernail, and wiped it deliberately on his trousers.

"Let me help you," Tim went on. "Jenny sent a text to her mother to say she was the only member of staff here and a customer wanted to take a car out, so she would have to go with him. Would Jenny normally do that?"

"Nah, not at all. There's a car missing too. Gary forgot to log a car that was brought in for a service, and now it's gone. I can't think why anybody would want to take out that old bone-shaker of a Volvo," Frankie said.

"Can you give us details of that car?" Tim asked.

"Old, blue, Volvo. That's all we know."

"Don't you have more details?"

"What part of 'Gary forgot to log it' do you not understand, big man?" Jamie asked Tim. "Mind you, Gary said someone was looking to buy it for £8,000. I can't think why."

Just then the door to the showroom opened. The man who entered made Tim, with his six-foot-four rugby player's frame, look petite. The man's girth darkened the room like a solar eclipse. He moved menacingly towards the group around the reception desk.

"I'm here for my car," he stated, flatly.

"You collecting a delivery or a repair, pal?" Jamie asked.

"I'm not your pal. My friend left it out the back in the garage."

"What car is it?"

"Blue Volvo, S60. My friend left it here. I've come to pick it up."

"Canny do that, pal," Jamie said. "No authority to release it to anybody except the guy who brought it in, or to the man we're told might want to buy it. Our mechanic was told the agreed price is £8,000. That's the problem, see?"

"I don't think that's gonny be a problem. I'll just take it. Now." The man moved forward forcefully.

Tim stepped between Jamie and the man.

"Who the hell are you?" the man asked Tim.

"DC Timothy Myerscough, may I also introduce my colleague DC Melanie Grant." Tim held out his hand to shake, and Mel could see that he pointedly crushed the big man's hand in his grip. "The management is right; unless your friend left authority for you to collect the car, they are not at liberty to release the vehicle to a third party."

"You bastard," the man growled at Tim. He stretched his fingers and rubbed his hand. Then he turned to Jamie, "I'll be back, and believe me, you'll find for sure I'm no your pal. This would never have been a problem in Mansoor's time." With that, the man turned on his heels and left.

"What's Mansoor got to do with this?" Tim asked.

"Nothing that I know about. He's in the big house, like your

40

pop," Jamie said defiantly.

Tim ignored him.

"He wouldn't mention Mansoor unless there was a link," Mel said. "And Mansoor is trouble however you want to dress it up."

"That's true, Mel. Can we see your CCTV, Frankie?" Tim asked pointedly.

"No film," Frankie said flatly.

"Is Gary here?" Tim asked.

Tim and Mel did not need to spend long with Gary to take his statement. It did not add much to what they already knew. The young mechanic wiped his hands on an oily rag and apologised for not having details of the Volvo.

"Who dropped the car off, Gary?" Mel asked.

"I don't know him. It wasn't any of our regulars."

"What did he look like?" Tim asked.

"The man who dropped the car off had black hair and a beard. Very smart. He said he knew Mansoor, that's why he brought it here. But that doesn't mean a thing now. Mansoor's away."

Tim and Mel left Gary and drove back to the station.

"You want to call the Boss and tell him what we learned at Thomson's Top Cars?" Mel asked.

"On his darts night? Over my dead body!" Tim replied.

"It might be," Mel laughed.

***

Jane gathered the officers for the door-to-door interviews. Their instruction: to interview and re-interview all neighbours, and find out where they were and what they heard between seven and ten in the morning of the day George was murdered. She told them she did not care if they, or the neighbours, thought it was relevant: Jane wanted every detail. Then she called in Colin, Nadia and Rachael.

"I need corroboration about the blue car and the man in the grey suit that Mrs Roberts mentioned, so I want you to examine the CCTV from the cameras leading to George's place. You need to cover the time span from seven to ten am," she said to Colin and Nadia.

"Not the CCTV, Sarge. It's the most boring job in the world," Colin complained.

"Perhaps not quite," Jane said. "Rachael, I want you to search for all reports of stolen blue cars."

"I think this calls for tea," sighed Rachael.

"Coffee for me," said Colin.

"Camomile," said Jane.

"Who included you? Slave-driver!" Rachael joked to Jane as she went to make the drinks.

Chapter Eight

DCI Allan Mackay called the room to order. "People, we have lost one of our own. We will solve this murder. Expeditiously. Do you hear me?"

"PDQ," said Bear.

"What was that, DC Zewedu?"

"I said we want to catch the bastard pretty damn quick, Boss."

"You're right, Bear," Hunter added. "I want my revenge. If I have my way, this murderer won't see freedom again."

"You'll find we get the job done quicker if you all stop blethering," Mackay snapped. "I'll have to call a press conference today and I must have something to say. DI Wilson, can you explain where we are?"

"Of course, Sir. DC Chan and I attended the post-mortem of George Reinbold. Doctor Sharma gave the death as occurring yesterday morning. George's alarm was set for seven and he was dead when the delivery girl arrived. Her statement confirmed her time of arrival as 10.30. George was dead by then. So we are estimating time of death at between seven and ten o'clock in the morning. The girl found the body and called the police. Forensics and the ballistics expert confirm he was shot at close range. The bullet appears to have been something like a .38. We are waiting for confirmation on that. The bullet certainly mushroomed upon impact. George didn't stand a chance." Hunter looked at the floor.

"Mel and I visited Thomson's Top Cars yesterday afternoon, Sir," Tim said. "The receptionist, Jenny Kozlowski, is missing. Also an old blue Volvo is unaccounted for."

"Yes, and a large, angry customer stormed in looking for it while we were there. He said it was an S60," Mel added.

"Apparently it was put in for a service and then the customer said there was someone interested in buying it for £8,000. That in itself is strange, because a Volvo that old is likely only to be worth £3,000 - £4,000. I checked," Tim said.

"A blue Volvo? One of my witnesses saw a blue car stop near George's home around nine in the morning," Jane said.

"Mel, you liaise with DS Renwick about the car. Jane, you get the door-to-doors finished today too," Mackay said.

"Sir," Jane nodded.

Mackay turned to Rachael. "DC Anderson, I want to know more about George's cases."

"Yes, Sir."

"How are you getting on examining the CCTV, DC Reid?"

"Slowly, Sir," Colin Reid replied. "There is no CCTV at George's house, but there are cameras on the street that we can check from both directions. DC Chan is observant, so we just keep looking on."

"What next, DI Wilson?"

"I am going to get a valuation of the books in George's collection, today, Sir."

"That will cost a fortune, man!"

"Not where I'm going, Sir. Tim you're with me."

"You remember I'm off this afternoon, Boss?"

"Yes, this won't take us more than a couple of hours. We'll leave the books and collect them with the valuation later."

"Do we know yet if George has family?" Mackay asked.

"I haven't been able to find evidence that he was married, but I haven't finished searching for children," Mel said.

"And in Germany?" Hunter asked.

"In his home there were many journals and scrap books," Bear answered, "but they are written in German. I think that we may need to have them translated, in order to piece together George's life, and possibly what led to his death."

"Call Doctor Gillian Pearson from the modern language department at Edinburgh University, Bear. She's always our first port of call when we need a translator. Amazing linguist. If she can't do the job, she will know someone who can," Hunter said.

As the meeting broke up, Mackay and Hunter agreed that the Press Conference would be arranged for noon, then Hunter and Tim headed for the car park. George's books were still in the van. Hunter shuddered at the thought of the potential value of the contents as he climbed into the driver's seat.

"So, Boss, who on earth will give you a cheap valuation for a haul of valuable books like this?" Tim asked.

"Aha, well, young Myerscough, it so happens that my father has collected rare books all his life. There is nobody who knows this market better."

"I thought he was a man of the cloth?"

"He was indeed. He was a Church of Scotland minister before he retired, but his other love has always been books."

Hunter drove quietly and calmly across the city. He was often amused how the driving habits of the good citizens of Edinburgh adjusted to the sight of a vehicle with POLICE emblazoned across it. He watched as each car reduced its speed to the legal limit; traffic lights were scrupulously obeyed, and *Give Way* signs afforded exaggerated attention. He smiled and indicated to turn right. He was waved across by another driver, although they had right of way. No big surprise. Hunter just raised his hand in thanks and drove across.

"Do we even really need a valuation?" Tim asked.

"Maybe not, directly, but you saw the security in George's house. I want to know why he was so security-conscious. It may just have been as a protection for his valuable library, or it might have been much more personal."

Tim nodded. "Yes, I see. Rachael said the insurance company confirmed they had required a burglar alarm and five lever locks on the back and front doors, but not the level of security Bear identified in George's home."

"That's what I suspected," Hunter said.

They pulled up outside the new town property in Coates Crescent. Tim grabbed a box of books as Hunter went to ring the bell.

"Nice place," Tim said.

"I told you, sound bookish investments. Some of these things can be worth a fortune," Hunter replied.

The door was opened by a man with a ram-rod-straight back and white hair. He looked exactly like an older version of Hunter Wilson.

"Christian!" he said in surprise. "Either it's your mother's birthday, or you want something. Eileen, our elder son is here."

"Christian, my dear. How lovely, and you've brought a friend!" A chubby little woman with greying brown hair bustled towards them.

"Hello, Mum." Hunter smiled as he hugged her and introduced Tim.

"I read about your father, Tim. Very sad. I'm so sorry," she said.

They followed Hunter's parents to a neat room where the walls were covered, floor to ceiling, with bookcases filled with obscure old tomes. The further up the wall they were, the dustier they got. Tim smiled and laid the box he was carrying on the table.

"Shall I bring in the rest of the boxes, Boss?"

"Yes please, Tim. You are right, Dad, I do want something. One of our own, the Crime Scene Investigation Manager, has been murdered. I hoped you could help me by valuing his collection of books."

"You know I will, lad, but I need something in return."

Hunter smiled but looked quizzical.

"Stay and have a cup of tea with your mother."

"Has she made scones?"

"Is the Pope a Catholic?"

Tim enjoyed the visit with Hunter's parents and enjoyed the scones even more. They chatted about George and his importance to Hunter as a friend and colleague, they touched on Tim's father and his incarceration in such a way that Tim knew they cared about both him and his father as people, and lastly they turned to the books Tim had brought up the stairs into their living room.

"These are exquisite, Christian!" Reverend Wilson said, cradling the children's book by Leyb Kvitko, *Di Bobe Shlak un ir Kabak*. "Is it inscribed to your friend? No! He would be too young."

"Possibly his grandfather?" Tim volunteered.

"Yes, lad, you are right. That is much more likely,"

The old minister laid the book down gently and accepted the recently-delivered copy of *Winnie the Pooh* from Hunter.

"A first edition. Lovely. My goodness, it is signed by both A A Milne and E H Shepard. That is most unusual, and in such excellent condition. I will enjoy looking at these for you, Christian." Hunter's father smiled.

Tim and Hunter did justice to the scones, fruitcake and cinnamon biscuits Mrs Wilson had made. She asked quietly after her grandson, Cameron.

"He is getting on," Hunter said. "I wish I could do more for him, but rehab is a very insular experience, I understand. I'll keep you posted, Mum."

The hour they spent together went by very fast. When they got up to leave, Tim noticed that Hunter shook his father's hand, but hugged his mother tight.

"Your mother is a fine baker, Sir," Tim said, as the door closed behind them.

"That she is, young Myerscough. That she is."

"How is Cameron really getting on in rehab?"

"He's on a twelve-week residential course. It's costing his mum and me a fair whack, but when he's through, the idea is he'll go and stay with his sister for a while. My daughter, Alison, lives in Shetland. It will keep Cameron out of the way of his old associates, and then he'll transfer to Edinburgh University next year and stay with his mother or me."

"If money is an issue, Sir…"

"Take your hand out of your pocket, son. We'll manage without your money. Anyway, you don't want to look slovenly on duty. Now, back to the ranch for us," Hunter replied firmly.

Curiosity overtook Tim on the drive back to the station.

"Christian, Boss?"

"Christian Cyril Hunter Wilson. What would you call yourself? One word of this to anybody and I'll have your balls for doorstops."

"Yes, Sir." Tim grinned. They drove the rest of the way

back to the station at Fettes in silence.

When they got there, Tim jumped out of the van and into his large, comfortable BMW. It had been his treat to himself when he took full control of the multi-million-pound trust fund his mum had left him when she died. He did love this car, large enough for him to be comfortable; hybrid to be green enough for his conscience. He drove across the city to HMP Edinburgh in the west of the city. The prison, popularly known as Saughton Prison (after the area in which it stood), was one of Tim's least favourite places on earth, but he would never miss a chance to visit his dad. Tim knew how much the time meant to his dad too.

He went through the usual security checks with everybody else and sat down in the waiting room. The room was covered in tiny marks and graffiti, but always smelled and looked clean. Tim's guess was that the prisoners cleaning this room always took longer doing it, as they hoped to see something or somebody out with their usual routine.

"You again?" Tim's reverie was disturbed as a familiar voice wafted across.

"Hi, Jamie," Tim smiled. "You here to see your old man too?"

"I'm not here for your company, fuckin' polis."

Tim blushed, but ignored the jibe. "What happened to your arm?"

"That fellow looking for the blue Volvo, the one who came in when you and DC Grant were with me and Frankie, well he came back with his friend, Lenny The Lizard Pratt. Broke my arm on the reception desk when they found we'd lost the car, didn't he?"

Tim was puzzled. "A ten-year-old-Volvo wouldn't seem to merit that kind of punishment. And I thought The Lizard was dating your mum?"

Jamie shrugged. "What can I say? I'm all sorts of lucky. I'll have to go back when the swelling's down a bit. The docs have to put a pin in here, 'cos' it's a bad break, hospital said." He pointed to his forearm and grimaced.

"You need to report it, Jamie. That's a nasty assault."

"Yeh, big man, like I'm going to tell you lot? I really want a stooky on my other arm as well."

It was Tim's turn to shrug as they realised the doors were unlocked for the start of the visiting hour.

As Tim strode towards his dad, he noticed that Jamie was not the only person who had recently suffered injury. Sir Peter's nose was strapped to repair a break, and his left eye was surrounded by a rainbow-coloured ring with a dark purple centre and yellow edges. The knuckles on both of his hands were grazed.

"Dad, what the hell happened to you?"

"Sit down and don't make a fuss. Former Chief Constables are only marginally more popular than child sex offenders. I've had to take a couple of beatings, but I'm not in bad shape, and if it's one-to-one I can pretty well hold my own. I'd look a whole lot worse if Ian Thomson hadn't stepped in."

"Thomson? Surely he doesn't owe you any favours?"

"True, but you got rid of Mansoor and the drug dealing out of his showrooms. By his beliefs, you did good by him, so he's paying you back by looking out for me."

"Does he have a cork eye?"

"He can't shadow me, son! Anyway, if I catch them, I can give as good as I get." He nodded towards an angry black-haired guy who looked as if he ate raw chickens whole. "Apparently I framed his brother."

"Did you?"

"Thanks for the vote of confidence. No, I did not. Now stop your nonsense and get us a coffee and some chocolate out of the machines."

***

Visiting time always seemed to go too quickly. It was not long until it was time for visitors to clear the room and for the prisoners to be searched for contraband before returning to their cells. Ian Thomson raised his head as Tim walked passed him on his way out. He saw Tim acknowledge him with a nod.

"Mansoor's men have targeted the showroom and my Jamie," Ian Thomson growled. "I don't want fucking drugs around my business again, and I don't want them playing fast and loose with my boy. Mansoor's got Lenny The Lizard Pratt and Big Brian Squires involved. You sort that out. I'll keep your old man safe, otherwise the former Chief Constable will find prison a very dangerous place, believe me."

Chapter Nine

"Janey, you must be getting excited, too?" Rachael asked.

"Nervous more than excited. It's all right for you – you have a family to help take the strain. I just have me."

"My family is your family, Janey."

"That thought makes me even more nervous," Jane laughed.

Jane had been brought up in the care system and had passed through several children's homes and foster carers. That beginning had been brutal. She never knew what she had done to deserve it. Jane knew she had family. She just didn't know who or where they were. Joining Rachael's large, close group of relatives her parents, her sister, aunts, uncles and cousins – felt foreign and exciting to Jane. It was good to be accepted as one of them, just as she was.

"I don't blame you. Imagine how I feel! Anyway, Dad insists he's walking us both down the aisle," Rachael said.

"There won't be an aisle, we're getting having a blessing of our civil partnership at the hotel. We're not really getting married," Jane smiled.

"As good as. You want to contradict him?"

"Not much."

"To me this is our wedding." Rachael hugged herself.

"Darling Rachael! When are we due at the dress shop?"

"Our appointment is 12.30 so that my sister can join us during her lunch break," Rachael smiled.

"Sarah works quite close to the shop, doesn't she?"

"Yes, and Mel has the day off, so she'll be there too, but Colin's wee girl Rosie will be at school, so Maggie and Colin will take her to get her flower girl dress at the weekend."

"And will our best men, Bear and Tim, be wearing their kilts?" Jane asked.

"The famous Zewedu and Myerscough tartans! Otherwise known as Scottish tourist. They'll be there in style. Those men are far too pleased with their own legs, if you ask me," Rachael joked.

"Sounds good. Let's go, shall we?"

"Yes, and we can stop at the car-hire company to pay the balance we owe on the way home.""Do you think it's silly to have cars just to drive around the block, Rache?"

"Very! But as this is our special day and it's what we want – so it's what we're going to do."

"I'm glad you said that. I agree." Jane smiled.

"It was good that Sarah and Mel were there to comment on our dresses. It is so difficult when we can't see each other," said Rachael as they drove past Edinburgh Airport on their way to pay the car-hire company.

"Outfits."

"What?"

"Outfits," repeated Jane. "Who said we're wearing dresses?"

"Aren't you? Oh shit!"

"Does it matter that much?"

"Janey, look!"

"I'm driving."

"Just. Stop!" Rachael shouted.

Jane did an emergency stop, as the cars behind her sat on their horns, shook their fists and swore. She ignored them all. Now she had seen what Rachael had seen. Jane grabbed her phone and rang the station while Rachael got out.

They stood and stared at the burnt-out car. The front of it was completely destroyed. Only the back of the car displayed anything recognisable.

"What do you bet it's the car taken from Thomson's Top Cars?" Rachael said.

"It's certainly been a blue Volvo. Let's wait till the crime scene investigators get here."

"That's all we need – an extra shift when we're meant to be using our day off to arrange our wedding."

"You take the car and drive over and pay for our wedding

cars. I'll wait here till the uniforms and CSIs get here," Jane suggested.

Rachael took the car keys from Jane and glared at her. "Do you always have to let work get in the way, Janey?" she said angrily as she flounced off.

***

Traffic always moves fast on the roads around Edinburgh Airport, but today cars were reducing their speed to a crawl. Drivers craned their necks to try to see what had resulted in all the police activity. Jane instructed some uniformed officers to take their places and move the cars along.

A young PC approached Jane, looking nervous. "Sarge? I think there's something you ought to see."

Jane frowned and approached the rear of the burnt-out car. It did not take long before she detected a familiar but noxious odour. Once you have smelled burnt human flesh, it is not a smell you ever forget.

Jane glanced at the young officer, who nodded. She looked into the boot of the car and saw the body of a young woman bundled into the cramped space. Her hair was singed as a result of the fire, and the synthetic fibres on her clothing stuck to her charred flesh, but her features were visible. She had been bound and gagged. Jane realised she must have been terrified.

"What a bloody awful way to go. I have a horrible feeling I know who that is, or was," she sighed. Then she peered into the boot of the car. "What's that?" She pointed to a packet under the spare wheel. It was protected by charred wrappers that had clearly withstood the worst of the heat when the car was burning.

"I don't know, Sarge. The whole car needs to be moved and examined, but after the lassie's been taken away, I s'pose."

"Yes, you suppose correctly, officer. Has anybody phoned the pathologist?"

"They have indeed, Jane." Dr Meera Sharma walked up behind them, dressed head to foot in her protective clothing.

Chapter Ten

Hunter and Tim pulled the car up in Gorgie, outside the tall, grey tenement where Jenny's mum lived. They noticed that none of the neighbours seemed curious when the police car stopped. The small homes built over one hundred and fifty years ago had originally had no bathrooms or toilets, but had been modernised with the benefit of substantial grants from the local authorities in the mid-twentieth century. Now, the three or four homes on each of the four floors of the building boasted internal bathrooms, kitchens and one or two bedrooms. They would make excellent starter homes, if the prices hadn't risen so fast.

"Such a lot of homes in this area," Tim commented. "It's always busy, isn't it? I remember going to the Gorgie City Farm once as a little boy." He pushed open the tenement door and jogged easily up the stairs without waiting for Hunter's reply. He was waiting at the door when Hunter finished climbing the four floors to Miss Kozlowski's door.

"Young Myerscough, nobody likes a show-off," Hunter said.

"No, Sir" Tim rang the bell.

Jenny's mum answered the door. She was wearing a loose-fitting shirt and jogging bottoms, and was towelling her dark hair dry.

"You?" she said. "You must have news that is either very, very good or bloody awful."

Hunter made to show the woman his identification.

"Don't bother with that. I know you both from the cop-shop."

"May we come in, Miss Kozlowski?" Hunter asked.

"Shit. It's bad. How bad?"

"Perhaps we could talk inside?" Tim said softly.

Ishbel Kozlowski began to cry as she led them along the narrow corridor to her living room. She collapsed on to the worn floral sofa and looked at them hopefully. The room smelt of stale cigarette smoke and furniture polish. A heady mix. Hunter sat down on the chair opposite her and told Tim to find the kitchen and make some tea.

"Where is the kitchen?" Tim asked.

"Through the wall, son. There's no' that much choice in these wee flats." Ishbel Kozlowski blew her nose on the towel round her neck and looked back at Hunter. She picked up her cigarette from the overflowing ash tray and took a long drag.

Hunter could have done with a drag himself, even if he had given up the weed ten years ago. He could see the hope and desperation in her eyes. He knew this was her only child. Hunter's stomach churned. Giving news this bad never got any easier.

"Miss Kozlowski, I am sorry to have to tell you that we have found the body of a young woman. We believe it may be Jenny, but I will need you to come down to the morgue to identify her. I am so very sorry." The end of Hunter's sentence was drowned by the screams of the distraught woman.

"No. No. You must be wrong, she's only eighteen. She's just a wee lassie. She's a good girl." The woman was distraught. She got up and wandered across the room. She picked up a photo of Jenny and held it tightly to her chest. Her tears rolled silently down her cheeks.

When Tim re-entered the room, he guided her back to the chair.

"Have a seat Miss Kozlowski. I don't want you to burn yourself."

"I've more important things to worry about than that, lad."

But she sat and accepted the mug of tea Tim handed her without even looking at him. She stared fiercely into Hunter's eyes before her own welled up with tears again.

"She's all I've got!"

"I'm sorry," Hunter said.

"Where did you find her?"

"We can't be sure, yet, that it is Jenny. That's why I need you to identify the body. But we suspect that it is your daughter. The body was found in the boot of a burnt-out Volvo car on the road to the airport."

"The airport? What the hell would Jenny be doing near the airport? She'd no business there, she was going to Nando's with her pals."

"Miss Kozlowski, the body is that of a young woman with long brown hair. She was slim and about five foot three inches in height."

"Oh God!"

"May we have Jenny's hairbrush or toothbrush please?" Tim asked gently. "It will allow us to get traces of her DNA and compare that to the DNA of the young woman we have found."

The woman nodded and stood up. She dragged her feet as she scuffed back along the corridor and returned carrying a small red hairbrush. She placed it into the evidence bag that Tim held. Then she lifted her jacket from the back of a chair and followed the men down to the car.

***

Hunter was pleased that it was Meera who greeted them and led the way to the viewing room. He thought it was good for Miss Kozlowski to have another woman present. Meera explained that the body had been found curled up in the boot of the car. The victim's hands and feet had been bound with gorilla tape, and a scarf had been wrapped around her mouth. Death had occurred approximately forty-eight hours previously, but a full post-mortem would be required.

Meera stood with her right arm around Miss Kozlowski's waist and her left hand on the other woman's shoulder.

"I just want you to confirm if you recognise the victim," Hunter said.

"Are you ready for my colleague to pull back the curtain?" Meera asked.

The woman nodded.

Dr David Murray pulled the cord to reveal the body.

Ishbel Kozlowski let out a horrified scream, then fainted. Meera's slight frame could not hold her, but with sportsman's reflexes Tim caught Ishbel and carried her easily all the way back to the car.

***

Hunter and Tim returned to the morgue to witness Jenny's post-mortem. They watched the procedure in silence. When Meera and David had finished their work, David began to clear up the workstation.

"You've had a long day, Meera," he said. "You get off, I'll sort this place out."

"I really appreciate that, David. I'm exhausted. It was awful, watching that poor woman when she saw her daughter."

"I will have more peace here than at home with Chrissie and the kids."

"Not my fault you have five children," Meera joked.

"It'll be six by the end of the year," David grinned.

"Your wife is a game girl, David. But don't you be asking for a raise in your salary to support all those wee ones!" Meera turned to Hunter and smiled. "DI Wilson, I hear you enjoy a good curry."

"I do indeed, Doctor Sharma."

"Want to see if we can get a table somewhere nice? The Cavalry Club, over in Coates Crescent, perhaps? It's my favourite."

"That sounds like an excellent idea." Hunter handed the car keys to Tim. "Back to the ranch with you, young Myerscough. I'm going out for dinner."

Chapter Eleven

When Hunter woke up, he felt really uncomfortable. It was early, he knew that, but he was not at all sure where he was. He moved his hands. What? His pillows did not have floral covers with frills around the edges. He leaned up on one elbow to try to get his bearings. He glanced to his right and caught sight of warm chocolate-brown eyes, surrounded by a mop of black hair, smiling up at him.

"I think I have time to complete one more examination before I have to get up. Pay attention, Detective Inspector Hunter Wilson," Meera purred as she drew him towards her.

***

Hunter arrived at the morning briefing with no time to spare, nursing a strong black coffee and a stupid smile. His mind wanted to wander back to Meera, but Allan Mackay interrupted his reverie by calling the briefing room to order.

"I need your attention, now. All of you! We have much to discuss this morning. Not least of all is the wonderful news that Superintendent Miller will be taking a short leave of absence..."

A loud cheer went up around the room.

"... to allow him to travel to London and collect his MBE," Mackay finished his sentence with a growl. "We are all justly proud of and delighted for our hard-working senior officer who does so much for The Scottish Police Benevolent Fund."

"More like another example of *My Boys' Efforts*," Bear whispered to Mel.

"You have an opinion, DC Zewedu?"

Bear shook his head. "I just said we need to find George's

58

murderer after all his efforts for us."

"Good. Yes. Of course. Now, where are we with that?"

"We have a witness who noticed a blue car outside George's home," said Jane.

"And a blue Volvo missing from Thomson's Top Cars," Tim added.

"And a body in the boot of a burnt-out blue Volvo on the way to the airport," Rachael whispered.

"All the same blue car throughout?" Mackay asked.

"We're still gathering that information, Sir," Tim said. "There is a break in the identification chain."

Hunter moved to the front of the room. "The body in the boot is confirmed to be that of Jenny Kozlowski, who worked at Thomson's Top Cars. Identification was made by Jenny's mother, Ishbel Kozlowski. Jenny and the Volvo went missing the night before George was murdered. She accompanied a customer who claimed to want to test-drive the car and she was the only member of staff available to accompany him. Doctor Sharma conducted the post-mortem of the young woman yesterday. We should get the written results this afternoon. The car has also been sent for forensic examination, because Sergeant Renwick noticed a packet secured under the spare wheel. Jane?"

"Yes, Sir. It looked as if there had also been other packets already removed from the boot. Whoever removed the other packets probably couldn't easily get to the one under the spare tyre because of the way Jenny was lying. The poor girl had been bound and gagged, and the car was burnt out at the side of the road, on the way to Edinburgh Airport. The fire had been started at the front of the car so the boot was least damaged. Still, Jenny didn't stand a chance. And it must have been a horrible way to die."

"It would be ghastly," Rachael commented, with a shudder.

"You noticed the car when you were just driving by, off duty, didn't you?" Nadia asked.

"Yes, that's right," Rachael said.

"We are never off-duty, DC Chan," Hunter said sharply.

"At least do we know if the car taken from Thomson's, the

car your witness saw and the car the body was found in are one and the same?" DCI Allan Mackay asked.

"Not yet, Sir," Tim said. "The CCTV in Thomson's Top Cars doesn't work, and they hadn't made a written note of the car details."

"Why am I not surprised?" Hunter sighed.

"But Forensics might tell us if fingerprints from Thomson's staff are on it," Colin suggested.

"Not if they were destroyed in the fire," Tim commented.

"And my witness didn't get a registration number," Jane added. "She doesn't even know the make of the car. Just that it was blue."

"Fabulous!" Mackay groaned sarcastically. "Colin, Nadia, check the ownership of the burnt-out car. See if you notice it on any of the CCTV leading to or from George's home. Hunter, can you call in a couple of favours to put salt on Forensics' tail?"

"I can try, Sir."

"Just one other thing, Sir," Tim said. "I saw Jamie Thomson yesterday, and some goon broke his arm over that car missing from his garage. So it must be important to someone, because they obviously want it back."

"Does he know who did it?" Hunter asked.

"The goon who came into the showroom when Mel and I were there is a chap called Brian Squires. He was the monkey who broke Jamie's arm, but the organ-grinder was Lenny The Lizard Pratt."

"Really? I thought he was living in Spain with Jamie's mum, the lovely but rather high-maintenance Janice?"

"He is, normally, but he's here right now, and he was furious they couldn't get the car back."

"They wouldn't want it back with a corpse in the boot," Hunter commented. "Jane, see how much more Uniform can find out about your blue car in their door-to-doors. Your witness saw a man in a grey suit too, didn't she?"

"Yes, Boss."

"The goon, Squires, who turned up at Thomson's when we were there, was wearing a grey suit, wasn't he Mel?" Tim commented.

"Yes, but that's not the first thing you would say about him," Mel replied. "The first thing I noticed was that he made you look like an anorexic dwarf! And Gary the mechanic said the man who dropped off the car had black hair and a beard. The photos I have seen of The Lizard make it look as though he has light brown hair."

"And although that can be changed, surely Jamie would have recognised The Lizard if he was the one who brought the car in to them?" Tim said.

"So why would The Lizard have any claim on the old Volvo, if it wasn't his in the first place? And why break Jamie's arm about it?" Mel asked.

Hunter spoke again. "Tim, you and Mel get back down to Thomson's Top Cars and find out all you can about Jenny's last hours, Jamie's attacker and that fucking car. For a car about ten years old, it seems to be getting a lot more interest than makes sense to me."

The phone next to Bear rang.

"Sir," Bear said, "your translator contact, Doctor Gillian Pearson, is here. She says she'll need a quiet room to work on George's scrap books, journals and private papers. Can I offer her the small room beside the coffee machine?"

"Good idea, Bear. You sort that out. I want to take another look around George's home."

As the briefing broke up, Gillian Pearson walked into the room. Hunter greeted her fondly and introduced her to Bear.

Hunter caught sight of Tim and smiled. It was clear he had noticed Gillian too. She was almost as tall as Hunter, with long legs, and she walked with an elegance that was devoid of affectation. She had blonde hair held back from her face in a loose bun, but the flash of green in the fringe of her hair emphasised her emerald eyes.

Tim did not hesitate to introduce himself to Gillian.

"I can show Gillian to her room, Bear," Tim said. "You don't mind, do you?"

"Apparently not," Bear smiled.

***

As Hunter walked up the pathway leading to his old friend's home, he paused and looked at the windows. The level of security inside was belied by the ordinariness of the entry. It was impossible to tell from here that the windows were triple-glazed, and what looked like old-fashioned lace curtains were bomb-proof. He could not see the bolts and linings that secured the doors. Still, as he entered the space that George Reinbold had occupied for so many years, it became instantly clear to him that the old man was very afraid of something. The manner of his death had proved his fears had been well-founded.

Hunter felt sad. He had never visited George here when he was alive, and now, as he wandered from room to room, he felt like a voyeur.

Just as he was about to leave, he noticed a postcard tucked behind the clock on the mantelpiece. Hunter picked it up. It showed a scene of the Elbe near the German border with the Czech Republic. The message on the back was handwritten in capitals, and appeared to be in German. Hunter cursed himself for having touched the card, and dug a small evidence bag out of his pocket. Gillian Pearson could translate the short message for him before the card was sent off to the forensic lab.

***

Mel and Tim walked into Thomson's Top Cars to find Frankie, alone, behind the reception desk.

"I never thought I'd say this," he said, "but I'm right glad to see you, cops."

"What's up, Frankie?" Tim asked.

"Jamie's arm's right bad and he's to get it seen to at the hospital and re-set with a metal bit in. And Gary's quit since we've heard Jenny's dead. And that big fat guy youse met the last time has been back and said he'll kill my twins if I say ought about him. And it's all fucking grim."

"What's to say about him? We saw him here and heard him threaten Jamie. You don't need to tell us that. Right?" Mel said.

"Right."

"Do you know his name, Frankie?" Tim asked. "We believe he is Brian Squires, who lives in Spain, but he's not on our books."

Frankie shook his head.

"Okay, you don't want to say anything?"

Frankie gave a thumbs-up, picked the spot on his forehead, and wiped the contents of his fingernail on his sleeve.

Tim grimaced, then said, "Is the man new to town?"

Frankie nodded slightly.

"Does he live in Scotland?"

Frankie shrugged.

"Do you know anything about him?"

Frankie gave another thumbs-up.

"How about you jot it down on your notepad, Frankie and go and make a coffee?" Mel suggested.

Frankie grinned and scribbled briefly before leaving the desk.

Tim and Mel looked at the note. They chatted quietly as they waited for Frankie to return.

"So, the big man *is* Brian Squires. He runs a bar in Spain with Lenny The Lizard Pratt, doesn't he?" Mel commented.

"That's what I've heard," Tim said.

"Looks like he's come over as The Lizard's muscle man. The only reason The Lizard would need muscle is if he's up to no good," Mel said.

"The Lizard is breathing, of course he's up to no good!" Tim said. He began to wander around the showroom.

"I think this is the only showroom in the city where you would find this Bentley next to that Porsche," he said to Mel.

Mel shrugged. Tim was the only person she knew who could afford either car, or both if he wanted them. She turned and noticed Frankie was only carrying one cup.

"I meant you could make a coffee for each of us too, Frankie," Mel said as he walked back towards them from the office.

She saw Frankie had the good grace to blush.

"Is Jamie's mother still dating The Lizard out in Malaga?" Tim asked him.

"Yeah, but I've heard The Lizard's over here to visit his mam. She's poorly and in hospital."

"Interesting. The Lizard is in Scotland visiting his mother, is he indeed? Well, well, well," Tim said.

"I wonder if he has any other reason to visit, apart from his dear old mum?" Mel said.

"Frankie, we're going to have to do some investigating. We'll do our best to keep your name out of it, but do you want some security around the girls?" Tim asked.

"Tim, way above our pay grade to offer that, pal," said Mel.

"I will provide it, if the force won't," Tim said quietly. "It needn't come out of the public purse. If your kids need protection, Frankie, say the word; I will pay for it personally. Family matters."

"I don't want anything to happen to the girls. I need them to be safe. And the lassie who minds them."

"I'll see to it that that gets sorted this afternoon, one way or another. Phone me if you need me, Frankie." Tim handed Frankie his card, and he and Mel left the showroom.

"Tim, I know you've got your Mum's trust fund money now, but do you really want to spend it on Frankie Hope and his sprogs? They're not your problem."

"Maybe not," Tim said firmly. "But family is important, and Frankie and I haven't got that much family left. It is my bloody money and I'll spend it as I see fit."

"Up to you," Mel said solemnly, "but it's not a good idea."

Chapter Twelve

Hunter made Gillian his first port of call when he got back to the station. He handed her the postcard and asked the meaning of the brief message on the back.

"It means, *Beware your sins will find you out*," she said. "The postmark is back in 2010, but it's not signed. I don't suppose you know who sent it?"

"Unfortunately not. But I am going to send it over to see if the card itself can offer any forensic evidence that might be useful to us. The problem with a postcard or envelope is that so many people touch it, so we are not likely to get anything. Still, it's worth checking."

Tim came into the room and smiled at Gillian. "A few of us are going out to the Golf Tavern in Morningside this evening, if you fancy joining us, Gillian?"

"That would be nice. I'd like that," Gillian said.

"We'll meet at the door and I can give you a lift up," Tim said.

"If I may interrupt your social life, young Myerscough, why are you here?" Hunter asked.

Tim smiled at Gillian before speaking seriously to Hunter. "When Mel and I were at Thomson's Top Cars today, we spoke to Frankie Hope. He's had the frighteners put on him by The Lizard and his gigantic side-kick, Brian Squires. Apparently The Lizard is back in town to visit his ailing mother."

"Is he indeed? I'll get Colin and Nadia to check the airports and sea ports and perhaps even Eurostar to find out when The Lizard arrived here. Do we know where he's staying?"

"Not yet. Maybe at his mother's house?"

"Get me an address, will you, Tim?"

"Of course. Just so you know, Boss, I've offered to provide safety for Frankie and his girls, since Lenny threatened them."

"Alright, son. Not your call, but seen as it's The Lizard, I agree. I'll get some of our boys allocated while we sort this out. But remember, young Myerscough, never let it get personal."

"Family is important, to me, Sir."

"I know, lad. Just don't make it personal. Not with my Cameron, not with Jamie Thomson..."

"Not with George Reinbold?" Tim asked.

"Don't be smart, that's different!"

Gillian spoke. "DI Hunter, I have noticed that George Reinbold's recent scrapbooks show that someone by the name of Heinrich Reinbold has been appointed as General Manager to the European chain of hotels which have opened in Scotland. See, this scrap here."

"What is the chain called?" Hunter asked.

"*Gemuetliche Erholung*. It means Comfortable Rest. I think the first branches in Scotland opened in Edinburgh, Glasgow and Aberdeen at the beginning of this month. The family Bible has an entry for a son born to George's twin sister, Ingrid. The child's name was Heinrich. There is no entry to show she ever married."

"Well-spotted, Gillian. I'll get Colin and Nadia to check on this manager too. Thanks, I'll leave you to it. How long will all this take you?" Hunter asked.

"I will be quicker if you stop finding me extra pieces of paper to translate!"

"Fair play." Hunter turned and looked at Tim. "Don't just stand there with your mouth open, young Myerscough. You're seeing her this evening. Don't you have work to do?"

***

Colin enjoyed working with Nadia. She was clever and organised, and took her turn to make the coffee. She also didn't drop crumbs all over the desk. He thought she was a great improvement on John Hamilton, his previous partner.

"Thanks Nadia," he said, taking a fresh mug of coffee from her. "Do you have that registration number?"

"Yep, we got it from the Edinburgh airport incident, and it appears the car was reported stolen by the owner in Folkestone."

"Folkestone? That's a long way away. I see it was reported about a week ago, and Folkestone is near the entry to the Channel Tunnel, isn't it?"

"Hmmm. It is. But the car came north, Colin."

"Let's just check the film on CCTV. In that length of time it could have gone south first, you know."

"I suppose so," Nadia said doubtfully.

"We better check."

The two of them watched CCTV coverage of the entry to and exit from the Channel Tunnel until their eyes hurt.

Suddenly, Nadia punched Colin's arm. "Look! There! We've got the bugger, it's on its way to France. Pause that screen. Let's print it off."

"Now all we've got to do is find it coming back." Colin rubbed his arm as he picked the sheet off the printer. "It's not a great picture of the driver, is it?"

"Looks like a man, maybe. The angle of the camera makes it impossible to see under the hat. Does he have a beard or is that a shadow?" Nadia screwed up her eyes to try to see more clearly.

"I don't think pulling faces will help you see him any better. Even if he has a beard there, he might not have by the time he drives back!" Colin laughed.

"Let's study the cars coming the other way, so we get this one on its way back, shall we? Oh, and it's your turn to get the coffee. But we can have tea and a piece of moon cake to go with it this time?"

"Isn't that the cake with the hard-boiled egg in it? I think I'll pass." Colin grimaced.

"I bet you've never tried it. You don't know what you're missing."

"True and true." Colin said.

Colin went through to make the drinks. He made Jasmine

tea for Nadia, and grimaced as he and cut her a generous slice of moon cake. No way was he eating that. He made himself a coffee and determined to choose a piece of fruit out of his desk to have with it.

Nadia looked up from the computer and grinned as Colin handed her the tea and cake while holding his coffee firmly in his other hand.

"Let's take a break. My eyes are getting tired," she said.

They finished their snacks and then turned back to the screen.

***

"You got a minute?" Gillian asked as she looked into Hunter's office to speak to him before she left for the evening.

"Just one minute, literally. I'm refereeing the Boy Scouts versus Boys Brigade Under-Fifteen football match tonight. I'll be called all the names under the sun by the parents anyway, without being late as well!"

"No, it's just an interesting point. The scrapbook contains mostly pictures, magazine and newspaper cuttings. Some in English, some in German, some in Russian. I'm almost finished with them. I think the translation will just take me another day, and then I'll get my notes typed up for you and start on the journals."

"Great. Thank you."

"Yes, but they will take longer. There are more of them, and there is more handwriting," Gillian explained.

"Understood. What have you found that you wanted to show me today?" Hunter asked.

"It's just that it seems there was a Stasi officer killed in George's home village a few months before George arrived here. The officer's name was Hans Merkel."

"Merkel, the same as the German Chancellor's name?"

"Exactly, she is Angela Merkel. But I don't think there's a connection. At least there's not one mentioned."

Tim poked his head round Hunter's door. "Boss, that's me and Bear off to the pub. See you tomorrow."

"You don't usually tell me when you are leaving, Tim." Hunter winked at Gillian. "You go, Gillian, I'll have a think about this and we'll talk more tomorrow."

"I thought I heard Gillian mention the name Merkel," Tim said. "There is a German art dealer, Max Merkel. It's common knowledge his father was in the Stasi."

"That's interesting."

"I thought the information might help." Tim blushed slightly.

Gillian nodded. "The Stasi was the official state security service of the old German Democratic Republic. Hated and feared in equal measure."

"I have to get out of here. We'll pick this up tomorrow. The ref cannot be late." Hunter strode past Tim to get to the car park.

Chapter Thirteen

Rachael couldn't think of a time when she and Jane had had so many days off together. It was lovely. Today, they were going to stop by the hotel in Belford Road, where they had chosen to have their blessing.

There were plenty of fancier venues than the three-star Bruce Hotel, in Belford Road, on the banks of the Water of Leith. But this hotel was within easy walking distance of one of Jane's favourite attractions in the city: The Scottish National Gallery of Modern Art. Rachael had agreed to the choice because she knew Jane would like guests to be able to visit the gallery if they wanted to.

"Janey, did you notice the hotel has been sold to a different chain?" she asked.

"Yes. I don't think it will really affect us, but I want to visit and see for myself."

"May be not, but the chain's name is totally unpronounceable."

"The hotel is still called The Bruce Hotel; it's just the company that owns it which has changed. The hotel still has the same rooms for our guests who are staying over, and the function suite for us. It will be fine!"

"As long as the honeymoon suite is still as nice, that's all I care about," Rachael said.

"We'll check! I want to take another look at the bar and the restaurant and make sure our cake is organised."

"One fruit tier for you and one chocolate tier for me."

"Yes, my little peasant." Jane laughed and pushed open the door to the hotel reception.

"What cheek! But I'm glad we have time off and can do this together, Janey."

"And guests should get parked easily on the big day."

***

Jane and Rachael went to reception to ask for the Events Manager. They were both relieved when the same woman they had made all their arrangements with came out to greet them.

"Hello, ladies. Jane and Rachael, isn't it? Not long to wait now! Are you getting excited?"

"Ooh yes," Rachael said.

"Your wedding planner has been in touch to finalise access and arrangements, but would you like to see the function suite again? It has been redecorated since our takeover by *Gemuetliche Erholung*."

"So that's how you say it. I'm glad they haven't changed the name of the hotel," Rachael smiled.

"That may change, but not yet. Hang on and I'll just get the rest of my keys." The lady disappeared into a room behind the reception desk.

"What are you doing, Janey?" Rachael asked.

"Reading the guest forms on the desk," Jane replied quietly.

"Why?"

"Because I'm a cop and I'm nosey. Look, it seems Lenny The Lizard Pratt is staying here."

"He must be feeling the cold today, it's a bit brisk. Doesn't he live in Malaga with Jamie Thomson's mum now?"

"Yes, that must be expensive. From comments the boss has made, I believe Janice is a bit high-maintenance. But it looks like he's here today. Lucky us."

"Look at that notice-board, Janey."

"Goodness, the General Manager is a Heinrich Reinbold. I wonder if that is a coincidence?"

"The boss doesn't like coincidences."

"Neither do I, Rache."

After looking around the function area and having another look at the luxurious honeymoon suite where they would spend their wedding night, Jane and Rachael joined the Events Manager for coffee in the bar and paid the balance of their bill.

"We are going to have such a fun day, aren't we, Rache?" Jane said, as the Events Manager went to get their receipt.

71

"And it is forever?"

"Of course!" Rachael reached out for Jane's hand, but noticed she was looking towards the far side of the bar. Two men were sitting with their heads close together, whispering.

"You might pay attention to me when I'm being romantic, Janey. Oh, is that Lenny The Lizard you're looking at?" Rachael asked.

"Ssssh." Jane moved seats to sit opposite Rachael. "Make it look as if you are taking my picture, but get those men in the shot," she whispered.

"Well, at least smile." Rachael took a couple of photos. She could tell that the men in the background never noticed.

***

Colin was glad nobody else was around when he and Nadia jumped up and punched the air above them. He appreciated her determination to see each detail of the task through.

"We've got it! Nadia, we've got it. I thought my eyes were going to bleed."

"Yep, we've got it. And do you see how much lower the car is sitting on its axle than it was on the way out?" Nadia pointed to the screen.

"Well-spotted. No, I hadn't noticed that. There must be some weight in it for that to happen to a Volvo."

"Still can't see clearly who's driving, though," Nadia said.

"No, but you can see the man's jacket and tie."

"Didn't Jane say one of her witnesses saw a man wearing a grey suit? The jacket is quite a light colour," Nadia said.

"Yes, but a grey suit in the street on a weekday morning in Edinburgh could be anybody from a doctor to a…"

"Policeman?" Nadia joked.

Chapter Fourteen

The following morning, the sky was clear and blue: the temperature was slightly warmer than on previous days and the spring flowers responded by pushing out more blooms.

Tim went for an early-morning run before he went to the station. His route from his father's house in East Steils, Morningside, took him down the hill, through the beautiful park, Hermitage of Braid. He ran steadily, not at speed, all the way to the end of the path in Liberton and back again. His playlist, firmly tucked into his ears, protected him from having to converse with any dog-walkers or other joggers. It was especially refreshing to experience the beautiful city in Spring, and Tim treasured this time to himself.

***

Hunter was already sitting at his desk when Jane knocked on the door.

"Come in," he growled.

"You all right, Boss?"

"Yes, I got punched yesterday by an irate father who was not happy with my penalty decision. I thought it was a stroke of genius, it meant honour all round in a two-all draw."

"I hope you bloody booked him!"

"No, Jane, I didn't. Anyway, what can I do for you?"

"You know Lenny The Lizard Pratt is in town?"

"Yes, I'd heard from Tim and Mel he'd been round with Brian Squires to put the wind up the boys at Thomson's. We're keeping an eye on Frankie and his girls. Jamie is still in hospital right now."

"Well, I know where he's staying. The Lizard's staying at

The Bruce Hotel on Belford Road."

"Where you're having your big day?"

"Yes. That's how we found out. Rache and I went there yesterday to finalise the arrangements, and we saw him in the bar, deep in conversation with another man. I didn't recognise the other guy, though."

"Pity."

"So we took a picture."

"Good thinking." Hunter grinned.

"Do you know this man, Sir?" Jane handed Rachael's phone to Hunter.

"No, I don't, but get that printed off, and we'll get Nadia and Colin to add him to their list. Those two are making a good team."

"Oh, just one more thing, Boss. The hotel has been taken over, and a new general manager has been appointed. His name is Heinrich Reinbold."

***

Jane left the room and nearly walked into Tim as she stared at the phone. He winced.

"You seem as precious as the boss today," Jane said.

"I went for a run this morning, I'll have you know. I should make it a more regular thing: I'm not as fit as I like to think I am. I'm feeling a bit tender, that's all."

"Are you sure it doesn't have more to do with you and Bear showing off to Gillian and Mel in the Golf Tavern last night?"

Tim smiled and shrugged. "Possibly. But, anyway, what are your eyes glued to that you didn't notice me?"

"I saw The Lizard yesterday and he was talking to a fellow I don't recognise. The boss says I've to print the picture off for Nadia and Colin to trace him."

"Let me see?"

Jane handed the phone to Tim.

"I can save you all a bit of time. That's Max Merkel. German art dealer. Does a lot of business in America and the Far East, as well as Europe. Very determined dealer. Ruthless.

He has quite a reputation, but he gets what his clients are after. He follows the money and demand. Dad bought a most vibrant painting by Kerry James Marshall through him some years back."

"I'd love to see that."

"Remind me next time you and Rache are at the house. You'll love it."

"But are you sure that's him?"

"Yes. See how he has a thick beard but not such a good moustache? He was attacked when he was a child and has a wide scar. He tries to grow a moustache to hide it, but it never works very well. He is sensitive about the scar, so nobody ever mentions it."

Jane smiled and went to break this news to Hunter, before the briefing started.

***

DCI Allan Mackay banged on a desk with his folder. It brought the room to some semblance of order.

"Are we any nearer to finding out who killed George Reinbold?" he asked loudly.

Colin was chewing on an apple, while Nadia, Tim and Bear finished their bacon rolls. Jane sipped her camomile tea and wondered if anybody apart from herself and Rachael still ate breakfast at home.

Hunter stood up. "I think we are making progress, Sir. Jane, can you start us off?"

Before Jane had time to draw breath, Gillian Pearson knocked on the door and entered the incident room. She looked around the room and gestured to Hunter.

"DI Wilson, I am very sorry to interrupt your briefing, but I have found information in George Reinbold's scrapbooks that I believe your team should be aware of."

"Come in, Gillian. What's up?" Hunter asked.

"What is so significant that we must be aware of it right now?" Allan Mackay said sharply. "This is an important, confidential briefing."

"I'm sorry to interrupt, DCI Mackay, truly I am, but I have been going through the various scrap books that George Reinbold made up from newspaper cuttings. The ones found in his flat?"

Mackay nodded. "So? They can wait."

"I've found newspaper articles from just before Mr Reinbold arrived in this country. They indicate that he was being sought by the authorities in connection with a murder."

"A murder? George was suspected of murder?" Hunter interjected incredulously.

Gillian nodded. "It seems he killed a Stasi officer, Hans Merkel, then fled the country, and, I suppose, he ended up here. There are other articles that tell of the execution of George's father and brother. He had a twin sister. She gave birth to a son, Heinrich Reinbold, about nine months after George fled. My guess would be that the child was the result of rape by the Stasi, but we'll never prove that now."

"Good God!" Mackay exclaimed. "Come with me, DI Wilson. We must get to the press conference now or we will be late. We are going to keep this as short and factual as we can. A man has been murdered in his home in Gilmerton. We'll give the date and time and ask that any member of the public who has information calls the helpline."

"And get every nutter in the city admitting to anything from cross-dressing in their girlfriend's clothes to killing the dinosaurs," Hunter said, as he followed Mackay out of the room. "Great! Tim, don't go far. After this press conference, we're off to The Bruce Hotel."

Chapter Fifteen

Hunter and Tim entered The Bruce Hotel. The clean, comfortable, modern reception area made a favourable impression on the officers, who moved steadily towards the desk. An immaculately-manicured young woman looked from one to the other and settled her gaze on the tall good-looking one with the broken nose.

"Can I help you, gentlemen?" she asked Tim.

Hunter showed his identification and asked to speak to the manager. A nervous, balding little man appeared from the office behind the desk.

"Brownlee, Barry Brownlee. How may I be of service to Her Majesty's finest today?"

Hunter explained that they had reason to believe Lenny The Lizard Pratt and Max Merkel were guests at the hotel.

"Oh, I couldn't possibly breach the confidentiality of our guests, you understand, gentlemen."

"Of course, I understand. Myerscough, arrest him for perverting the course of justice."

Tim made to grab the man's arm, but he moved it quickly.

"Now really, I don't think this is necessary," he objected.

"No, it's not, if you choose to assist us. I only want to know if these two men are registered here, and when they arrived. Alternatively, I can station officers outside your premises until I know one way or the other. Do you understand?" Hunter spat the last word.

"Yes. Yes, I do." The little man nodded nervously. He pulled up a screen on his computer, wrote down the information and handed it to Hunter.

"Thank you. Also, I believe you have a new General

Manager since the hotel changed hands, Mr Heinrich Reinbold?"

"Yes, yes, Mr Reinbold."

"Well. Is he here?" Hunter asked sharply.

"Not at the moment; he is in Glasgow this morning."

"No problem, thank you again," Hunter said.

The detectives turned on their heels and left the premises as swiftly as they had entered.

"You couldn't arrest him for that, Sir?"

"No, all nonsense. Just my little joke," Hunter smiled.

"I didn't see Mr Brownlee laughing, Sir."

"People watch too many cop programmes where everything happens in an hour. You drive."

Tim winced as he caught the keys.

"What's wrong?" Hunter asked.

"Pulled muscles. I went for a run this morning."

"You have pulled muscles, I got punched. Good Lord, who would want to join the boys in blue? Anyway, let's get back to the ranch."

Tim shrugged. They got into the car and drove back to the station.

***

Hunter was greeted in his office by his phone ringing.

"DI Wilson." His face grew sombre as he listened quietly to the voice at the other end of the line. "Understood." He hung up the receiver and went to find Mackay.

"Sir, I just had a call from the Forensics boys. They have some interesting news for us."

"Oh, good. Have a seat, Hunter. Tea?" Hunter accepted, more for the politics than out of a desire to drink tea with a senior officer.

"That package Jane Renwick spotted in the burnt-out car held high-grade cocaine from Peru."

"Peru? That's different."

"The drug squad knew a new source of coke was making its way into the country, but they didn't know the route. It seems we came across it accidentally. The route seems to be coming into Europe and across the Channel through the Tunnel."

"Do they know who's behind it?"

Hunter shook his head. "But we do know The Lizard is in the city, ostensibly to visit his sick mother."

"Aye right!" Mackay said sarcastically. "Could he be running the drug operation in Edinburgh for Mansoor while he's in prison?"

"I don't know, Sir. I wasn't aware they were that close. I do know The Lizard is bad news wherever he is, and Tim said something about him laying claim to the old blue car that went missing from Thomson's Top Cars. He had Brian Squires break Jamie Thomson's arm when he learned the car wasn't in the showroom. We know now that the burnt-out car found near the airport had cocaine in the boot. We also know both cars are old Volvos, we don't know, yet, if they are one and the same vehicle. I am having Colin and Nadia liaise with Jane on registration numbers."

"It's true, there is more than one old Volvo in the world; those cars are well-made and last forever. The one Jane spotted didn't even burn all the way through when it was set alight. But it is a hell of a coincidence that we find a burnt-out blue Volvo with cocaine in the boot, and The Lizard is laying claim to an old blue Volvo that has gone missing."

"I don't believe in coincidences, Sir"

"Neither do I, Hunter. Neither do I."

"We do know The Lizard is staying at The Bruce Hotel in Belford Road. Jane and Rachael saw him talking to an art dealer from Germany, Max Merkel."

"Never heard of him."

"No, me neither, but Tim Myerscough has. He identified him from a photo Jane and Rachael took while they were in the hotel sorting out their arrangements."

"What a lucky break they saw The Lizard."

"I always tell them, Sir, *Never off duty* – and some of them listen," Hunter smiled.

"Well said."

"Apparently this Merkel guy is a big deal on the art circuit.

And his father was in the Stasi."

"East German security in the old days?"

"Yep. Meanwhile, Gillian found the evidence that George was accused of murdering a man called Hans Merkel."

"And now George is dead, while a Max Merkel and The Lizard stay in an Edinburgh hotel. I really don't like this."

"In addition to that, the General Manager of the hotel chain has the same name as George's nephew: Heinrich Reinbold."

"Get to the bottom of this, Hunter. Do it quickly. The sooner we have a national force with a united Major Incident Team, the better."

"If you say so, Sir."

Chapter Sixteen

Hunter went to find Colin and Nadia. He found them in the canteen, eating lunch and looking at photos of each other's children. Suddenly, Hunter realised that he was hungry too. It was nearing the end of time for lunch service, but he joined the queue behind Mel and picked up a plate of dried-out fish and chips. It would fill a hole. The canteen was still busy, so Hunter walked over with Mel to join Colin and Nadia.

"That looks vile, Boss!" Mel grinned.

"It does, doesn't it?" Hunter agreed. "I know you have been putting in the hours over George Reinbold, and I appreciate it. Colin, Nadia, have you got the route sorted for the Volvo yet?"

"I think so. We can't trace on areas where there are no cameras, but we can pick it up again when there are. And it is the same one that Jane and Rachael found burnt out at the airport." Colin chewed the last bite of a banana that served as pudding.

"I want a timeline for the journey that vehicle took. As much information as you can give me, especially the registration number and the identity of the driver."

"Sure." Nadia took out her notebook.

"Anything else?" Colin said. "I'm feeling there's something we haven't been told yet."

"I need you to check the date of entry to this country by Lenny The Lizard Pratt, Heinrich Reinbold and Max Merkel. I want method of entry too, if you can get it."

"What about me, Boss?" Mel asked.

"Mel, I want all the contacts and associates for those three men. I want to know as much about them as you can find. Add Brian Squires to your list. I can make Bear and Rachael available to help you, if you need them. You can each take one of these characters."

"That would be five of us and four people to investigate, how does that add up?" Mel asked.

"You're resourceful, you'll manage. In the meantime, I'm off to Saughton with Myerscough," Hunter said, consigning the remains of his lunch to the bin.

***

"I want to interview Ian Thomson," Hunter said to Tim as they waited for Ian to be brought to the private consultation room. "I need to find out what he knows about The Lizard, and why that man is really in the city."

"You mean you want to find out what he knows, that he's prepared to tell us."

"Yes, but I don't think there's much love lost since Ian's wife ran into the arms of The Lizard and took off to Spain with him."

"No, probably not," Tim agreed.

"And we are protecting his son and nephew from the bad guys."

"We are, Boss. Very good of us!" Tim smiled.

"We'll make time for you to meet with your father while we're here."

As Ian Thomson entered the room, Hunter indicated to the prison officer that he should wait outside the door. He noticed how lean Ian Thomson had become. His muscular frame was clear underneath his ill-fitting prison clothes. He watched as Thomson sat down and stared across the table.

"This is a fine mess," he said shortly.

"What's that, Ian?" Hunter asked.

"Me in here, his dad" (he nodded towards Tim) "along the block and .Mansoor in solitary. Just as well The Lizard's back in town, or you'd have nobody to keep you busy. All the scum would be in here with me."

"Wish it were that easy," Hunter said.

"Well, what do you want with me? It's not the pleasure of me company, although thanks for looking out for Jamie and

82

Frankie. They're a pair of clueless buggers."

"You'll get no argument from me on that score," Tim replied. "But talking of clueless buggers, thanks for keeping an eye on my dad too."

Ian Thomson winked at Tim and turned his attention to Hunter.

"How do you know The Lizard's in town anyway?" Hunter asked.

"Word gets about," Ian Thomson said flatly.

"Aye, but you don't," said Tim.

"Arjun Mansoor said."

"I thought he was in solitary?" Hunter asked.

"He is now. The Lizard's stooge brought him a snowball and he was sharing it about like it was chocolate. Got caught. Got searched. Got banged up in solitary. Apparently it's brilliant stuff, though, from Peru."

"So I've heard. Did you try it?"

"You know me better than that, DI Wilson," Ian Thomson said firmly. "I don't have any truck with drugs. It's a mug's game – only brings misery to the users. You've got to be well up that food chain to make any money out of it."

"Who brought it in to the country?" Hunter asked

"Do I look like a grass to you? Piss off!"

"Who brought it in to the prison?"

"Use your loaf, Inspector. Mansoor was dealing in here, and he knew that The Lizard was back in Edinburgh, so it must have been a contact of The Lizard's who came to see Mansoor. But he never told me who."

"You don't like The Lizard, do you, Ian?" Hunter asked.

"Would you have a lot of time for the arsehole who shagged your wife as soon as you were in the big house?"

"No."

"They live in Spain most of the time now. She takes no interest in our Jamie. Fucking useless mam she is. But she must have burned her way through a lot of The Lizard's cash, because I've heard he's doing business over here right now. She's not a cheap date, my Janice. I could have told him that, but he never asked."

"Any idea about the kind of job The Lizard might have taken on here?"

"Well, it'll have to pay well and he won't need to be here long. He'll want to get back to sun, sangria and sex with my bloody Mrs, won't he?"

"Does The Lizard shoot?" Tim asked.

"Hedoes, but he's not the best marksman in the world. He's fine at close range, I suppose. Not squeamish. No conscience. You've met the type: scum that'll do anything to make a few bucks. Like Arjun Mansoor."

"Time's up, Sir," the guard said to Hunter.

"Always lovely to chat, gents, but if I was you I'd check the visiting book and the log of Mansoor's official phone calls."

Hunter asked the guard to bring Sir Peter Myerscough through to see Tim. Then Hunter went off to find somebody who could show him the visitors' book and Arjun Mansoor's phone transcript, while Tim spent a little private time with his dad.

Chapter Seventeen

Tim was glad to be having dinner with Jane and Rachael this evening. Instead of having a hen-do they were giving a pre-wedding supper for those helping with their big day. He was tired of dining alone in his father's large Morningside home.

Rachael had excluded her parents from the evening on the grounds that they would be too embarrassing, and Rosie, the little flower-girl, was represented by her parents, Colin and Maggie.

Tim arrived with Bear and Mel, to find Sarah, Colin and Maggie already chatting in the living room. Tim had never met Sarah before, but she bore a striking resemblance to Rachael, so there was no doubting her identity. Nevertheless, she approached him to introduce herself.

"I'm a detective, I worked out who you are," he smiled.

"As I'm the only person in the room you don't know," she nodded, "that doesn't make it such brilliant detection. But perhaps I could get you a drink, anyway?"

"Beer, please. Budweiser if they have it."

"I think you're on safe ground. I'll be right back."

Tim had the nagging feeling Sarah had been told he was single and to make a point of chatting to him. He spotted the two Samuel Peploe paintings he had given to Jane and Rachael as engagement presents. He knew the paintings meant more to the girls than they had ever done to him. He followed Sarah into the kitchen to claim his beer.

"Tim!" Colin called over.

Tim raised his bottle in acknowledgement and wandered over to talk to Colin and Maggie.

"I hear you are expecting more tiny footsteps, congratulations, Maggie. And you of course, Colin."

***

The meal was almost finished. Bear was just polishing off the lump of blue Stilton while Rachael picked at the grapes. Jane brought through another cafetière of coffee.

"The boss's real name is what, Tim?" Bear laughed.

"Christian Cyril Hunter Wilson. He told me himself." Tim grinned. "He swore me to secrecy, though."

"Like that was ever going to work!" Bear grinned.

"Christian Cyril. I knew his dad was a minister, but that's harsh!" Rachael smiled.

"Please let me call him Cyril, just once!" Mel joked.

"Why would you do that? Don't you like life?" Bear nudged her.

"Is he coming to the wedding, Jane?" Tim asked.

"Yes. With Meera, apparently."

"Our hotel's been taken over. I noticed the General Manager has the same name as George's nephew. And Mel has tracked down that his nephew works for this group." Rachael commented.

"It can't be a coincidence," Tim said.

"No, chances are it's that same man." Rachael said. "It's nice to feel there is a link back to George, although he doesn't have anything to do with us. He's too high up the food chain. As General Manager, I suppose he's in charge of all the Scottish hotels."

Suddenly, the room fell quiet and the mood became sombre.

"We are going to miss George so much on our big day," Jane said sadly. "Do you know he gave us a first edition of Ian Fleming's *Diamonds are Forever* as a wedding gift? Lord knows what it cost him, and now he's gone, I feel so guilty."

"You know the last thing George would want is to upset you," Mel said.

"I know, but we don't seem to be making any progress on finding out who murdered George or why he was killed," Jane said.

"Actually, I think the boss may be making some progress," Tim said. "He and I went to speak to Ian Thomson yesterday.

Thomson wouldn't say much, but he did know that The Lizard is here, and seemed to think that he's on a job."

"What kind of job?" Bear asked.

"Don't know, and Ian Thomson didn't say, even if he knew. But he hinted that The Lizard is available for hire and is pretty unscrupulous."

"We all know that," Jane said.

"We also know that George was accused of killing Hans Merkel – whose son Max is in the city talking to The Lizard." Rachael emptied the remains of a bottle of red wine into her glass.

"Shall I open another of these?" Jane asked, holding up the empty bottle.

"Why not? Maggie can't drink and is driving Colin home, and Tim's butler is taking us home as well as Tim!" Mel smiled.

"You have a butler?" Sarah asked Tim in an incredulous tone of voice.

"Long story. My father's staff really. I just live in his house for the time being. Anyway, I can't see Max Merkel getting involved in anything dubious. He is a very highly-regarded art dealer. My father knows him personally."

"Not much of a recommendation right now, Tim," Bear said.

Tim grinned. "Careful, Bear, or you'll be walking home."

***

"Clouseau! Come to join us for a pint, and are you going to manage to save this darts match for us?" Tom from the darts team called to Hunter as he walked into The Persevere Bar.

It was the first time Hunter had been there since he had spent the night at Meera's. He wondered if his friends would notice any difference in him.

"Thanks, Tom," he said, accepting his drink. "Is the whole team here already?"

"Are we never not all here by the time you arrive? I have never known a darts player play more final legs than you! On you go, then." Tom grinned at Hunter. "And stop smiling: this is a serious business."

It was almost impossible to stop smiling. Hunter was so happy that things with Meera were getting on track at last. Then he thought about George. He must have had such a sad, scared life: no family here, never married, just his job and his books for company. What a lonely life, what a dreadful death. What strange entries in Arjun Mansoor's prison visiting records.

"Hunter, focus!" Tom shouted.

Hunter pushed his thoughts aside to concentrate on winning the match for the team.

Chapter Eighteen

Hunter and Tim arrived at The Bruce Hotel, accompanied by two uniformed officers, in time for breakfast. The warmth of the hotel dining room combined with smells of bacon, coffee, disinfectant and furniture polish to make a distinctive smell. They spotted The Lizard alone at a table with a croissant and a copy of the *Financial Times*. He was smartly dressed in a grey pin-stripe suit and tie. They strode towards him.

"Didn't know you could read, Lizard," Hunter commented as he pulled out a chair beside him.

"Ha, ha, your jokes don't get any better, Detective Sergeant Wilson. Long time no see. It's been lovely."

"Never mind my jokes, and it's Detective *Inspector* Wilson to you." Hunter nodded to Tim to take the seat on The Lizard's other side.

"He's a big lad, isn't he? Must have eaten his porridge," The Lizard said. Then looking at Tim, he added, "You must be that lying cheating bastard, Peter fucking Myerscough's son. You look too much like him to be anyone else."

"I am, and I'm an even bigger bastard than my father, who's *Sir* Peter fucking Myerscough to you," growled Tim.

"I heard he's in the big house."

"Will your friends be joining you for breakfast, Mr Pratt?" The young waiter came over and started pouring coffee for Hunter and Tim.

"These are no friends of mine, Gustav, and they won't be staying for breakfast."

"Of course, Mr Pratt. You are looking very smart this morning, Sir. No tracksuit for your usual morning jog like before?"

"I had time to shower and change after my run today,

Gustav. That will be all, thank you." Lenny The Lizard dismissed the waiter with a wave.

"Good service here," Hunter commented.

Lenny smiled. "It is why I use *Gemuetliche Erholung* hotels whenever I can. The staff all know me."

"And do they know that your friends Arjun Mansoor and Ian Thomson are in prison?" Hunter asked.

"No friends of mine. I'm with Ian Thomson's old lady now. He's no too happy about it, but she's a fine woman. And Arjun's a fool."

"What makes you say that about Arjun? I thought he was a friend of yours?"

"He was an associate, that's true. He's not much of a businessman, though. Thought he could take over the supply of snow to Scotland. You can't do that single-handed. That's why he got caught."

"So how would you do it, Lizard?" Hunter asked.

"Goodness, me, Inspector, I'm not that kind of man."

"What kind of man are you, then? You've stolen your friend's wife, assaulted his son and threatened his nephew. That's not a nice kind of man. It's certainly not one who would think twice about making off with an old car as well."

"I did not steal the lovely Janice. Is it my fault if she could not resist my charms? And I was there when poor Jamie was injured, but he did not suffer at my hand. And Frankie, young Frankie, maybe he misunderstood what I said. Anyway, the stupid bastards lost my fucking car, didn't they? I only wanted to collect it after a bit of a service. You know, to give Ian a bit of business in his time of difficulty."

"What do you mean, it was *your* car, Lizard?" Hunter asked. "Jamie said the mechanic at Thomson's Top Cars was told there was a buyer willing to pay eight grand for the car by the customer who took it in. And that wasn't you. What would make you think you could get it for zip-all?"

"And why was a ten-year-old Volvo worth breaking the boy's arm for?" Tim added. "What was in the car that made it so valuable?"

"I always thought of the car as mine. Sentimental value,

only, really, for that old car. It belongs to my dear old mum."

"Funny name you mother's got, Keith Black," Tim said quietly. "When did she move to Folkestone? Was it for her sex change?"

"Well, perhaps I did leave out a few details." Lenny The Lizard had the good grace to blush.

"I think we'll need to chat about this in more detail down at the station. Lizard, my colleagues will drive you there. DC Myerscough and I have other business here."

The two uniformed officers led The Lizard to the police car outside the hotel.

***

"Now, young Myerscough," Hunter said, "let's find your friend Max Merkel, shall we? You take the lead, he'll recognise your family name."

"I don't know him, but I know of him, Boss. He and my dad have done business, so, yes, I'm sure he'll know the name."

The detectives went to the reception desk to find out which room was occupied by Merkel, and took the lift to the top floor. Hunter knocked on the door and stood back so that Tim was in line of sight. The door was opened abruptly by a man on the phone in agitated conversation. His English was highly accented and difficult to follow; his meaning was not. He was extremely angry about something.

Hunter and Tim entered the spacious suite and stood quietly waiting for him to finish.

"Apologies. Herren Katz and Roundall, is it not?"

"No, Mr Merkel," Tim glanced at Hunter. "I am Detective Constable Myerscough and this is Detective Inspector Wilson, we are from Lothian and Borders Police."

"*Mein Gott!* Not more problems. Can no fool in this country get anything right? What now?"

"What do you mean?" Tim asked. "Who has been creating problems for you, sir?"

"You don't know? Then no matter. I am trying to obtain a valuable book collection that I understood was to be valued by

Katz and Roundall, and it seems to have gone 'up into the air', I think you say. It does not fill me with confidence for the auction I try to arrange with them."

"A collection has gone missing? What kind of collection? This could be very serious," Hunter said.

"A valuable collection of first edition books was to be available from Katz and Roundall and it is now not. And there is no sign of it anywhere. Very odd. The owner died, you know."

"Indeed, that does seem odd," Hunter said softly.

"Anyway, how can I help the police, when I have just arrived in your country?" Merkel paused and looked at Tim. "What do you say your name is? Myerscough? You must be your father's son," the man laughed. "I mean you must be the son of my client Sir Peter Myerscough, you are very like your father in the face, but more tall."

"Yes, I get told that a lot," Tim smiled.

"We just wanted a brief word with you, Mr Merkel. Are you happy to speak here?" Hunter asked.

"Yes, we will sit at the table. Shall I order coffee?"

"Thank you, but I don't think we'll be that long," Hunter replied.

"Fine. Now, what is the matter?"

"You were seen yesterday in the hotel lounge speaking to a Mr Lenny Pratt. Do you know him well?"

"I did sit with another guest, we were alone in the bar and joined each other for a quiet drink. I do not think we exchanged names. I certainly have never seen him before."

Tim took out his notebook and jotted down Merkel's reply.

"I think your father died when you were very young, Mr Merkel," Hunter said.

"He was murdered when I was only three years old. It was a very bad act. Especially hard on my mother."

"Of course. It must have been. Did you know that George Reinbold, the man accused of that murder, lived here, in Edinburgh?"

"Lived? He has died?"

"He was murdered a few days ago."

92

"That is good news. I have waited a long time to know this," Merkel said defiantly.

"Do you know who committed this crime?" Hunter asked, in a measured tone of voice.

"I do not think of it as a crime. I think it is only karma for the justice that evil man ran away from decades ago."

"His family suffered," Hunter said.

"So did mine."

"Did you have anything to do with George Reinbold's death?"

"Sadly no, but I will happily reward the hero when you identify them."

"Did you arrange for George Reinbold to be killed?"

"No, I did not. How could I, when I did not know he was here?"

"What brought you to Edinburgh, then?"

"It is a beautiful city with many great art galleries and auction houses. I wanted to view, and perhaps secure, some articles before I move south to the galleries and auction houses of London, Amsterdam and Paris. I love Paris in the springtime." Merkel smiled.

Hunter nodded. "Just one more thing, do you know a Mr. Arjun Mansoor, Mr Merkel?"

"Indeed, yes. I have a client by that name. He has a wonderful eye for gold jewellery and Middle Eastern furnishings. His purchases are always most tasteful. Just like your father's," he looked at Tim.

"Thank you, Mr Merkel." Hunter stood up. "Will you be here long?"

"I had only planned to stay a few days, but now I think I may stay to watch that criminal's end. I would very much like to watch him burn here, before he burns in hell. When will the funeral be?"

"I couldn't say, sir. The body has not been released," Hunter said.

"No matter, after so many decades, what's a few days? Goodbye, gentlemen." Merkel held the door open for Hunter and Tim.

On the way back to reception Hunter turned to Tim and said, "I want to know when Merkel actually arrived in Edinburgh. It didn't feel to me that time had healed many wounds there."

"No, Sir, I think the milk of human kindness may have curdled. Funny what he said about that book collection. Do you think it was George's he was talking about?"

"I do. I'll find out from Jane exactly what she said to Katz and Roundall when she took the *Winnie the Pooh* book to be valued. I'm so glad I took the books to my father, for all sorts of reasons now. I'm not happy that he knows Mansoor. He is always bad news. Before we go back to the station, let's see if we can get hold of Heinrich Reinbold. I would like to talk to him, too."

***

"You were lucky to catch me, detectives; I was about to leave for a meeting in Glasgow, concerning our new hotel there. Again, it is very central, we are pleased with the move into Scotland." Heinrich Reinbold smiled a bright white straight-toothed smile that must have cost a fortune. His thick head of dark blond hair was not so much styled as coiffed, and his chin was covered in designer stubble. He looked high-maintenance.

"When did you arrive in Edinburgh, Mr Reinbold?" Hunter asked.

"I arrived here at the beginning of the month. First, I was in Glasgow. Then this hotel joined our chain last week. I wanted to be in Edinburgh to see the contract finalised and be here for that. Aberdeen is next month, but I plan to make Edinburgh my home base."

"Have you visited anybody since you arrived?"

"What do you mean? I have visited a real estate agent and signed on to the register of a doctor, and had a most agreeable visit with a young Vietnamese woman at The Empire Massage Suite in Lothian Road."

"Indeed, Mr Reinbold. Did you visit a Mr Arjun Mansoor or

perhaps any relatives?"

"I do not know that name, and I am the last living member of my family, DI Wilson. Due to an unfortunate incident before I was born, most of my family were killed or tortured by the Stasi. I am a soul all alone in the world."

"You are now, sir, but until a few days ago a man who I believe was your uncle, George Reinbold, was alive, and had been living here since he was a young man. Did you know that?" Hunter stared into Heinrich's eyes.

"My uncle was George Reinbold, but how could I know that? He escaped from the *Deutsche Demokratische Republik* and was never heard from again. It was particularly hard on my mother. She was his twin sister and loved him very much. She was always loyal to him, but she had me, so life was not easy. She forgave him; I never could."

"He was well-respected here, but he was violently murdered, only a few days ago, after you arrived here. Do you know anything about that?"

"No. Had I known my uncle lived here I might have made a point to meet him. Or maybe instead I would have taken the job in Paris." Heinrich's voice became increasingly quiet. He avoided meeting Hunter's searching gaze.

Hunter drew the meeting to a close. He was now sure that Heinrich was George's nephew. He did not think any of the three men were telling him the whole truth or even all they knew, but at least he had a chance to have another go at The Lizard.

***

Hunter and Tim were on their way back to the station when a call came through to inform them of a person of interest who had been stopped at Edinburgh Airport on his way into the country.

"It seems they had a tip-off that somebody on the flight from Paris was a cocaine courier," Hunter said to Tim. "This fellow was stopped at immigration. He was sweating profusely and did not look well."

"With reactions like that, he sounds like an internal carrier," said Tim.

"I agree, but the interesting thing is he doesn't have much English, but he does have a name and address on a note inside his passport."

"What was it?"

"I don't know that, yet. He's been taken over to the Western General Hospital for a scan, so let's swing over there, before we head back to the ranch."

"No problem, Boss," Tim said as he changed direction and headed for the hospital. But what about The Lizard?"

"The Lizard can wait."

***

When they arrived and found their way to the Outpatients Department, a couple of uniformed officers were standing near the traveller. He looked sleepy.

"Do we know his name?" Hunter asked them.

"His passport says Hadi Akram, but he won't say anything."

"What was the name and address on the note he was carrying?"

The Constable got the piece of paper out of his jacket pocket and handed it to Hunter.

"Tim, isn't that Arjun Mansoor's old address?" Hunter passed the note to Tim.

"Yes, it is. I suppose his wife still lives there."

"But the name is different: Kasim Saleh. Maybe I'll pay them a visit."

"Do you want me to go and check on The Lizard's mum while we're here, Boss?"

"You do that, I'll check with the doctors and find out if Mr Akram is likely to survive. I'll meet you back at the car. Good work, officers."

Hunter left the PCs to guard Mr Akram.

Chapter Nineteen

It was early evening when Jamie clambered out of the taxi that had brought him home from the hospital. He was glad to be out; the nurses weren't as pretty as the last time he had been in, and with his arm in this cast, he couldn't do much. He was also glad to see Frankie had got someone guarding the house. He didn't care what the neighbours thought. He was sick about his Jenny: dead in the boot of a car. He knew her mam hadn't liked him before – she must hate him now.

He wandered up the path and unlocked the front door, nursing his broken arm. He slipped off his jacket and went first to the kitchen where he got a can of beer out of the fridge. Then he heard Frankie coming down the stairs.

"Thanks for coming in quietly, cuz. That's the girls off to sleep at last," Frankie said. "Suppose I'm making tea again? What do you want to eat? Fish and chips, pie and chips or sausage and chips?"

"Dunno."

"Baked beans or peas?"

"Don't care."

"Jamie, you've got to eat. Starving yourself'll no bring Jenny back."

"Aye."

"How about pie and baked beans and chips?"

"A Govan salad?"

"Okay."

"I wonder why The Lizard and his muscle Brian Squires were so angry about that fucking old Volvo? I mean, who cares about an old car like that?" Jamie asked.

"Was it The Lizard that brought it in?"

"No. I'd have known him. He's with my mam."

"That's what I thought. So why us? Looks like they used the showroom as a collection point again, do you think?"

"That's the sort of thing fucking Mansoor would do, cuz. Let's eat and think about this. I'll phone that pretty little copper after."

***

When they had finished their meal, Frankie cleared the plates away and went to wash the dishes. He didn't want his twins growing up in a dirty home, and he knew by now, after living with Jamie for a few months, the only way to have the place clean and tidy was to do it himself.

"You okay to tidy up and do the dishes while I phone Mel at the cop-shop, Frankie?"

"Aye, like you're gonny do it if I don't," Frankie grumbled.

While Frankie went to make himself busy, he saw Jamie take out his phone and call Fettes Police Station. He saw how awkward it was for Jamie with only one hand, but didn't offer to help. Jamie never offered to help him, so let him struggle.

***

Calling the police to offer them help was not something Jamie had ever really seen himself doing in the past. But it wasn't the cops who broke his arm, and they did seem to be trying to do right by him and Frankie. Anyway, DC Mel Grant was pretty, and that big blond one, Myerscough, had been decent to him and Frankie when Brian Squires came in shouting the odds. Pity he hadn't been there when the oaf came back with The Lizard.

"Aye, hello, can I speak to Mel? Aye, DC Grant, that's her. Well, can she call me back? It's Jamie Thomson. It's important. Oh aye, she's got my number pal. We're tight." Jamie left his number anyway and flung himself down on the big, black reclining chair that he thought of as his seat. He had no sooner talked Frankie into getting them another beer when the phone rang.

98

"Yep," Jamie said as he picked up the phone. "Mel, darlin'! How lovely to hear your sweet voice. I knew you couldn't resist calling me back."

"Jamie, you called me saying it was important. What's going on? You and Frankie haven't got into any more trouble have you?"

"No. Not at all. I'm doing you a favour. Not the one I'd like to do you, but a favour anyway."

"Get on with it Jamie, I'm a busy person."

Jamie could hear she was getting irritated, so he stopped playing the smart arse and began to explain his thoughts.

"Yes. Well, do you remember the big fat guy who came into the garage when you and Blondie were there?"

"DC Myerscough. Yes."

"Well, Squires came back with The Lizard and broke my arm when he heard we'd lost the old Volvo."

"So I heard. My guess is it wasn't your beer-drinking arm. You on the mend?"

"I'll get there. I'll soon have two arms to put around you, darlin'."

"That won't be happening any time soon, Jamie. But this is all old news. What's so important?"

"Well, I was there when the car was brought in, and it wasn't Squires or The Lizard that brought it. I knew it wasn't Squires when he tried to get it back the first time he came, when you were there. And I'd have recognised Lenny The Lizard anyway. He's with my mam now."

"Who was it?"

"I don't know. Not anybody I knew. I've been trying to think. I can't remember much, but it was a guy with a foreign accent."

"What did he look like?"

"Black hair, beard, ordinary really."

"Do you remember what he was wearing?"

"Dunno. Just a suit, I think. Nothing special, but smart enough. A suit. Looked like a businessman who needed to get his car seen to. What do they look like?"

"Businessmen don't usually run around in ten-year-old cars.

Not successful businessmen, anyway, do they, Jamie?"

"Well this one did."

"What colour was his suit, Jamie?"

"I don't know. Dark, grey, something like that, I suppose. It was nothing special."

"Who took the car for the test drive with Jenny?"

"If I knew that, I wouldn't be calling you. I'd have killed the tosser myself."

"Would Gary have seen the man who went out with Jenny?"

"No, he'd gone home by then. He's left altogether since Jenny was found. Frankie saw the man though, I think. Wait." Jamie put his hand over the mouthpiece. "Frankie, did you see the man who wanted to take the Volvo for a run?"

"Aye, but I didn't know what he wanted cos I was leaving as he went in. But I suppose it was the same one. Jenny said she'd help him and I could just go. I wish I'd stayed now."

"Jamie, can I speak to Frankie?" Mel asked.

"Okay. I suppose so, but no flirting," Jamie teased as he handed the phone to his cousin.

"Frankie, what did the man you saw look like?" Mel asked.

"I don't know. About my height; maybe, five nine, five ten-ish, light brown hair, a beard. Sharp dresser, nice grey suit, light grey shirt and a tie. Don't see a tie so much now, really," Frankie said thoughtfully.

"I'll need a statement from you about this, Frankie. I'll call over to the showroom tomorrow. Pass the phone back to Jamie, will you?"

Mel arranged to see Jamie at the showroom the following day too, then ended the call.

"Hey, Frankie, if that pretty wee copper is coming to the showroom tomorrow, I'll need to take a shower and so I'll be all smart and looking great: she won't be able to resist me," Jamie said.

"I only see two problems with this, Jamie: one, she has managed to have no trouble resisting your chat so far, and two, you need to keep your cast on that arm dry."

"That's where you come in, my man. Can you get a black plastic bag and some packing tape out of the kitchen and help

100

me cover up me cast?"

"Aye, hang on," Frankie murmured.

He came back with the bag and tape that Jamie had asked for and a sharp pair of kitchen scissors. The young men bickered and argued.

"You need to take your shirt off, you'll no get it over the bag," Frankie said.

"Aye, and you'll need to tape the hand end as well as at the elbow. Don't stick that tape to my skin, it'll rip all my skin out and take my hair off and hurt tae buggery."

"Shut it, Jamie! You wake the twins and you'll be sorting this yourself."

The rest of the procedure was conducted in silence. When Jamie was happy that the results would keep his arm dry, he crept upstairs to take his shower.

***

Frankie watched Jamie climb the stairs then glanced at his own face in the living room mirror. His acne was not as bad as it had been before the twins were born, but the pimples and blackheads that stared back at him still caused him grief. Then Frankie had an idea. A stroke of genius. While Jamie and the girls were upstairs he had the kitchen to himself, so he would give his face the scrub he was sure would sort the problem. He rummaged around under the kitchen sink and found one of those little sponges for washing the dishes. It was soft on one side and rough on the other. Frankie smiled as he set about his plan. He lathered the washing-up liquid in his hands. It cut the grease on the dishes; he hoped it would work on his skin as well. He stood at the kitchen sink and rubbed the lather over his face and neck and then picked up the little sponge. He rubbed the rough side firmly down the sides of his nose and across the crease of his chin. It hurt. It must be doing him good.

Frankie went back to peer at himself in the mirror in the living room before he decided to continue with his plan and rubbed the rough surface of the little sponge all over his face again. The pimples on his forehead and chin burst, but the spots on his cheeks were harder to rub away. Still, he scrubbed until his eyes watered with the pain and rinsed his face to wash away the muck. Rivulets of blood and a clear, sticky stuff dribbled from the lesions. Frankie grabbed a clean tea-towel out of the drawer and patted his face dry. When he went back to the living room mirror, his face looked red, raw and sore. Maybe this had not been one of his best ideas.

When Jamie returned to the room, he was clean and freshly-shaved in anticipation of seeing Mel the following day. His dressing gown covered his modesty because he would need Frankie's help to remove the makeshift cover from his cast.

"Frankie! What the hell have you done, man? You look like a scraped pig!" Jamie shouted when he saw his cousin's face.

"Sssh. You dope, you'll wake the twins, Jamie."

"You've done that to your face and say I'm the dope? I don't think so," Jamie replied.

"I just thought I'd do my best for tomorrow too and give myself a good scrub," Frankie whined.

"Well, I can see you've done that, but it's not a good look, Frankie. Don't look so miserable, lad, we'll think of something."

"What?"

"I've got it! Go and get the bag of stuff you keep for the twins."

Frankie looked at him doubtfully, but went to get the bag.

"Is this what you use for their arses?" Jamie asked, taking their cream out and holding it up.

"Aye," Frankie said.

"Well, Frankie, lad, if it can keep the wee ones' nappy rash under control, your scrubbed face should be a dawdle."

Frankie rubbed the antiseptic cream all over his suffering skin. Then he sat for the rest of the evening trying to ignore Jamie's jibes that he looked like a spooky clown with the thick layer of white cream covering his face.

***

102

Mel was pleased with the new details she had learned from the boys. Getting it out of Jamie and Frankie might have been like pulling teeth, but it could be important. She was looking forward to sharing the information at tomorrow morning's briefing.

***

Hunter decided he would ask Jane to accompany him to Arjun Mansoor's home. If the wife was living there with only her young son, it might be better to be accompanied by a female officer.

Finding a place to park in Gillespie Crescent was never simple at the best of times, and the double red lines on the corner between Gillespie Crescent and Bruntsfield Place didn't make it any easier. Hunter had to go up and down the street twice before successfully squeezing into a space. He rang the doorbell, and Jane had hardly swept a non-existent piece of fluff from her jacket before the door was opened promptly, almost aggressively. The frown on the face of the occupant changed instantly to bewilderment.

"Who are you?"

"Mr Saleh? I am Detective Inspector Hunter Wilson, and this is my colleague, Detective Sergeant Jane Renwick. May we come in?"

A small woman bustled from a room at the end of the corridor. The only word she said that Hunter understood was 'Kasim'.

"Mrs Mansoor, I hope you are well," Jane said in a conciliatory tone.

Neither Hunter nor Jane understood the words the woman spoke as she disappeared again, but they knew she was not pleased to see them.

"Mr Kasim Saleh, may we come in?" Hunter said again.

The man waved Hunter and Jane into a sumptuously-furnished sitting room and closed the door.

"You are Mr Kasim Saleh?" Hunter asked. He looked at the man solemnly. He was shorter than Hunter's five feet eleven inches, had black hair and a well-trimmed beard, and wore brown chinos, a light blue shirt and a navy cashmere jumper.

"How do you know my name?" the man asked.

"A traveller from Paris carried your name and this address, Mr Saleh. He does not speak English. He became ill at the Airport and has been taken to hospital."

"Who is he?" Saleh asked.

"His passport bears the name 'Hadi Akram'."

The man looked down and did not meet Hunter's gaze. "I am not familiar with that name. I will go and ask my sister, maybe she knows the man."

As he left, Jane whispered to Hunter, "So he must be Mansoor's brother-in-law?"

Hunter held his finger to his lips and nodded.

"No she does not know the name either," Mr Saleh said as he re-entered the room. "Maybe a friend or a relative gave out the name and address and forgot to tell us. It happens with our family."

"That must be it. Thank you for the explanation, Mr Saleh," Hunter said. "I am sorry to have troubled you. Thank you for taking the time to see us and helping to explain the note the traveller was carrying."

"I am happy, of course. The traveller, he will recover, I hope?"

"I'm sure he will, but he was taken to hospital because he was suspected of carrying a great deal of cocaine in his body. If that is found to be so, he will be in hospital for a while, then he will spend a long time in prison for drug trafficking. Anyway, thank you, and please apologise to your sister for us. We did not mean to cause Mrs Mansoor any distress."

"How long will you be staying here, Mr Saleh?" Jane asked as she followed Hunter towards the door.

"I will stay with my sister while I am taking care of some business for her and her husband, while he is unable to deal with matters freely. Then, of course, I will return to my wife, my home and my own business interests." The man stood at the door until the detectives climbed into their car and drove away.

104

Chapter Twenty

DCI Allan Mackay called for silence in the briefing room. He was always curious as to why every briefing room he had visited, up and down the country, smelled of coffee and bacon. He watched Bear lick some grease off his fingers and smiled. Colin popped an apple core into his mouth and crunched on it. Mackay watched him with a grimace. That couldn't be good for you.

"We have a lot to cover this morning. DI Wilson, I think you can start us off?"

"Thank you, Sir, Yes." Hunter stood up and cleared his throat. "Tim and I went across to The Bruce Hotel in Belford Road, yesterday. Jane and Rachael had noticed that Lenny The Lizard Pratt was staying there. Jane?"

Jane explained what she and Rachael had seen, and added, for the others' information, that they had taken a photo of the two men and that Tim had been able to identify the other party as the art dealer Max Merkel.

"I brought The Lizard in to finish questioning him," Hunter continued, when Jane had finished. "He was not helpful, and he's out on bail."

"On what grounds did you bring him in?" Mackay asked.

"Assault to severe injury, Sir," Tim replied. "He and his goon Brian Squires badly broke Jamie Thomson's arm at Thomson's Top Cars Showroom, but we couldn't hold him so he has been released on bail. He says he's only here to visit his poor old mum in the Western General Hospital."

"Do you believe him?" Mackay asked.

"Well, I've checked, and there is a Mrs Pratt in Ward 51."

"But The Lizard is bad news anytime, where ever he is," Hunter said. "He's always up to something."

"My view exactly." Mackay turned back to Hunter. "Where's Squires?"

"Back in Spain before we caught up with him, I believe. But I've marked his card, and the Spanish police will pick him up for us, if necessary. Anyway, next time he comes home to the UK he will be flagged up as being wanted in connection with an assault. My guess is The Lizard plans to be here, playing the doting son until his mother is fit to go home."

"Well he'll not be going back to Spain if he's only out on bail," Mackay said.

"That's the idea, sir," Hunter replied.

"Sir, Jamie Thomson phoned me yesterday with information," Mel said. "The Lizard had claimed the missing Volvo car from Thomson's Top Cars was his. When he discovered it had gone missing, he instructed Squires to break Jamie's arm as punishment. It was pretty harsh for an old car."

"Yes, Mel? What did the bold boy, Jamie, have to say?" Hunter asked.

"Well, Sir, Jamie said it wasn't Squires or The Lizard that brought the car into the showroom. It was a businessman with black hair and a beard."

"Can't be much of a businessman if his car's ten years old," Hunter observed.

"That's what I said," Mel added. "What I want to know is how The Lizard even knew the car was there, and why it was worth assaulting the wee muppet, Jamie."

"That is odd," Mackay agreed. "And what's the link between The Lizard and the man who took the car to Thomson's?"

"I don't know, Sir. By the descriptions Jamie and Frankie gave of the man who brought the car into the showroom and the man who asked to test-drive the Volvo, they were clearly different men. One had black hair and a beard, the other light brown hair and a beard."

"But they don't know who they are?" Jane asked.

"No, but they did say they both wore grey suits." Mel looked up from her notes.

"Fabulous!" Jane rolled her eyes.

"We were also informed of a passenger on a flight from Paris to Edinburgh. The man was found to be carrying a quantity of cocaine internally. We went to see him at the hospital. He was carrying a card with the name 'Kasim Saleh' on it, and Arjun Mansoor's address."

"How interesting," Mackay commented. "Did you manage to speak to the passenger?"

"He claims to speak no English, Sir. So Jane and I went to Mansoor's home. I thought it would be best to attend with a female officer in case Mrs Mansoor was alone in the property."

"Very wise, Hunter."

"Thank you, Sir. We did see Mrs Mansoor there, but also the Mr Kasim Saleh named on the card. It transpires he is Mrs Mansoor's brother. He says he's here on business for Arjun Mansoor, while Mansoor is inside."

"What kind of business?"

"Well, Sir, he didn't volunteer, and I didn't press him. You see, I didn't want to arouse his suspicions. Because when I had a look at Mansoor's prison visitor records, I'd noticed that the only four people who have ever visited Mansoor are his wife, his lawyer Donald Blair, Lenny The Lizard Pratt and Kasim Saleh. I plan to go over to Saughton again to find out anything more I can about Saleh."

"Keep me in the loop, Hunter. Now, anything on Merkel?"

"Tim and I found Merkel in his suite at The Bruce Hotel and spoke to him. He had certainly not mellowed in his feelings towards George Reinbold over the passage of time. And Mansoor is one of his clients."

"Really? That man is everywhere, like a bad smell," Mackay said.

"What has Merkel got to do with George, again?" Nadia Chan asked.

"Gillian Pearson discovered that before George came to this country, he was accused of killing Merkel's father," Hunter replied.

"Goodness! I thought George was one of the good guys?" Nadia said.

"He was," Hunter answered. "He was only a kid when the charge was made. And life in East Germany was no picnic when George was growing up. The Stasi controlled the country with a mixture of violence, fear and misinformation."

"Probably why he came to Scotland. To get away from the Stasi," Tim said.

"I know I would, if I'd been in East Germany," Bear added.

"We also managed to speak to George's nephew, Heinrich Reinbold," Hunter continued. "He has come to Edinburgh as General Manager of the hotels his company is opening in Scotland. The Bruce is one of the ones they have taken over. He claimed not to know that his uncle lived in the city and that he thought he was the only surviving member of his family. But he could not meet my gaze."

"Why is he here?" Mackay asked.

"New promotion, Sir. His company runs a chain of hotels and they are spreading into Scotland this year. The company is called *Gemuetliche Erholung,* and The Bruce is the hotel in Edinburgh that has been bought by the chain. They haven't changed the name of the hotel; it's just the ownership that has transferred. Heinrich certainly had no warm, happy memories of his Uncle George."

"I see," Mackay said.

"Jane, I want you and Bear to gather photos of The Lizard, Squires, Merkel and Heinrich Reinbold. Show them to your witness. I know she is elderly, but they might just help jog her memory. I am sure there will be photos on line you can download," Hunter said.

"Yes, Sir,"

"Mel, you and I will go and have a chat with Jamie and Frankie to see if they recognise anyone from photos too."

"Yes, Boss."

"Nadia and Colin, I want you to trace that Volvo as closely as you can from when it comes back through the Channel Tunnel all the way up the road to Edinburgh. You must be able to get a look at the driver at some point."

"Yes, Sir," they said in unison.

"Tim, you and Rachael take over finding out all you can

108

about Max Merkel and Heinrich Reinbold. Liaise with Gillian Pearson in case her translations can add anything to our knowledge." Hunter paused, and then continued, "Jane, when you went to Katz and Roundall, did you say the *Winnie the Pooh* book formed part of a collection that we would need to have valued?"

"I think I said something about there being more books. Why, Sir?"

"Did you give George Reinbold's name?"

"No, I didn't have to. It was on the packaging. One of the assistants wrote it down, along with his address."

"Did they indeed?"

"I just thought it was procedure, Boss. I didn't think anything of it," Jane said

"You weren't meant to, Jane." Hunter looked across at Tim. "But that's our leak."

Chapter Twenty-One

Meera stared at the results she had received from Forensics. Hope died inside her: the skinny little corpse found tied up in the boot of the car was without doubt Jenny Kozlowski. DNA confirmed that. Meera already knew – the reaction of Jenny's mother had left her in little doubt – but now the strands from Jenny's hairbrush were compared with DNA from the corpse, and the evidence was complete.

The cause of death (suffocation) did not surprise Meera, but what did surprise her was the high concentration of cocaine in Jenny's system. The young woman had no history of drug abuse, but she had been bound and gagged and put in that boot with cocaine packed all around her. The high quality Class A drug flowed into her lungs with every breath she took. The beast who left her there, before he torched the car, knew she would die – and had even left a sealed packet of cocaine rather than move her. Callous brute. When as the car burned and the oxygen was sucked away from Jenny, she must have been terrified: gasping for air, struggling, trying to scream. What a horrible way to die, Meera thought. George's death was wicked, but at least it was quick. She sent a copy of the forensic report to Hunter.

All of a sudden Meera did not like her job. She felt helpless, when all she had ever wanted to do was help.

***

In contrast to Meera's misery, Colin and Nadia were almost dancing around the office. There was no doubt about the car: the registration matched that of the burnt-out vehicle Jane and Rachael had found, and they now had a picture of the driver.

They had sat for hours in front of the screen with a bag of dried apricots between them, munching their way through the CCTV footage, and it had eventually yielded the information they needed. The driver had managed to drive from Folkestone to York without them getting a clear picture of him. Now they had one. Excellent. Unfortunately they did not know who he was. But at least they had his picture.

They watched as their glee turned to dismay when the driver parked in the multi-storey car park at Edinburgh Airport. They watched him exit the car park and walk smartly into the terminal. They followed his progress into the gents, but they never saw him leave.

"Fuck, fuck, fuck, fuck, fuck!" Colin's shout increased in volume as he stretched back in his chair.

"The big beard was a disguise, wasn't it?" Nadia asked quietly.

"He was probably wearing a wig too. Who went in and who went out of that gents' lavvy? Fuck!" Colin shouted again.

"Let's see who picks up the car, shall we?" Nadia suggested.

They both looked at the screen and saw the car leave the airport premises. It was driven by a smartly-dressed man with a neatly-trimmed black beard and short black hair. He wore a grey pin-striped suit. Again, Colin and Nadia did not know the man, but they followed the car on the CCTV footage as he drove directly to Thomson's Top Cars. The CCTV in the garage was not working, but they saw him turn off the main road towards the showroom. At that point Colin and Nadia decided to take a break.

"Shall I begin write this up for the boss, and you make the tea?" Colin suggested.

***

Jane and Bear visited Florence Roberts.

"Come in!" the old lady called from her living room.

"Good morning, Mrs Roberts," Jane said.

"Oh it's you, dear, how nice to see you. Just come in and

take a seat. I leave my door unlocked during the day, that way I don't have to get up if anybody comes."

"It's not very safe, Mrs Roberts," Bear said softly. "It could be anybody."

"It is anybody: I don't know you."

Jane smiled. "Mrs Roberts, let me introduce my colleague, Detective Constable Winston Zewedu."

Bear went over and shook the old woman's hand. She was sitting by the window in a large green chair decorated with old lace antimacassars. The window ledge was covered with plants that looked as if they needed a good watering. In front of her, Mrs Roberts had a trolley on wheels that bore the dishes from her most recent meal, her glasses, and more pens than Bear thought she could ever have use for. The old lady was neatly dressed in black trousers, a pink twin-set and pearls. Although the room was suffocatingly warm, she also wore a dark green blanket draped over her shoulders.

"Would you like to make us a cup of tea?" Jane asked Bear.

"Of course, Sarge. How do you take your tea, Mrs Roberts?" Bear asked.

"Just like you, son – sweet and black," the old woman giggled.

Bear smiled and shook his head as he went away to make tea.

"Mrs Roberts, would it be all right to show you some photos to see if you recognise any of the men in them?" Jane asked.

"What, like the one what went to the door of the old man that died?"

"Yes, exactly like that. It could help us a lot. Would you mind having a look?"

"Ooh dear, you know I didn't really see his face very well? But I was looking out for my carer, so I wasn't wearing my glasses. Still, I'll try my best if you think it will help."

"That's all we ask, Mrs Roberts. We appreciate your help. I'll just wait until DC Zewedu comes back," Jane said.

"He'll be a witness to what I say, won't he? I watch Judge Judy and Judge Rinder so I know about that sort of thing."

112

Jane smiled and they waited for Bear.

"Here's your tea, Mrs Roberts," Bear said as he came back into the room.

The old lady sipped the tea Bear handed to her and frowned in concentration as she stared at each of the photos in turn.

"Does this look like the man you saw?" Jane asked showing Mrs Roberts a photo of The Lizard.

"I don't think so. The man I saw had a beard. This one just looks like he's no' shaved."

"He could have had more of a beard and just shaved it in that picture, perhaps?" Bear suggested.

"Not sure," Mrs Roberts said.

"What about this man?" Jane asked, showing a picture of Brian Squires.

"Good Lord, no! He looks like he's had the first one for lunch! It's no him."

"That's fine," Jane laughed, but was disappointed when Mrs Roberts wasn't sure about Max Merkel or Heinrich Reinbold either. So there were still three men of interest in relation to George's murder.

***

Tim took Max Merkel and Rachael took Heinrich Reinbold. They sat down with computers and phones and set a challenge between them as to who could find out most on their given suspect first.

Rachael did not take long to discover that Heinrich Reinbold's promotion to General Manager in Scotland had been offered rather than sought. When she spoke to the Human Resources department of *Gemuetliche Erholung* it was clear the man was held in high regard. He had been working for the company in a managerial role for over six years. When the plans to open establishments in the UK and Scandinavia started to come to fruition, the European General Manager's role was split between North and South. Heinrich Reinbold was offered the Northern role.

"And it will probably be split again between East and West

when we start opening in the Czech Republic, Poland and so on," the woman with faultless but slightly accented English told Rachael.

"Did Heinrich ask for the post that covered Scotland?" Rachael asked.

"It does not say so here. Heinrich was appointed to the Northern role. He did say he had family in Scotland, though, when he secured the position."

"Did he say what family?"

"We would not hold that detail, unless it was relevant to his work in some way, like for insurance, such as a wife or children. No, it does not say."

"Heinrich seems to be spending a great deal of his time in Scotland."

"With three hotels opening there in the next two months, that does not surprise me. He will have a great deal to do. I have no doubt, after that, when we have a hotel opening in Oslo and one in Bergen, he will be in Norway for large periods."

"I understand. That makes good sense. Thank you for your help, Magdalene." Rachael rang off and turned to Tim.

"I thought you said Heinrich Reinbold didn't know George was here."

"That's what he said to the boss and me."

"When he got his promotion to the new General Manager position, he told the company he had family in Scotland."

"He told us he believed he was the only surviving member of his family. So he lied to someone. How did he arrive here?"

"He travelled by Eurostar from Paris. Apparently, he chose to travel by train because of the amount of luggage he had."

"Yes, could be. It would also be easier to dismantle a gun and hide bits in different pieces of luggage to avoid detection," Tim mused.

"You have a devious mind, Tim Myerscough."

"I thought we went to special detective classes to develop just that," he smiled.

"Any info about Max Merkel?"

"Not much. He arrived by plane from Frankfurt to London,

initially, then flew up with British Airways, via Heathrow. Two large suitcases and one piece of hand luggage. Met at the airport by a pre-arranged limo driver who took him to The Bruce Hotel in Belford Road where he had reserved the suite on the top floor. That's where he was when we spoke to him."

"So everything hangs together for him?"

"Not quite. He said he didn't know that George lived here, but he asked his driver to take him to the hotel via Gilmerton."

"That's a strange route."

"The driver told him that, but Merkel was adamant he wanted to go that way."

"Merkel asked the driver to stop in George's street. He said an old friend of his father lived here and he wanted to be able to find the place again."

"Really?"

"The driver said he took a picture of a front door as they moved away."

"George's door, no doubt."

"I'd think so. But the driver couldn't be more specific than that. You want a coffee before we write this up?"

"Tea for me, please, Tim."

***

Hunter and Mel strode along George Street towards the Edinburgh office of Katz and Roundall. They would visit them before stopping by to see Jamie and Frankie.

The wide New Town streets were busy for this time of day. In the elegant New Town, where the buildings that were now shops, bars and offices had originally been built as fine Georgian town houses. People of great wealth and influence would have lived in those homes where the buildings lined broad avenues and open squares. The bustle of the city seemed civilised in these elegant surroundings. They watched shoppers going in and out of the upmarket boutiques and designer stores, and office workers and affluent residents going to enjoy food and drinks in chic hotels and atmospheric cocktail bars.

Hunter had always liked the New Town area of the city.

Today, he enjoyed the feeling of the fresh spring air on his face. Perhaps the cool breeze would calm his rage. He was angry. He was sure that somebody within the respected auction house of Katz and Roundall had let slip about George's book collection. He didn't know what their ulterior motive was, but he was sure they had one – and that thought made him furious.

His calm expression belied the turmoil he felt inside as he entered the auctioneer's elegant office. The quiet interior contrasted starkly with the bustle of the street outside. Hunter showed his identification at the desk and introduced Mel. The office manager appeared promptly to remove the police detectives from public view.

Hunter explained that Katz and Roundall had valued a book at this office. It had been delivered to a murder victim, and the police needed to confirm the valuation shown on the insurance declaration.

"Your staff were made aware that further valuations might be required, as the victim owned an extensive collection of first edition books."

"We would always take an interest in such a collection, and are delighted to be able to assist the boys in blue with such valuations as might be needed," the bumptious little man laughed.

"That's as maybe. Why did your staff member take a note of the victim's name and address?"

"That would only be required if we were asked to carry out the formal valuation, Detective Inspector Wilson. I have no note of that instruction, and those details are not on our file, so I think your colleague was mistaken. We have taken no such information."

"May I speak to June Dormer, who carried out the valuation, please?" Hunter asked impassively.

"I'm sorry, she's not available."

"Why not?"

"She is advising on art works for a new hotel chain in the city. Her husband also has important business here, so I do not expect her to be back this afternoon."

"Is she working at the *Gemuetliche Erholung*, who took

116

over The Bruce Hotel in Belford Road?"

"Possibly. What makes you think that?"

"Get her to call me as soon as she is available," Hunter handed over his card, then he and Mel left promptly.

"Would you like some lunch, Mel?" Hunter asked. "We could pop into The Livingroom? My treat."

"That's really kind of you, but won't that take a bit too long, Boss? It's a bit fancy, and waiter service."

"I am certainly due many hours from when I have worked through my lunch breaks, and I believe you are too. Let's stop in. It won't be the full three courses and coffee, mind," Hunter smiled.

"That would be very nice, Sir, thank you."

They walked into the busy restaurant and were shown to middle of the room where their small table had a crisp, white table cloth and linen napkins.

Hunter chose the fish & chips washed down by a large diet coke, while Mel settled on a salad with a side order of fries and a soda water and lime. As they waited for their meals to arrive they chatted quietly about Jane and Rachael's forthcoming union. Then Hunter suddenly fell silent and stared across the room. Mel's eyes followed his gaze.

"Who is that, Sir?"

"That is Kasim Saleh having lunch with The Lizard. Blow me down!"

"It doesn't look friendly. The Lizard seems to be very angry."

***

Hunter and Mel ate quickly so they could leave The Livingroom without The Lizard or Saleh noticing them. Hunter drove them to meet with Jamie and Frankie at Thomson's Top Cars.

"Mel, darlin' always good to see you!" Jamie called over. The lad completely ignored Hunter.

"Good afternoon, Jamie." Hunter said. "Is Frankie in too?"

"Yes, why? Am I not enough for you now, DC Grant?"

"Jamie, we have some photos," Mel said. "We wondered if either of you had seen any of these men before."

"We'll have a look. I'll go get Frankie."

Jamie went to the office at the far end of the building and walked back across the showroom with his cousin beside him.

Mel watched the two young men walked together, in step, and noticed that Frankie was wiping a fingernail on his trousers. She saw a small spot on his chin was bleeding, always a sign he was nervous. What did he have to be nervous about? She noticed he looked at the ground as he walked, that contrasted with the confident swagger in Jamie's step. Then, as Frankie got closer, she saw his face was red and sore. Poor Frankie and his bloody acne.

"Right, Frankie, let's see what we can do to help the police," Jamie smiled.

"We don't say that very often in our house," Frankie said.

"It's all for you, DC Grant," Jamie said to Mel.

Both Jamie and Frankie immediately identified the first two photos as Brian Squires and Lenny The Lizard Pratt. These were the men who had broken Jamie's arm. Hunter already knew this.

"Okay, Jamie, those are the easy questions," Hunter said.

Jamie then surprised Hunter by identifying the third photo as being the man who came into the showroom to test-drive the Bentley.

"Are you sure that's the same man?" Hunter asked for confirmation as he stood staring at the photo of Heinrich Reinbold.

"He didn't do ought wrong," Jamie said defensively. "He had a driving licence and he only wanted a test drive."

"Is it all right with you if we decide who broke the law, Jamie?" Mel asked.

"No need to be smart," Jamie frowned.

"My thoughts precisely, Jamie. Now, have a look at these photos, will you, boys?" Hunter asked.

"Never seen them," Jamie said.

"He was the one who came in as I was leaving," Frankie pointed to a picture of Max Merkel. "Or could it be him?"

Frankie asked pointing back to the picture of Heinrich Reinbold.

"Well which was it, Frankie?" Mel asked gently.

"It canny be him, he was with me, mind," Jamie said, pointing again to Heinrich's photo.

"No, I think it was this man, if he had a beard. Could he have had a beard and shaved it off?" Frankie asked.

Hunter stared miserably at the picture of DC Colin Reid that he had put in to cause confusion. He realised now that, with Frankie, artificial confusion was not required.

"No, I think it was him," Frankie pointed again to Merkel, but not in a way that left Hunter with any confidence.

Mel arranged to stop by the showroom the following day for Jamie and Frankie to sign their statements.

***

Hunter was pleased to make his escape back to his flat. He had so many overtime hours accrued to him that he did not feel a bit guilty clocking off an hour or so early today. He wanted everything to look as good as it could for this evening, himself included.

He tidied the living room, ran the vacuum over the floors, washed all the dishes that were lying in the kitchen and changed the bed. He thought about polishing the furniture, but settled on spraying the polish into the air to give a fresh smell. There were limits to his housework enthusiasm.

Hunter was taking Meera out to the cinema this evening. He would let her choose the film: he hoped she might go for *Welcome to the Punch* or *Parker,* but he really didn't mind. He was looking forward to spending the evening with her and, perhaps a bite to eat afterwards. Now that he had tidied his home, he could even invite her back at the end of the night.

When all the work was done, Hunter felt a bit sticky and sweaty all over. He should really clean and tidy on a more regular basis, but housework always came very low on his list of priorities. He doubted that would change, even for Meera, any time soon.

He jumped into the shower, washed himself thoroughly, and chose to wear a smart cotton blue-striped shirt, a brown V-necked sweater and smart blue chinos. He looked at himself in the mirror and nodded.

"That will have to do," he muttered, as he jogged down the stairs to the car.

He wanted to make sure he was at the cinema complex (Vue, on Leith Street) far too early, so Meera was not left waiting for him on her own. The place was always crowded, and not everybody was pleasant. He was beginning to feel quite protective about Meera. But she was so independent that he was sure she wouldn't approve of that, if she found out.

Hunter parked in the St James car park and crossed the street to the venue. As he looked across the busy foyer he was surprised to catch sight of Tim Myerscough smiling and laughing with Gillian Pearson. Hunter looked away, sharply. That was their own business, in their own time. Soon he noticed Meera arrive, and didn't give Tim or Gillian a second thought.

Chapter Twenty-Two

Today was going to be a busy day. Jane and Rachael had less than a week to finalise the arrangements for their wedding. They had made an appointment to see the florist early, before they went into work. The morning sky offered a pale blue background to the clouds bathed in pale pinks, greys and yellows, and the sun blinked through the strands of clouds, promising a lovely, warm spring day.

"I hope the sun is shining on our wedding day," Rachael smiled.

"Me too," Jane agreed. "Maybe one day we can get married for real, and not just this blessing of our civil partnership."

"This is our wedding, Janey, please," Rachael said firmly as they entered the shop.

"Trisha, it is so good of you to let us come in so early," Jane said to the florist.

"No problem. I have to get to the flower markets early anyway, and I have a complicated wreath to make for a funeral later in the week, so I wanted to get it started, sketching the design."

"Well, we appreciate it," Rachael said.

"Ooh, is this the design?" Jane asked.

"Yes, it is really unusual. The client wants me to put a copy of A A Milne's *Winnie the Pooh* in the centre, surrounded by yellow carnations and petunias. I rarely get asked to use these flowers because of their meaning."

"Gosh, do flowers have different meanings? What do these ones mean?" Rachael asked.

"The petunia is said to symbolise resentment and anger, while the yellow carnation is for rejection and disdain."

"Goodness! Don't use them in our bouquets. Who ordered

that, then?" Rachael asked.

"The man paid cash. I don't know his name."

"It must be quite an expensive wreath," Rachael said.

"Well above average. So I told him about the flowers, of course. He said they were favourite flowers of the deceased and nobody would care about the meaning. So I just do what I'm asked. First time I've ever had to put a book in a wreath, though. I'd have thought it would get destroyed quite quickly, given our weather!"

"What did he look like? What are the instructions for delivery to the funeral?" Jane said.

"He came in yesterday. He said the details of the funeral hadn't been fixed yet, but he'll phone me as soon as he has them."

"A bit vague for an expensive wreath like that," Jane said.

"Yes, if he hadn't paid up front, I wouldn't be doing anything yet. Now, let me try to remember: he was medium height, light brown hair, nothing special, a bit of a beard. The thing I noticed most was his accent. It was European, maybe German or Swiss, or even Belgian. Why are you so interested?"

"We have an interest in a case involving *Winnie the Pooh*," said Jane.

"Did he steal your honey?" Trisha joked.

"Not quite," Jane smiled.

"Come on now. No more talk of funerals. Let's see that you are happy with the style of bouquets for your big day."

***

"Right, people, can we have a bit of quiet?" DCI Allan Mackay called the briefing room to order. "Does anybody know where DI Wilson is?"

"Just behind you, Sir. I had to take a call." Hunter came in quietly carrying a large mug of coffee. There was no doubt, from the delicious smell, that it came from the coffee maker in his office, and was not the instant coffee available to most of those in the room.

"Jane, did Mrs Roberts identify the man she saw?" Hunter asked.

"No, Sir, but she did rule out Brian Squires."

Hunter nodded. "I think Squires only comes into play when The Lizard needs muscle. So he doesn't have to get his own hands dirty."

"We did learn something strange from our florist, though," Rachael commented.

"And?" asked Mackay.

"She has had an order for a funeral wreath with a copy of *Winnie the Pooh* in the centre and flowers meaning *I hate you* around the outside."

"That can only be for George's funeral. Do we have a date for that yet, Sir?" Hunter asked Mackay.

"No, but it's easy enough to tell a florist that a funeral has been postponed."

"Well, Sir, he told the florist that he didn't know the details of the funeral yet, but wanted to be sure the wreath was ready in time," Jane said.

"I don't suppose they paid with a credit card?" Mackay asked.

"No, Sir, cash."

"Did the florist remember anything about the customer, DC Anderson?" Mackay asked Rachael.

"Medium height, medium hair, beard and foreign accent."

"Could be either Reinbold or Merkel," said Hunter.

"It doesn't mean either of them killed George, Boss. Just that they're glad he's gone," Bear said.

"Well, I'm not!" Hunter slammed his fist on the desk. "I want to get the bastard who murdered that frightened old man. Whatever he did as a kid, he didn't deserve for anybody to be judge, jury and executioner."

"Take photos down to the florist and see what she says, will you, DC Anderson?" Mackay asked.

"What else did we find out? Colin?" Hunter asked quietly.

Colin smiled. "We did okay, I think, Boss."

"We followed that car all the way to Edinburgh Airport from Folkestone," Nadia said. "It was a black-haired man with a well-trimmed beard who drove north, but we lost him in the airport."

"How did you do that? There's CCTV all over the bloody airport!"

"I know, Boss, but not in the Gents. He went in, but never came out."

"Disguise?" Hunter asked.

"Must have been." Colin said.

"A different foreign-looking man drove the car from the airport to Thomson's Top Cars," Nadia added.

"Mel, have a look and see what you can find, will you? A fresh pair of eyes might help. Tim, any luck your end?"

Tim nodded and swallowed the last piece of his bacon sandwich. He took a mouthful of coffee to wash it down. That earned him a frown from Mackay.

"Heinrich Reinbold and Max Merkel both arrived here recently. Merkel flew in from Germany, Reinbold came on Eurostar, both came through London. Reinbold came to take up his promotion. We have no specific proof of why Merkel is here, but he said it is to examine works of art. That certainly makes sense, given that's what he does for a living."

"Both have told us they did not know George was here," Rachael added. "But Reinbold told his bosses that he had family here, and Merkel asked his chauffeur to stop in Gilmerton on the way to The Bruce Hotel."

"The driver says Merkel took a picture of George's house," Tim said.

"How did the driver know it was George's house?" Colin Reid asked.

"Well, he took a photo of a house in that street, my guess is it was George's place," Tim replied.

"You know how I feel about guesses, Tim. What do we know about the timeline at Thomson's?" Hunter asked.

"It was a dark-haired man who brought the car in, and a brown-haired bearded man who arrived later when Frankie was leaving, and Jenny told her Mum she was going for a test-drive with a customer," Mel said.

"Surely that wasn't within Jenny's job remit?" Hunter

asked.

"I doubt it, but she was the only one there. I suppose she thought she was doing the right thing. She wouldn't think about the age of the Volvo he was asking about," Tim commented.

"Mel, go down and show Jamie and Frankie the photos of Merkel and Reinbold again. And take a copy of the images Nadia and Colin got from the car's journey north this time, too. They might recognise the driver."

Hunter ensured that every member of his team had all the information that had been gathered. Then he went downstairs to find PC Angus McKenzie and PC Neil Larkin. He would require them to track down June Dormer from Katz and Roundall by going round to her home. So far, the woman had managed to avoid Hunter's request for contact. His patience had run out.

**

"Boss, can I have a word with you?" Rachael asked.

"Of course," replied Hunter. He led the way to his office and closed the door behind her. "What can I do for you, Rachael? Not last-minute nerves, is it? Jane will be gutted!" Hunter joked.

"No, Sir. We are really looking forward to the big day. And we have time off for our honeymoon, you know."

Hunter smiled. "I won't block that leave."

"I know, Sir. I am also aware that after we get back, we, that is Jane and I, should work on different teams. Jane enjoys working with you and the team, but she would love to transfer to the Major Incident Team when Police Scotland comes into being next month."

"Jane is a great detective. I am glad she's considering a move to MIT. She's exactly what they're looking for."

"Several of the team are thinking about it."

"I know. It will be interesting to see how the new single force develops," Hunter said.

"But I have decided that I want to apply to join the Witness

125

Support Team. Will you approve my application, Boss?" Rachael asked.

"You will be an excellent member of that group, Rachael. I am sure that is a good move for you. I will be delighted to support your application, but you do know there will be special training involved?"

"Oh yes, Sir. I'm ready for that."

"I will be sorry to lose you."

"Thank you, Sir. Before I go, I want to help find out who killed George. And Jenny."

"Let's get that done, and stem the flood of cocaine pouring into our city. In the meantime, go and speak to your florist. See if she recognises any of our suspects."

Chapter Twenty-Three

Jamie was on his way back to The Western General Hospital. He had to get his arm checked to see if the pins were holding. It was irritating him that he couldn't drive. Everything took so much longer when he had to use public transport. Still, he had now got the knack of buying a day pass on the buses and jumping on and off them just like the old folk did. It was all right for them; they got some kind of coffin-dodgers' bus pass that got them free bus travel. It wasn't fair that he had to pay for his ticket.

As Jamie got off the bus, inside the hospital grounds, he started to look around to see exactly which way he should go. Then he caught sight of The Lizard walking up from the car park carrying a bunch of corner-shop flowers. Jamie got his bearings and walked away, head down, ignoring the bully who had overseen the breaking of his arm. It was his bowling arm. He might never throw a strike again, but at least he could lift a pint with the other one.

But The Lizard must have spotted him, because he called out, "Jamie, young Jamie, good to see you. Your mam'll be right pleased I've seen you out and about looking so well."

"Was she right pleased you broke my fuckin' arm, ya bloody wanker, Lizard? Out of my way, or I'll put this cast to good use and shove it down your throat."

"Now, that's not a nice way to speak, is it lad? I had nothing to do with your poorly arm. If you recall, it was Brian Squires who did that. He has an uncontrollable temper."

"That's not quite right though, is it, Lizard? You were there. You're the boss and you ordered Squires what to do. We both know that Brian Squires couldn't wipe his arse without being told what to do by you, Lizard. Why were you so worried about that old car, anyway?"

"No reason, lad, no reason."

"Well, word on the street says it was blowing a snowstorm in that Volvo, and your name was all over it. If they're right, that would explain a lot."

"Don't believe all you hear, Jamie, lad. It might not be good for your health," The Lizard sneered menacingly.

"Piss off, Lizard." Jamie nipped into the hospital and went straight to reception so The Lizard couldn't follow him and punish him for his cheek.

***

The Lizard growled after him, but did not follow Jamie. The lad was not worth any grief to him today, but he didn't like the sound of that rumour the lad had heard.

Lenny The Lizard turned into the Anne Ferguson Building and took the stairs up to Ward 51. He did his best to keep fit. His mother was receiving treatment for her heart, and that weakness might be hereditary. The Lizard had no desire to make an early exit from this world. He and Janice were having way too much fun, even if that did come at a high price. No wonder Ian Thomson had got into robbing banks; that woman was an expensive luxury.

Every time he went to visit his mother, he was more and more impressed by the patience and dedication shown by the nurses. They had told him not to expect too much, but his mother thought she was on the mend. Who was he to disabuse her of that? The poor old bat looked so frail. He knew she wouldn't be getting home any time soon. He knew that she wouldn't get out of hospital until care could be put in place to allow her to continue to live at home. So he gave her the flowers, and pretended to listen to her grumble about the food, the draught from the window and the uncomfortable bed.

In reality, Lenny The Lizard sat and thought: working out what could possibly be arranged about the cocaine from the car that was unaccounted for. He didn't want the rumour Jamie had heard spreading any further, but he had already spent the money he was due.

128

Chapter Twenty-Four

Tim was glad to have a day off. He had a busy day planned. His first task was to meet his sister, Ailsa, from the airport. She worked so hard, as a doctor in Accident and Emergency at King's Hospital in London, that Tim was glad she was flying north for a few days off so that she could attend Jane and Rachael's celebrations.

Edinburgh Airport was busy as Tim waited for Ailsa to come through to the Arrivals area. He was glad her flight was on time; he didn't like waiting for anything, not even Ailsa.

As he glanced around the crowds of people mulling about, Tim was shaken out of his reverie when his phone rang. He was surprised when Hunter's number came up on his screen.

"Boss?" Tim answered his phone.

"Tim, before you ask, I remember you are off today, but I wondered if you could do something for me. Are you going to see your dad?"

"Yes, with my sister. Our visit is sanctioned for this afternoon."

"That's what I thought. We've had a call from the prison governor, Elliott Smith. More cocaine has found its way into the prison. Can you stop in to speak to him while you're there?"

"Sure, Boss." Tim tried not to sound as angry as he felt. Some day off. He didn't even notice Ailsa walking towards him.

"You look thrilled to see me," she said, as she took his arm.

"Sorry, Sis. I've just had the boss on asking me to speak to the prison governor while we're at Saughton."

"Never off duty, huh?" Ailsa said. "Come on, let's grab a coffee here before we make our way over to see Dad. You can fill me in on all I need to know."

***

Visiting his father was always difficult. Partly because of the humiliation of seeing his dad amongst the criminals, and partly because he worried about the beatings his dad suffered, from the criminals his dad had put away, and those who saw him as an easy target when Ian Thomson was not around.

Tim was aware that this was the first time Ailsa had been to the prison. He found the frisking and searching they had to endure unpleasant. He also knew his sister well enough to know that she would find it most unnerving.

"That was the most humiliating experience I have ever had to endure," she whispered to him.

"And it won't get any better any time soon," Tim said. As They walked into the visiting room, Tim saw his statuesque blonde sister blush. The wolf whistles and nudges were obviously not for him.

"Ailsa, darling." Sir Peter kissed his daughter lightly on the cheek.

"Dad," she said, and took a chair opposite him. The room was stuffy but smelled of disinfectant and soap. Loud, threatening calls and noises invaded her ears. Ailsa stared at her father's bruised face. The brightly-coloured identifiers that all the inmates were required to wear clearly marked her father out as one of the prisoners. Suddenly, she was overwhelmed. Tears pricked the back of her eyes.

"Oh, Dad. How did all this happen? Why did you let it happen?" she asked.

Her father reached out to hold her hand and comfort her, but a prison officer corrected him.

"No touching. You know better than that, Sir Peter," he said.

"Are you okay, Dad?" Ailsa asked.

"I'm fine, keeping my head down, Ailsa. Don't worry about me."

"I'll get us coffee from the vending machine. You want a Kit-kat, Dad?" Tim got up without waiting for a reply.

When Tim returned to the table, he found his sister listening patiently to their father's grumbles about life behind bars. He noticed Ailsa's eyes had glazed over, and knew the conversation had been all about their father. Prisoners are, to a man, self-absorbed and self-obsessed. Tim had forgotten to warn Ailsa about that

"Ailsa, have you told Dad your good news?" Tim said to change the subject.

"Not yet, I've been hearing Dad's news," she said. "I'm moving, Dad. I have a new job in A & E at Edinburgh Royal Infirmary. I'll be moving up here in a couple of months, so Tim won't be rattling about in your huge home all on his own."

"That's good. But he's not on his own; Kenneth and Alice live in anyway."

"Having staff is not the same as having company, Dad," Tim said.

"You have Lucy."

"Lucy is a cat, Dad. It will be lovely to have Ailsa around in Edinburgh again."

"Talking about staff, Ian Thomson has been taking good care of me here. I only got tripped up in the gym once yesterday."

"Good to know," Tim smiled.

"I hope you're looking after his boy, Jamie?"

"The force is looking out for him. Dad, have you heard anything about a new supply of cocaine coming in here?"

"I'm in counselling. I don't use any more."

"I understand that, but have you heard anything?"

"As far as I know, all drugs, including cocaine, that come into the prison run through Arjun and his heavies. He is the drug lord in here. I keep away. It's easier."

"Of course. But how does he get supplies?"

"It's delivered to him, but I don't know how it's done because he hardly has any visitors except for his wife, her brother and his lawyer. Oh, and I heard Lenny The Lizard Pratt came in to see him. That's got trouble written all over it."

"Well, it isn't unheard of for any of those kinds of contacts to make the drops," Tim said.

"Ah, but he's not just supplying the jail. He's working the city from here, son. Mansoor has a team on the outside dancing to his tune."

"Do you know who's in charge of that?"

"He calls him Bill," Sir Peter Myerscough whispered.

"Bill? Thanks, Dad. I'll see what more I can find out."

***

Tim stopped by to speak to the prison governor, Elliott Smith. He was keen to tell the governor what he had learned from his father.

Mr Smith greeted Tim near the gate and took him up to his office through the front door. Tim reflected how much nicer it would be to visit the prison this way every time he came. As he took a seat opposite Mr Smith, he was amazed that such a short, skinny little man should be in charge of so many dangerous prisoners. He looked down at his hands and noticed he was sweating.

He spoke softly to explain. "My father does want to atone for his crime. He is most repentant."

The governor smiled. "Everybody in here is either not guilty, set-up or repentant, DC Myerscough. Nobody likes getting caught."

"I suppose that's true," Tim said.

"We know that Arjun Mansoor is the ringleader of the drugs gang, and I believe he organises most of the distribution, certainly of cocaine, throughout Edinburgh, even from here. We have not managed to catch him in the act or find his phone, but he must have access to at least one unauthorised mobile phone." The governor shook his head.

"He is a very slippery character," Tim agreed.

"And a very persuasive one. He's good at getting the weaker and more vulnerable people to do what he wants of them. He uses a mixture of threats and promises."

"I know."

"Everything comes to a stop when he is in solitary, but unfortunately we cannot justify keeping him in solitary all the time. Human rights and all that, DC Myerscough."

"No of course, I understand that. I'm told that Mansoor has very few visitors apart from his wife, her brother and his lawyer."

"That's true. His Iraqi Consul has been in to see him once. Mansoor has dual nationality. Apart from that, his only visitors are his wife, and, more recently, his lawyer, his brother-in-law and an old family friend."

"I take it they were all subject to the usual searches?"

"More thorough than most, I assure you. Of course the lawyer is exempt, but he is well known to us and represents many different clients without issue. Donald Blair, his name is. Very well respected."

"Of course. Thank you, I will inform my boss." Tim got up to leave.

"I was sorry to hear about old George Reinbold's death. He was a fine gentleman."

"Yes, that he was. He and his expertise will be much missed."

***

Waiting in the car, Ailsa wept. Seeing her father in prison had hit her hard. She remembered fondly the confident, larger-than-life character he had been.

She thought about how much he had enjoyed the kudos of being married to Louise Wills, the tobacco heiress. He had revelled in being the powerful Chief Constable of Lothian & Borders Police, and he had delighted in accepting the role of Justice Secretary after he was elected to the Scottish Parliament.

Never for a moment had she thought her father had needed the crutch of cocaine to get through life after her mother died. Then, of course, addiction was followed by blackmail and fraud. What an unholy mess!

***

133

"I've invited Bear and Mel to join us for dinner tonight," Tim told Ailsa when they got home. He lifted her suitcase out of the car.

"Good, it's too long since I've seen Bear. When is he going to make an honest woman of Mel? They've been together for years now."

"And I hope you don't mind, but I've also invited Gillian Pearson, the interpreter who is working with us on a case."

"No problem, you've talked about her so much, it'll be nice to meet her. It's good to know you're dating again."

Tim blushed. "It's not exactly dating; just a bite of dinner with friends."

"Yes, right. And I believe you. What are we having to eat, anyway?"

"Alice is cooking, so we're having her special."

"Lentil soup, Beef Wellington and Eve's Pudding with custard," Ailsa laughed.

"Young Miss Ailsa, how good to have you home," Kenneth said as he opened the door of the house.

"Kenneth, lovely to see you." Ailsa smiled broadly and gave the butler a hug. "And darling Lucy." Ailsa picked up the elegant Persian Blue cat and nuzzled her face into the creature's beautiful coat. "You must be loving having your man to yourself, Lucy," Ailsa said as she carefully replaced Lucy onto the carpet.

The cat immediately wound her body around Tim's legs and purred loudly, rubbing her neck against his calves and marking him with her scent to show that he was her person.

"Yes, you better watch your step, or I'll tell Lucy on you, Sis," Tim joked.

"Now I am going to have a shower and get changed before your guests arrive. I don't want to let my big brother down."

"Are you going to need Alice and me this evening, Master Timothy?" Kenneth asked Tim.

"No, thank you, Kenneth, I just have a phone call to make before I get ready for my visitors."

"The dining table is set and the house is ready for your guests. Check the rooms and let Alice or me know if you need anything else done."

"Thank you, Kenneth." Tim went into his father's office and called Hunter to inform the DI of the information he had gathered from his father and from Elliott Smith.

"And your dad says Mansoor calls his contact on the outside, Bill? That's new, thanks Tim. Rachael's florist identified the customer who commissioned the special wreath too, and I was right, he has contacted her to say the funeral has been postponed."

"Has it even been arranged, Boss?"

"No, a curious lie. Still, at least we are making progress. Anyway, you have a good evening."

"You too, Sir,"

"Darts match at The Persevere Bar tonight. We are taking on an East Lothian team, they have beaten us the last three times we've played, so this is a real grudge match," Hunter chuckled.

"Good luck, Sir."

Chapter Twenty-Five

Hunter was in the incident room staring at a photograph. When Tim opened the door, Hunter barely looked up.

"Ah, young Myerscough, there you are. Who is this man?"

The question made Tim glance at his watch to check if he was late. It was thirty-four minutes till his shift started. One day he would be in the office before the boss, but not today. Tim sometimes wondered if Hunter slept there when he was working on an important case.

He walked over to Hunter and picked up the picture. He shook his head and was about to put the photograph back on the desk, when he took a second look.

"Goodness, Boss, isn't that the guy Hadi Akram? The one who took ill at the airport with all those baggies of cocaine on his body? He's still in the Western General Hospital, isn't he, Sir? What made you take his picture?"

"I didn't. This is the photo Colin and Nadia produced from the Volvo's drive north."

"Really? So our mule is the driver?"

"It looks like it."

"I don't fancy his chances of a long life."

"Agreed. And it is strange, because the methods of transporting the drugs are too different in style. It's as if he were working as a courier for two different bosses. So, I plan to go over to the hospital today to speak to Mr Akram. Want to join me, young Myerscough?"

"Yes, I would. Thanks, Boss. By the way, how did the darts match go?"

Hunter laughed. "We hope to break their winning streak next time."

Hunter and Tim arrived at the hospital to find The Lizard standing over Hadi Akram, screaming abuse at him.

"Hello there, Lizard. Why are you shouting at my prisoner?" Hunter asked.

"Your prisoner? My goodness, I must be in the wrong room."

"Please don't tell me you thought this was your mother. That is not the kind of language anybody should use to their mother, not even you."

The Lizard smiled. "Don't be ridiculous. My mother's moustache is grey, not black."

"You're a funny man, Lizard. But I understood Mr Akram does not speak or understand English. Do you know differently?"

"No, as I say, I am in the wrong room. I'll just pop up and spend some time with my mother. The old girl is still quite poorly. Goodbye, detectives."

Hunter caught Tim's eye and shook his head as Tim made to stop The Lizard from leaving. The Lizard watched warily as Tim stepped out of his way and took his chance to leave quickly.

"Let's speak to Mr Akram," Hunter said to Tim before turning to the prisoner. "Mr Akram, now that I know you understand English, tell me why you are in this photo."

The man in the bed shrugged and looked away.

Tim moved to the other side of the bed.

"I have lots of pictures of you, Mr Akram," Hunter continued. "In each of them you are driving an old blue Volvo, that I now know had a boot full of cocaine. You drove it all the way from Calais to Edinburgh Airport."

The man glanced at Hunter, then at Tim, then stared at the ceiling.

"Mr Akram, you drove that car full of cocaine all the way from France, through England, to my city. You dropped the car in the airport car park. I don't know yet which flight you took out of here, but I will find out. Believe me, I will find out,

137

because you came back. You came back by plane, and this time, when you arrived here, you had a body full of that muck. There was so much of it in your system that you collapsed in the airport. You should be dead by now, and were it not for the excellent work of our doctors and nurses, you would be. Why should they bother with you, Mr Akram?"

The man shrugged again and closed his eyes.

"Let me put it this way, Mr Akram," Hunter went on. "I don't really care about you. In fact, I don't care about you at all. I do care about who you are working for. Who is that?"

The man shook his head.

"Okay, let me tell you about the other people I care about. I care about the young woman who was found dead in the boot of the Volvo you were driving. And I care about the old man who was shot after he helped me jail Arjun Mansoor last year for drug trafficking. I care about those two innocent, murdered people – and I am going to get my revenge. If you won't help me, I'll take my revenge on you."

The terrified man stared silently at Hunter.

"Tim, book him. Two counts of murder and one of drug trafficking." Hunter turned his back.

"No!" Akram shouted.

Chapter Twenty-Six

The last fitting Jane and Rachael had for their wedding outfits was bad-tempered and loud. The serene surroundings of the wedding boutique were shattered by the women as they bickered and argued in such colourful language that it made the assistants in the shop blush.

"I'm not sure whether Jane and Rachael are just having pre-wedding nerves or whether they are genuinely as furious as they sound," Mel said to Sarah.

"Have you never heard them have a full-on argument before?"

"No. Never even a cross word," Mel said. She looked concerned as she looked over at Sarah.

"I'm surprised," Sarah said.

"No, I've never heard those two argue. The occasional meaningful glance, but certainly nothing like this."

Sarah looked at her with wide eyes. "Really?" she said. "They fight like cat and dog sometimes. Have you heard the way they shout at each other when they are out on a jog? Or when they go round an art gallery together and Jane is trying to study the paintings and Rache gets bored and makes childish comments? This is nothing."

"Let's allow them get on with it, then. We'll just try on our own things to make sure they fit," Mel said.

"Good idea, then we'll just go and they can argue in private. I have to get back to work."

"Where do you nurse, Sarah?" Mel asked.

"I work in the wards for care of the elderly. Usually Ward 51 or 52 at the Western."

"Oh, have you been nursing Mrs Pratt, then?"

"Yes. Well, I did."

"Oh. Was she moved? Or did she not like you, or something?"

"I have no idea whether she liked me or not. She died yesterday."

"I didn't know that. Poor old girl," Mel said.

"It was very sudden. An aneurysm."

"The way to go."

Sarah nodded. "Given a choice, yes."

"Your dress is really pretty, Mel."

"The colour is lovely on you too."

"It is a flattering style. Is that us done then?"

"Yes. I'll go and tell Rache and Jane that we're leaving."

Mel had become unaware of the racket the brides were making until Sarah came back and there was silence.

***

Mel called Bear to tell him the fitting was over and she still liked her dress.

"Oh, and Rachael's sister was nursing Lenny The Lizard Pratt's mother, but she died suddenly yesterday."

"I'm not sure the boss knows that. He saw The Lizard at the hospital when he was there with Tim, yesterday. I'm going to let him know. Speak later, babes." After making sure nobody was listening, Bear blew her a kiss.

***

"Dead?" Hunter asked Bear. "How did she die? When? She was alive when I spoke to her horrible piece of work of a son yesterday. He left us to go and spend time with her, he said."

"I don't know; Mel just told me. She'd been speaking to one of the nurses who said it was sudden, yesterday."

"Okay. I think I am going to need to have a word with our friend, The Lizard. Do you fancy a trip to The Bruce Hotel, Bear?"

140

Chapter Twenty-Seven

"Gentlemen, good afternoon," Hunter greeted The Lizard and Merkel. "How fortuitous you are both here. Lizard, I was sorry to hear about the death of your poor old mother."

"How do you know about my mother? And who the hell is he?" Lenny The Lizard tossed his head towards Bear.

"This is my colleague, DC Winston Zewedu," Hunter replied sourly. "Back to your mother. The end was very sudden, I hear. When will the funeral be?"

"Give me a chance, Inspector. Mum's not been dead 24 hours."

"Of course. And what will your plans be after the funeral? Remember, you are on bail. You must keep yourself available, Lizard."

"I'm well aware of that, Inspector."

"And talking about funerals, Mr Merkel, why did you order a very expensive wreath for George Reinbold? You did do that, didn't you? Why did you do that? The choice of petunias with yellow carnations around a copy of *Winnie the Pooh* was not very subtle. Now I want to know if you murdered our colleague. I think that is best discussed at the station," Hunter said.

"How on earth did you find out about the wreath? I paid cash! In your view, detective, I may be guilty of bad taste, but sending a few specially-chosen flowers and a book to a dead man does not make me guilty of murder."

"Paying cash is not foolproof, Mr Merkel. There are ways other than credit card payments that we can identify people."

"How could you track down that tiny, obscure shop? There are hundreds of places to buy flowers in this city. Did you ask them all?"

"I think we will discuss this further at the station, don't you?" Hunter said softly.

"I hardly think that is necessary," Merkel said.

"Bear, escort Mr Merkel to the car, will you? See you soon, Lizard." Hunter ignored Merkel's protestations.

"How did you know, Boss?" Bear whispered Hunter after Merkel was secured in the car. He was keen to know what Hunter had spotted that he had missed, but equally keen that Merkel did not hear them talk.

"Just confirming the florist's identification. It would either rule him in or out," Hunter replied quietly. Then in a normal speaking voice he said, "Now, come on, Bear, let's get back to the ranch."

Back at the station, Hunter led the way into the stale-smelling interview room and stood to the side as he watched Bear and Merkel follow him. Merkel's nose wrinkled as Hunter motioned him towards a blue plastic chair that was bolted to the floor next to the heavy metal table with the official recording equipment. Hunter began asking questions about George, Merkel's father, and the limousine drive from the airport to the hotel. Merkel clearly felt uncomfortable, but declined to answer any of the questions put to him.

Hunter spent enough time with Merkel to know he did not like him. He had spent enough time questioning him to know the art dealer was hiding something, and he also knew he could not arrest this man for paying cash for an ornate funeral wreath. He could not arrest this man for taking a strange route to his hotel, nor could he arrest this man for taking a photo of George's front door. Hunter had Bear drive Merkel back to the hotel. Hunter could not be sure that the art dealer was guilty of George's murder, but he put ports and airports on notice so that he would know if the man tried to leave the country.

***

Jamie was pleased the customer came into the showroom. He recognised the man as the one who had asked to test-drive the Bentley. The one who was in that photo the cops showed him. Jamie stood up a little straighter and tried not to lean on his broken arm.

"Hello, again," Jamie said.

"Good afternoon, young man. You have so many fine vehicles for sale, I have been tempted back."

"Good, that's right good. I'll ask Frankie to come over to help you too." Jamie had decided that any man whose photo was being shown around by the police probably wasn't Santa Claus. Jamie wanted some back up, and Frankie was all he had.

"What's up, Jamie? Oh," said Frankie.

Jamie could tell that Frankie also recognised the man from the photos. Out of the corner of his eye, he spotted that the man had caught the glance between himself and Frankie.

"So, I remember you had a run in the Bentley. Is there anything special you would like to take a look at today?" Jamie asked the man.

"Maybe I shall have a look here." The man stepped towards the Porsche.

"It's a bit different from the Bentley you drove last time you was in," Jamie commented.

"I like all nice cars," the man said, in a strange foreign accent.

Jamie was keen to make a good sale. He did not understand that this customer made Frankie feel uncomfortable. He was angry with Frankie when he spoke to the customer in a grumpy tone of voice.

"We're not a car rental, you know. We sell these; you don't just come and drive them for the hell of it."

"I did not mean any offence. I am wanting to buy a car while I am here," the man said.

"Calm down, Frankie. He didn't mean anything by it, man," Jamie whined, looking at the customer then glowering at Frankie.

"Well, I don't like him. You do what you suits you," Frankie said quietly. He turned on his heels and marched towards the office. He slammed the door.

"Look, I'm really sorry," Jamie turned to his customer, only to see that he, too, was walking away.

Jamie was furious. Another possible sale lost. He marched into the office. "Frankie, you have been a real twat. I'm going to tell my pop you're a wanker."

"Say what you like, just remember you live in my house."

"I will say what I like, because you work in my business."

***

Hunter had never liked Sir Peter Myerscough. He didn't like him when he stood in the way of Hunter's promotion, and he didn't like him when Sir Peter had an affair with Hunter's sister-in-law and then dumped her. However, given what the prison governor had said about the cocaine flooding the prison, Hunter realised he could use an eye on the inside, and Tim's father was the closest thing he had to a nark. He told Tim what he wanted to ask of his father, and Tim accepted that they should ask, but warned Hunter that he was not sure his father would agree.

"My dad is having a hard enough time in there as it is, Boss. If Ian Thomson didn't look out for him, he'd be chopped liver. You know yourself that former cops aren't overly popular in jail, so you can imagine that former Chief Constables are even less so."

"I understand, young Myerscough, but I have to ask. He's our best shot if he will agree to help us," Hunter said.

Elliott Smith, the prison governor, arranged a private visit for Hunter and Tim when Hunter explained his thinking.

***

When Sir Peter walked in he raised his eyebrows at the sight of Hunter with Tim.

"I thought it was a bit too soon to have another social visit from you, Tim, and as you are both here, it must be business."

"It is. Dad, we need your help."

Hunter told Sir Peter about Akram and the two methods by

which he smuggled cocaine into the country.

"It sounds to me that this man is working for two different traffickers," Sir Peter said.

"I think so too," Hunter agreed.

Hunter looked at his former Chief Constable. Prison was never a kind environment, but Sir Peter's famous blond hair was quickly turning white. His blue eyes both bore the remnants of bad bruising, and the man did not hold himself as tall and erect as he had done once. However, he had lost a lot of the flab of middle-age that had settled around his belly. Hunter guessed that Sir Peter was making good use of the prison gym facilities and that he would leave the establishment healthier than he had entered it.

"No individual gang would use two such different types of transportation. Poor bugger isn't going to last long if he's working for two outfits anyway, is he? He must be in trouble up to his neck."

"I agree." Hunter nodded his head.

"So, what do you need from me, DI Wilson? I take it Tim is just here to persuade me to do the right thing by you?"

"No, Dad, I'm not, but it is important."

"There are only three people who visit Mansoor regularly, and the governor knows Mansoor controls the prison supply of cocaine," Hunter said.

Sir Peter nodded. "That was true for weeks, but in the last day or two he has been having more visitors than Waverley Station."

"Really? Who's been visiting Mansoor, then?"

"Well, apart from his wife, his brother-in-law and his lawyer Donald Blair, there was Lenny The Lizard Pratt, and some guy with a strange European accent. But, if you want my opinion—"

"Not really," Hunter said flatly.

"Well, I'm giving it anyway," Sir Peter said firmly. "My opinion is, you should enlist Ian Thomson. He knows everybody in here and most things that go on. I only get told what the prisoners, and the guards, trust me to know."

"That's not a bad idea, Boss," Tim said. "Do you have the

photos with you?"

"Yes," Hunter tugged the photos out of his inside jacket pocket. "Sir Peter, is either of these men the European one?"

Sir Peter immediately pointed to the photo of Max Merkel. "It's him."

Chapter Twenty-Eight

Jane and Rachael had separate rooms in The Bruce Hotel the night before their blessing. They wanted to observe the tradition that the bridal couple should not see each other before the ceremony on the day itself, but there was no tradition to prevent them from having dinner together and then coffee and a night-cap in the bar on the night before.

Jane ordered a camomile tea instead of coffee.

"Do you have decaf?" Rachael asked.

"Of course," the waitress replied.

"Then I'll have a decaf latte please."

The women moved a little closer and held hands under the small table in front of them.

"Are you excited about tomorrow?" Rachael asked.

"Yes, it'll be funny being part of a big family. I was only three when I was put into care, and from then on I just went from children's home to foster care and back again. I've always had to stand on my own two feet. You don't know how lucky you are to have a loving family."

"Well, you will know soon enough how lucky I am, they'll be your family too in less than twenty-four hours. And don't you complain to me about it afterwards," Rachael smiled.

***

Hunter and Meera arrived early at The Bruce Hotel in order to take up Jane's suggestion of a visit to the National Gallery of Modern Art before the service. It was a beautiful spring day and the grounds around the gallery, with its mature trees, squirrels and birds, kept them amused. Hunter would quite happily have continued to enjoy the outdoors and given a body swerve to the paintings and exhibits.

Meera pointed towards a group of people in fine clothes entering the building. "Look, Hunter, those people look like other wedding guests. Perhaps we should go in too?"

"If you say so, but I am quite happy out here, you know," Hunter said, before reluctantly following her inside.

**

"Didn't the girls look radiant walking down the aisle?" Rachael's father said to Hunter as they stood at the bar. "I felt so proud. I am so glad Rachael has found happiness, she was a miserable teenager, you know. And their flowers were very pretty, weren't they?"

"They both looked beautiful, Mr Anderson. Relaxed and happy. It's marvellous."

Hunter glanced around the bar. It was crowded while the furniture in the hotel function suite was being changed around after the meal to accommodate an evening reception of dancing and drinking in celebration of the new couple. Hunter watched guests taking the opportunity to get photographs, buy drinks and catch up with those they knew who had not been sitting near them at the wedding breakfast. There was a feeling of joy in the air.

"And it was a good spread for the meal," Rachael's father added as he turned away to walk back to the table with his drinks.

"Yes. I've heard this band is excellent, too. I'm looking forward to the evening, Mr Anderson." Hunter moved to follow the man back to the reception guests, praying he would make it without tripping and spraying alcohol over anybody.

As he was leaving the bar, Hunter saw Tim wander up with his hand in his pocket.

"Can I just put this behind the bar for the wedding guests?" Tim handed the head barman an envelope. "Take drinks out of that until it is finished."

"How much is here?" the barman asked.

"One thousand pounds," Tim said.

148

"I can't guarantee it'll be only wedding guests, but we'll do our best."

"That's good enough," Tim grinned.

"Let me count it with you, then," said the man.

Hunter went back to the table, glad he had bought drinks before Tim's money was there. Hunter liked his independence. He found Tim's spontaneous generosity embarrassing, but noticed that Tim had done this quietly and at a time when most people wouldn't notice. Sir Peter would have wanted the glory, whilst his son just wanted to do a nice thing for his friends. They didn't need to know.

The band were starting to play as Hunter got back to his table. He distributed the drinks and sat down to put his arm around Meera.

Jane and Rachael started the dancing in traditional fashion. They had chosen *Amazed* by Lonestar as their first dance. All eyes were on them. Family and friends smiled and clapped and joined in as the song progressed.

So many photos were taken that Rachael felt like a film star in her pretty, tailored, elegant, white dress that showed off her long neck, slender arms and long, blonde hair. Rachael clearly felt beautiful and happy.

Jane also looked lovely in a short ivory coloured dress that flattered her toned legs, but she had never been comfortable getting her photograph taken. Ever since she was a little girl, she associated it with moving to a new childrens' home or having to find yet another new foster family. It was never good news.

Today, however, Hunter saw her put those thoughts aside and hold Rachael close. He was so happy for her. Jane had had such a difficult childhood, but now she had her forever partner whom she adored, her forever home where she was safe, and her forever job that she knew she was good at.

Hunter smiled at her as she smiled for the cameras and she and Rachael danced to their song. He watched as they were joined on the dance-floor by Bear and Mel, Tim and Sarah, Rachael's parents, and Colin and Maggie holding wee Rosie the bridesmaid in their arms. Hunter thought about his own marriage, and wished Jane and Rachael so much more happiness than he had had.

Jane was so happy she started to cry and laid her head on Rachael's shoulder. "This is the happiest day of my life, Rache," she whispered.

As the dancers left the floor after the first dance, Hunter said to Meera, "It was unkind of you to look so good, you shouldn't outshine the brides, it's twice wrong, today."

"And that is twice corny, whenever," she replied, with a grin.

"But did it work?" Hunter asked.

"Shut up and let's dance." Meera stood up and straightened her dress, but immediately she stopped. Hunter was gazing out of the function suite and towards the bar,

"What's the matter, Hunter? What are you looking at?"

Hunter was silent. There were three men at the bar. He watched them carefully. Without saying anything he wandered off, leaving Meera standing. Never off duty got old, to Meera, sometimes. He knew that. But he couldn't help it.

"You got a minute?" Hunter said as he approached Tim

"Yes, Boss. What can I do for you?"

"Come here, and look."

Tim followed Hunter to the door of the function suite. The three men had their backs to them, but there was no mistaking the fact that Lenny The Lizard Pratt, Max Merkel and Donald Blair were deep in conversation. The detectives were obscured by the dim lighting in the reception area, but the bar was brightly lit. Hunter and Tim could see into the bar clearly.

"Can you hear what they're saying?" Hunter asked.

"Not above the noise of the band, Boss, no."

"They know who we are. Let's find Colin and ask him to go over and buy a drink so he can listen in. They don't know him."

Colin left the group he was speaking to when Tim and Hunter came over to him. He listened carefully as Hunter spoke to him quietly.

"Colin, you see those three men standing at the bar?"

"Yes, Boss, Lenny The Lizard, Max Merkel, but I don't

know the bald one."

"Donald Blair. He's a solicitor, and we have information that he is working for Arjun Mansoor. I'm concerned he may be involved in the cocaine finding its way into the prison. Can you go up and stand near them to hear what they're talking about? I'd go, but they'd recognise me or Tim."

"Sure, Boss. I just hope they keep talking." Colin made his way towards the bar and did as he was asked. Colin was aware that Hunter was watching him. He took his time choosing the type of beer he would have, discussing ales and the benefits of real ale to bottled beers with the barman as he listened to what the men were saying.

"Well?" Hunter asked as he got back.

"The drinks were free. That was a nice surprise. Someone put a thousand pounds behind the bar."

Tim blushed.

"And that young barman knows his beers. He's a member of CAMRA."

"Really? Do I look like a man who cares?" Hunter said crossly.

"The men were talking about Mansoor and the jail just when I got there. I didn't really catch much of that. Except apparently Hadi someone is in hospital after catching something."

"Getting caught, more like. Go on."

"The Lizard said he is going back to Malaga after his mother's funeral. He said the showroom boys are thick and being difficult."

"Which boys?" Hunter asked

"The boys at Thomson's Top Cars, I think. He mentioned Jamie being a dick about his arm," Colin said.

"To be fair to the lad, he was assaulted by The Lizard and his goon, Squires. His arm was badly broken. I'm not surprised he's not co-operative in relation to anything The Lizard puts to him. Anyway, The Lizard's only out on bail. He's going nowhere fast, no matter what he thinks. Did you catch anything else?"

"Donald Blair said the governor at Edinburgh Prison is a

pushover, but some guy Mansoor had hoped would help had turned him down."

"I doubt the governor is that. And who turned them down for what?

"I don't know."

"Is that all?" Hunter asked.

"Merkel said he is due down in London next week for an exhibition he is putting on in the city, and he's going to an auction at Christie's and some artwork The Lizard has given him will clean up well. He has clients selling a couple of pieces in this auction. Still, there is someone up here who will let him know when the date of George's funeral is confirmed. He is determined to be at George Reinbold's funeral. As soon as his friend tells him when it is, he says he'll come back for it. The Lizard and Blair said they would be there too, to see that the old bastard is gone."

"Who said that?"

"I don't know, Boss. I was so intent on not being caught out, I didn't look to check which of them was speaking."

"No problem, Colin. Thanks."

"Can I get back to the reception, Boss? The Mrs wants a wee dance before we take Rosie home to bed."

"Of course," Hunter said. "I'd better get back to Meera."

***

Jane and Rachael got up early and managed to enjoy a quiet continental breakfast together before they called a taxi to take them to Edinburgh Airport. They were standing near the doors of the departure area looking at the board and waiting for their flight to Crete to be allocated a check-in desk. Jane turned to look around the crowded area at all the people milling about to see if there was anybody she knew.

The airport was busy with groups, couples, families and businessmen all struggling with luggage, talking on phones or waiting to check in for flights. In many ways, although Edinburgh is the capital of Scotland, because of its comparatively small population the feel of the city is like living in a large village. It's hard to go anywhere that you don't recognise someone, especially if you are an observant police detective. Jane's eye caught sight of a familiar face.

"Look, Rache, over there. Who is that? I recognise him?"

"That guy in the queue for the London flight?"

"Yes. He looks familiar."

"He does. Isn't it that the art dealer Tim knows, Max Merkel?"

"That's what I thought, too"

"What are you doing now?"

"Phoning the boss."

"Fucking hell, Janey, we're on our honeymoon."

"We're police, Rache. We're never off duty."

Chapter Twenty-Nine

It was a fairly sleepy looking group of detectives that sat around in the incident room for the following morning's briefing.

"It's all right for Jane and Rachael, they'll be halfway to their honeymoon destination by now," Bear complained as he gulped at his second coffee of the morning. "Anyone know where they're going?"

"Crete, I think," Tim said. "By way of consolation, I brought doughnuts, I thought we'd need the sugar rush, although Ailsa didn't approve."

"First class honours degree in Medicine from Cambridge, what does your wee sister know?" Mel asked. "You got a chocolate one?"

"Help yourself and pass them round. There's an apple doughnut for you, Colin. It was the closest I could get to a piece of fruit in Krispy-Kreme."

Colin yawned and gave him a thumbs-up as Allan Mackay smacked a book on the desk to get attention.

"Quiet, calm down, folks. Lots to get through this morning," Mackay said. "Can we start with George's murder? I want to release his body for burial as soon as we can."

"We know he was shot, and probably by someone hired to do the deed. There are four men in our sights. Lenny The Lizard is always bad news, but he says he's here to visit his mother."

"Is she ill?" Mackay asked.

"She was before she died, sir. The Lizard has been a bit trigger-happy in the past, too. And we have information that he needs money, fast. We also have George's nephew, who bears him a grudge, recently moved to the city. Arjun Mansoor has his brother-in-law, Kasim Saleh working for him in the city. Arjun blames George for the fact that he got caught for drug trafficking last year. Last, but not least, the son of the man that George killed when he was young was recently in the city, on business, but he flew down to London this morning."

"How do you know that, Boss?" Mel asked.

"Jane called me from the airport. She and Rachael saw Merkel waiting at a check-in-desk with his luggage."

"Well spotted, DS Renwick," Mackay said.

"Yes, no way we would have known otherwise."

"Jane's witness said the man who went up George's path wasn't as big as Brian Squires, but she couldn't say between The Lizard, Merkel and Heinrich Reinbold. Too far away," Bear said.

"Thank you, DC Zewedu. Now, what about Jenny Kozlowski?" Mackay asked.

"Perhaps Colin and I can help with that?" Nadia asked, looking at her colleague for support.

Colin nodded, wiping sugar from his mouth with back of his hand. He rarely ate cakes but clearly enjoyed that doughnut.

"It took hours, but Colin and I got a good picture of the man who drove the car that Jenny was found in," Nadia continued. "He drove the car from Folkestone to Edinburgh Airport, and then, after changing in the gents lavvy, he got a flight back to Paris."

"He's the same man the boss and I saw in hospital," Tim commented. "He was taken there when he arrived back in the country by plane because he'd been carrying cocaine internally."

"The car was taken from the airport to Thomson's Top Cars by a different man. We finally got a clear picture of him too." Colin handed round the photo.

"I know that face, don't you, Tim?" Hunter smiled.

"Yes, indeed. That makes sense." Tim nodded slowly.

"Well done, Colin, Nadia. Now we have to tie the cocaine in that car to him, and we need to find out who took the car for its test drive with Jenny," Hunter said.

"Akram's information will help, won't it, Boss?" Tim asked.

"Akram is the mule?" Mackay asked.

"Yes, Sir. For two different dealers, it seems," Hunter said.

"Unusual," Mackay said.

"Yes Sir, I think he was cheap and vulnerable; he was 'hired' when he was living in the Jungle in Calais. His English isn't great, he says he didn't realise what he was getting into."

"Poor bugger. How did he end up working for two different groups?" Mackay asked.

"He got in tow with the first lot, then when he went to get his passport, he didn't understand what was being said to him and ended up agreeing to courier for a second gang," Hunter explained.

"That's grim. And do we know anything about the man who went on the test drive with Jenny?"

"Well, Sir, when we showed photos to Jamie and Frankie, Jamie identified Heinrich Reinbold as the customer who took the Bentley for a drive. Frankie identified Merkel, or perhaps Colin, as the man who came in to the showroom as he was leaving."

"What? When did I change teams?" Colin asked indignantly.

"Because of your build and colouring, I put a photo of you in to test our witnesses. With Frankie, I don't think the confusion was helpful. Sorry, Colin. Frankie did finally decide that Merkel is the man who took the Volvo out with Jenny. But it took him a while."

"And Merkel's now in London. You better not have lost him, DI Wilson," Mackay said gruffly.

"No, Sir. I've been in touch with Frank Armstrong in Southwark CID down in London. Armstrong has had men watching Merkel since his plane landed in London. I plan to gather more information, and by the time Merkel comes north for George's funeral we will know if there is a case against him or not."

"He deals in high class art, not battered old cars, Boss. He is very well respected."

"I know that, Tim."

"Mel, do you remember when we were in seeing Jamie and Frankie, Brian Squires came in?" Tim said.

"Yes; he said the Volvo was his friend's car," Mel replied.

"And when we caught up with Lenny The Lizard he more or less said Jamie deserved to get his arm broken because the lad had lost his car," Tim said.

"I'm getting the feeling Jenny Kozlowski was a 'wrong place wrong time' killing," Mackay observed. "I'm not even sure her attacker meant to kill her, just stop her getting in their way."

"I don't think that will cut any ice with her mother, Sir," Hunter said softly. "Her only child ended up dead."

"I think Jenny's death, whatever the intention of the killer, is tied up to the supply of cocaine to the city. If we solve that, we'll know who murdered Jenny," Mackay said.

"There seem to be two different gangs bringing cocaine in right now: one for the prison and one for the city generally. They both seem to centre around Mansoor, and poor, desperate Akram seems to have been used by both," Hunter said.

"My father and Ian Thomson are willing to assist us in snaring Mansoor," Tim commented.

"Why is Ian Thomson willing to help?" Mackay asked. "I hope he's not expecting any favours?"

"No, Sir. We did the decent thing by his son and nephew, and made sure The Lizard and Squires had to keep their distance. In Ian Thomson's mind, this'll pay us back for that, and we can't look for any more favours from him," Tim said.

"Yes, he also hates the drug trade and is furious with Mansoor for using his showroom for trafficking drugs last year," Hunter said.

"So why was it used it again?" Tim asked.

"It was easy?" suggested Bear.

"They knew where it was?" asked Mel.

"They didn't think we'd look there after last time?" said Colin.

"Enough!" Mackay shouted, thumping the table with a book. "Hunter, sort out the cocaine in the jail, and do it quickly. We have a captive audience there."

***

As the meeting drew to a close, Tim felt the mobile phone in his pocket vibrate. He did not recognise the number, but took the call and was surprised to hear his father's voice.

"Dad? Where are you?"

"That is the most ridiculous question I've been asked all day!"

"Well, how come the pre-recorded prison message didn't come on first?"

"You're a bright, lad. You work it out. Ian Thomson lent me a phone so I wouldn't be recorded."

"Ah."

"Just don't tell the governor. Anyway, I spent yesterday making a spreadsheet of everybody who knows about the drugs coming in to Mansoor. It makes interesting reading."

"Go on."

"Well, apart from the snowmen in here who stuff the coke up their noses, those who know about the drugs coming in must include whoever is bringing it in, and anybody turning a blind eye to it."

"The prison officers? I can't see that, Dad, it'd be more than their job's worth and they'd end up inside with you lot."

"Thanks, son. That's what I worked out, so the most likely source of bringing it in is Mansoor's solicitor, Donald Blair. He's the only person who visits Mansoor that gets privileged visits: he doesn't get searched. That's who you want to target. Do you want me to pretend I'm using again and set up a sting?"

"Only if you can do that without using cocaine again, Dad. I don't think Ailsa and I could cope with that."

"I promise you, I can. Now, this is my idea..."

Chapter Thirty

Sir Peter walked along the corridor to Ian Thomson's cell. Finding Ian was alone, Sir Peter returned the phone, with a packet of cigarettes in payment. He sat down and explained the sting that was planned.

"Yes, easier for you to pretend you're back on the snow than for me to show a sudden interest," Ian said. "No-one would believe that, because everybody knows my views about drugs."

"You're right. It would never work with you. It's also common knowledge you hate Mansoor. But nobody here has ever asked me what I think of him. I just steer clear."

"Until now."

"Yes, until now."

"Get a message to him through wee Mick."

"The Irishman in the cleaning team? Good idea, those boys go everywhere."

"You'll need plenty smokes up front to secure snow from Mansoor, though. He doesn't give credit."

Sir Peter nodded and went back to his cell. It would arouse suspicion if he spent too long with Ian Thomson.

***

Tim and Bear went to as many of the rugby internationals played at Murrayfield as their shifts allowed. Wild horses would not have kept them away from the Six Nations International match today, Scotland versus Wales.

Tim and Bear both felt at home at Murrayfield. It's a stadium where everybody gets a seat. So, although today would be a capacity crowd of over 67,000, the people making their way along Roseburn Street towards the venue were good-natured. Tim had decided to ask Gillian Pearson to join him. He was glad when she accepted, so they walked, hand in hand, chatting with Bear and Mel.

"When is Ailsa going home?" Mel asked.

"She flew back this morning, on the basis that if she didn't have a ticket for the match, she might as well benefit from a cheap flight," Tim replied. He was aware of comments about himself and Bear as the four of them walked along. The men were used to causing a stir. They were both tall, with the physiques of rugby players. Although they were now in their early thirties, and playing for the older players' team of Merchiston Castle School former pupils, their distinctive builds and vastly different colourings always caused people to look twice. Tim knew that Mel was used to it, but was aware that the glances were all new to Gillian (although she often got a second glance herself, due to the bright green flash at the front of her hair). As the four of them went into the Roseburn Bar for a drink before the match, a group of Welsh supporters were getting up to leave and Gillian managed to grab the table.

"That was quick. Well done!" Mel said.

Gillian grinned. "It comes from playing musical chairs with three older brothers."

Tim sat with the girls while Bear went to buy the round. He, Tim and Mel all ordered pints of special. Gillian asked for a gin and tonic and a bag of cheese and onion crisps. Bear caught Mel's eye and smiled.

"We have a lady present," he smiled.

"And that'll not be me, big man," Mel replied. "I know. Go on, get them in before I die of thirst."

"Oh, I'm sorry," Gillian said. "I've never liked beer."

"Don't worry about Bear, he's just teasing me. He always says a pint glass looks silly in my wee hands, but compared to him and Tim everybody in the world has wee hands."

It was Tim's turn to smile.

As soon as Tim saw that Bear had made it to the front of the queue around the bar, he got up to help and Bear passed the drinks back to him. They managed this above the heads of

160

everybody else and never spilled a drop.

"You big boys sure ate your porridge when you were young, didn't you?" a little Welshman said.

"That we did," Bear laughed.

"You two have done that before," Gillian said.

"More times than you would believe," Tim replied as he sat down.

"Myerscough, isn't it? Tim Myerscough and Winston Zewedu? My goodness, imagine seeing you here."

Tim and Bear stood up at the same time. Both of them dwarfed the newcomer. Neither of them smiled.

"Lord Buchanan," Bear said holding out his hand to shake the man's hand formally.

"Well, I never, Lucky Lord Lachlan Buchanan. What are you doing slumming it here?" Tim did not offer to shake hands.

"I'm just meeting a few friends. Fine pub, here, what? And I heard about your dad, Myerscough. Rotten luck getting banged up like that."

"Lucky! Oh, hello Tim, Bear," a familiar voice said.

"Sophie. Long time no see. May I introduce you? Gillian Pearson, meet Lady Sophie Dalmore, my ex-girlfriend," Tim said.

Gillian gasped and blushed. She brushed the green flash in the fringe of her hair and smiled.

"And my present one, of course." Lucky put his arm protectively around Sophie's waist.

"Of course," Tim said flatly.

The tension amongst the group could be cut with a knife. Tim could tell that Gillian was uneasy; the three men stood verbally scoring points against one another, whilst Sophie looked as if she wanted the earth to open up and swallow her.

"Good to see you boys. We must get together sometime," Lucky said insincerely.

"Of course," Bear said, sarcastically.

"Why?" Tim asked.

"Indeed. Well, I see my friends, I must go. Sophie, I won't be long. Will you wait in the Range Rover?"

161

"Range Rover? You had me folded up in a Fiat 500 so you could save the planet!" Tim said angrily.

Sophie looked embarrassed, but said nothing and turned to walk out of the pub.

As Lucky turned to walk away Tim made to sit down, but he noticed the group of men in the corner that Lucky was heading for.

"You should choose your friends more carefully, Lucky, or you may not be Lucky Lord Lachlan Buchanan for much longer."

"Jealously doesn't become you, old boy. And no hitting on Sophie, if you know what's good for you," Lucky sneered.

Bear made to stand up to defend Tim, but Tim shook his head. "He's not worth it, Bear."

"Who are his friends?" Mel asked, nudging Tim.

"Look over there," Tim murmured. "Donald Blair, Brian Squires and Lenny The Lizard."

"I know Squires and Lenny The Lizard, but what is the other man's connection?" Mel asked.

"Donald Blair? He's a lawyer."

"The one..?"

"Exactly."

"What are you two whispering about?" Bear asked.

Tim nodded at the group.

"I thought Lucky Buchanan was choosy about the company he keeps," Bear said.

"Aye, well, not this time, he's not. Of course, it could be perfectly innocent. The Lizard's mother gets buried tomorrow. Squires could just be back for that," Mel said.

"How do you know she gets buried tomorrow?" Bear asked.

"Sarah told me. The Lizard took a huge box of Thornton's chocolates in for the staff and told them."

"Does the boss know?" Tim asked.

Mel shrugged.

Tim took out his phone to tell Hunter the news.

"Can you and Bear make sure Squires doesn't leave the premises?" Hunter said. "I'll get somebody down there now to bring in him for the assault on Jamie. Then we might focus his mind on getting some information out of him."

"I think we can manage that, Boss. Donald Blair and another guy are with Lenny The Lizard and Squires. Do you want us to approach them?" Tim asked.

"No, not if you don't have to. Uniforms are five minutes away."

Tim casually took a photo of the four men before putting his phone back in his pocket. Then he whispered quietly to Bear and the two big men lifted their pints off the table and made their way to the doors of the Roseburn Bar. The pub was mobbed. It always was when an international match was on. But the mood in the bar was good-humoured and happy. Win or lose, the Scots and the Welsh fans enjoyed each other's company, a joke, and a song at the end of the night.

Lucky stood up and walked out just before the uniforms walked in. Bear nodded to Tim and the peer left without issue. There were wolf-whistles around the bar as the uniforms fought their way through the crowd.

"Entertainment for the ladies, the strippers are here!" one Welsh wag shouted.

Tim nodded towards the table where the three remaining men were sitting, and the officers made their way towards it. The Lizard and Brian Squires both tried to make a run for the door, but the place was far too crowded for that strategy to be successful. Then Bear stuck out his leg in front of Squires, and the man clattered to the ground.

"Fucking shit, me knee," Squires bellowed.

"Sorry, man, an accident, right?" Bear said in a most unconvincing Jamaican accent.

The officers winked at Bear then turned to their prisoner and formally cautioned him.

"Where did that ridiculous accent come from?" Tim laughed. "You're Ethiopian, not West Indian, although you speak better English than most Brits!"

"I blame the beer. Not enough of it, that is. And it's your round."

***

163

Gillian had never been to an International Rugby match. She looked around in awe as she entered the stadium with Tim, Bear and Mel. She felt Tim's hand holding hers tightly and smiled as he gave it a little squeeze.

"The stadium seems so much bigger than on the television. It is certainly a lot louder," she said to him.

They moved slowly along the row to their seats and she was delighted they were near the centre line. She noticed the score board, the big screens and the loud laughter and chatter rising from the crowd.

"This is going to be fun," she said to Tim.

"Can you see okay? You'll get close-ups of some of the action over there," he pointed to the screens.

"Yes these are great seats. I guessed that the screens would help with detail. It's all very loud, isn't it?"

"Sixty-seven thousand people can make a lot of noise, but don't worry. It's always good-humoured with the Welsh," Tim said.

At the end of the match, with the score 28-18 in favour of the Welsh, Tim was proved right. There were many Scots shaking their heads and showing no surprise that their national team had lost another rugby match.

***

"Well, at least Italy may save us from the wooden spoon," Tim said to Bear as they made to leave the stadium.

"Enough of that. Is Kenneth picking you up after the match?"

"Yes, we'll never get a cab, and it's too cold and windy to ask Gillian to walk."

"It is a bit chilly," Gillian said.

"Great, we'll all jump in and he can take us back to ours for takeaway pizza, if you can cope with that, Gillian?" Bear asked.

"We have wine as well as beer in the fridge," Mel whispered.

Kenneth stopped outside Bear and Mel's Marchmont home.

"When shall I come back for you, Mr Myerscough?" he asked Tim.

"Don't worry about that, I'll get Gillian safely home, thank you Kenneth. Then I'll make my own way. You just enjoy your evening."

"Thank you. You too, sir. Will you require Alice to leave you some supper?"

"No thank you, I'll raid the fridge if I need to."

"Ooh, she doesn't like when you do that, sir," Kenneth smiled.

"She never did, even when I was a child. But it's never stopped me yet." Tim grinned. He shook Kenneth warmly by the hand before he turned to go into the close that housed Bear and Mel's flat, bounding up to the top floor two steps at a time.

Chapter Thirty-One

Gillian was glad of the warmth in the flat. She was becoming increasingly fond of Tim. She gazed at him across Bear and Mel's cosy living room. His tousled mop of blond hair, startlingly blue eyes and relaxed demeanour made an agreeable package. Even his broken nose didn't spoil his good looks. She felt that she had known him far longer than she really had. More than that, she trusted him. She had not trusted anybody for a long time; not since she had found the cocaine belonging to her last boyfriend amongst her underwear.

However, she could see how important a friend Bear was to Tim, and she knew that, to be any part of Tim's life, she would have to be accepted into the group by Bear too. Suddenly she became aware that the others were all looking at her and were waiting for a response. She blushed.

"I'm so sorry, I was day-dreaming."

"Pizza. What kind of pizza would you like?" Tim asked with a smile. He put an arm around her shoulder.

"Oh, I'm glad it's not something more important," Gillian smiled back.

"What's more important than pizza, woman?" Bear joked.

"Garlic bread," said Mel.

"Chips," said Tim.

They settled on two large pizzas, one a *Quattro Stagioni* and the other a stuffed crust meat feast, and added four sides of chips to the order.

"It'll probably take for ever to get here because I doubt we will be the only people to have this idea today," Mel said.

"You're right," Bear said. "Would anybody like a drink?"

"Just a beer, thanks," said Tim.

"I think there's some white wine in the fridge. I'll have a

glass of that," Mel said smiling at Gillian.

"Could I just have a coffee, please?" Gillian asked.

Bear paused and then grinned, "Yes, coffee is a drink! How do you take it, Gillian?"

"Just milk. Can I help?" Gillian asked.

"Those three words are music to my ears. Come on through to the kitchen and we'll get everything sorted. I think we have a couple of garlic breads and some onion rings in the freezer. We can cook those through so we don't starve to death before the pizza arrives."

Gillian followed Bear through to the kitchen, and was surprised how bright and modern it was. The cosy living room had made her think the rest of the flat might also be more traditional. She was also struck by the fact the kitchen was spotlessly clean.

Bear noticed her glance. "Mel is OCD about hygiene. Cleaning the kitchen and bathroom are two of her favourite hobbies. It would be unkind of me to stand in her way." He winked at Gillian and they set about getting the drinks and snacks organised.

"How do you and Tim know Lord Buchanan?" Gillian asked.

"He was in the same year as us at school. He was at Fettes and we were at Merchiston Castle, so there's quite an old school rivalry."

"Unusual to have Merchiston Castle boys in the police force, surely, because it's such a posh school?"

"Not so unusual as you would think. I am thick and Tim is principled, that's how come we are here. And it's a great job. We both love it." Bear smiled.

Gillian doubted Bear was nearly as thick as he would have her believe, but she let that drop. When they went back into the living room with the drinks, Mel and Tim were deep in conversation.

"What is the boss's full name, again?" Mel laughed.

"I told you before: Christian Cyril Hunter Wilson!" Tim grinned.

"Save me, that's too funny," Mel squealed.

"You've got to be joking," Bear said.

When the laughter died down a bit, Tim turned to Bear suddenly and asked, "Bear, did you ever hear from the boss why George had those guns and precautions in his flat?"

"No, he never said. To be honest, I'd forgotten about the guns. One was the very old style that was used by the Stasi in East Germany, wasn't it?"

"I think I might be able to answer that," Gillian said. She was sitting on a sofa to Tim's left. Her feet were stretched out in front of her and she held her mug of coffee in both hands.

"What do you know about it, Gillian?" Tim asked her.

"Well, I can tell you how he got the old gun. George took it from the Stasi officer who he killed, when he ran away. George's diaries indicate that he carried it all the way across Europe in case he needed it to defend himself, but, even when he was attacked by dogs who savaged his leg, he never used it. My guess is he was traumatised by what happened and having to leave home. But he didn't say that; it's just my guess."

"What do you mean, he didn't say that? George is dead," Mel said.

"Yes, but when I translated his diaries, I felt like I got to know him."

"Did they say what he was so afraid of? His home was more secure than Fort Knox," Bear said.

"He remained a private and cautious man all his life," Gillian replied.

"This was more than cautious," Bear said. "He had bomb-proof curtains."

"George Reinbold helped with the conviction of many villains, some of whom had contacts that stretched all the way across Europe. Maybe further, but it was Europe he was worried about. I think last year he helped convict a drug dealer, Arjun Mansoor?"

Tim nodded. "Yes, he did."

"George's diaries from the time of that conviction show that Mansoor's car dealing was contaminated by his drug dealing. George was concerned that the contacts Mansoor worked with would be furious when he was taken out of the loop. It would make their businesses much less profitable, and they would also have to take time out to find a new willing contact."

"He couldn't have been so worried, because he didn't say anything," Bear said.

"He was private," Gillian said firmly. "He was cautious. George's view was that the fewer people who knew about him and his life, the safer he would be."

"That worked well, didn't it?" Mel said sarcastically.

"I only know what he wrote. He began getting postcards from all over Europe. All bore the same message in German: *Beware your sins will find you out*. But none of them was signed."

"Does his diary state the dates on which he received the postcards?" Tim asked.

"Yes, and the date of each postmark."

"Does the boss know about all this?" Bear asked.

"He has my translations. I very much doubt he's had time to read all the diary entries, though."

"I wonder if that's why Saleh had to come over?" Mel said. "To stop Mansoor's druggie contacts from finding someone new to work with and leaving him high and dry?"

"That would make sense," Tim said.

"Should we call the boss?" Bear asked.

"He's got a darts practice tonight," Tim said.

"Then let's tell him when we get in tomorrow," Mel suggested.

"Agreed!" Tim and Bear said simultaneously.

The doorbell rang. "Pizza!" Bear jumped up with ease and flexibility.

Mel organised more drinks. This time, Gillian accepted a large glass of chilled white wine.

Chapter Thirty-Two

Mick gave Sir Peter a note written by Mansoor. It instructed him to go to chapel on Sunday and bring two packets of cigarettes. Sir Peter had never been particularly religious in his life to date, especially since his wife had died so young. He was still angry with God for taking her. He missed Louise more than he could ever admit. She was the brightest and best person he had ever known, or (with the exception of Tim and Ailsa) ever would know. Although their children bore his looks, long limbs, athletic physique, blond hair and blue eyes, they were their mother's children: athletic, sociable, intelligent and charming.

However, since his incarceration, while he could not claim to have 'found God' as so many did, Sir Peter did make a point of going to both the religious services provided by a local Protestant minister and the Catholic priest. He went to the gym when permitted to do so. He went to change his books at the library regularly. He even went walking around the exercise yard in the rain. Indeed, Sir Peter did whatever he was permitted to do that took him out of his cell.

So being asked to attend chapel was not a problem. His name was already on the list, and, thanks to Ian Thomson's warning, he had added three packets of cigarettes to his shopping request for 'essentials'. It was many years since the then Chief Constable Peter Myerscough had given up smoking. However, he had discovered that cigarettes, and chocolate, were currency in his new abode. Tim always made sure that there was money in his father's prison account, so he could afford a few extra supplies of both.

He was searched as he lined up at the door of the block to be escorted over to chapel. He was glad he had given one of the packets of cigarettes to Ian Thomson to carry for him. The men going for worship walked in a straight line, single file. Men from each different block sat in the rows specified for them by their prison officers.

Sir Peter was lucky; Mansoor was only two rows in front of him. He noticed the imperceptible nod from Mansoor as he sat down. The cigarettes were passed forward in silence during the service. Nothing was returned, and Sir Peter was becoming anxious. But as they all lined up to leave, Mansoor leaned over and shook his hand.

"No hard feelings, Sir Peter," he said, slipping the wrap of cocaine over without further comment.

When Sir Peter spoke about this to Ian Thomson, the man explained Mansoor's actions.

"There's no way he would risk passing snow back through the men to you. There would be a less than fifty percent chance that it would reach you."

"Even coming back only two rows?"

"Did you see who was behind Mansoor? It was Muscle. No way could Mansoor be sure he'd pass it back. So, anyway, what now? You're not going to take that stuff?"

"No. I need to borrow your phone and tell my son I've got it. Then his boss can question Mansoor with a view to finding out the external supplier."

"Good luck with that," Ian Thomson said doubtfully.

***

When Tim told Hunter about the cocaine his father had scored from Mansoor, he could sense the DI's delight.

"Good. Your father is a new customer, so his request would not have been included in any previous supplies Mansoor had."

"But, Sir, won't he have extra cocaine in case he needs it?" Tim asked.

"Where would he keep it? He's not manager of Thomson's Top Cars any more, with its unlimited hiding places. No, he will get the supplies for the orders he has, and then get rid of the gear as quickly as he can, so he doesn't get caught with it."

"That makes sense."

"Now all we need to do is find out who visited Mansoor in the last week."

Hunter lifted the phone and dialled the prison governor. At the end of the conversation he turned to Tim and said, "Mansoor has only had one visitor in the last ten days. I think we have our man."

"Excellent news, Boss. What now?"

"Will you ask your father to order another wrap? The governor will inform us the next time the supplier arranges a visit to Mansoor."

"Of course," Tim said.

"I'll admit, lad, I never thought I'd see the day when I was working co-operatively with your father."

"Yes, Boss. I mean, no Boss." Tim grinned sheepishly.

"Get out of here, Tim. Go and phone your father and arrange for Jamie Thomson to be there too. He will be willing to play along, and the supplier will never suspect he's co-operating with us."

Tim hesitated.

"Now!" Hunter smiled.

Tim went back to his desk and dialled the mobile number that had come through on his phone when his father called. Tim found himself speaking to Ian Thomson.

"I can't get your dad just now. We're in lock-down. Something kicked off. A stabbing about a love rival," Ian Thomson said.

"Is my dad okay?"

"Yes, he was in the gym and was brought back and locked up. I saw him coming back. I'll give him the message when I can."

"Thanks, Mr Thomson." Tim rang off and went to tell Hunter.

"Fine, now it's just a waiting game."

"Have you read the diary entries Gillian Pearson gave you from George, Sir?" Tim asked.

"There are fifty years of diary entries. What do you think?"

Hunter asked crossly.

"Well, she was talking about some of them yesterday. Maybe we should read them? At least for the last year. She says they show George becoming increasingly security-conscious."

Hunter picked the files off the floor and handed them to Tim.

"Briefing's tomorrow is at ten. Make sure we know the relevant details by then."

"Sir?"

"Divide and conquer, young Myerscough. Spread the load amongst the team so that by tomorrow's briefing, we know all that is relevant."

Tim tucked the heavy files under his arm and walked slowly back to the incident room. He was fairly sure his first experience of delegation was not going to make him popular amongst those in the team.

Chapter Thirty-Three

Meera agreed to release Jenny's body for burial. She doubted there was more the poor girl could tell her. However, just in case the body was required to provide evidence in the future, the coroner insisted that the body be buried and not cremated. Meera knew Jenny had been overpowered, tied up and bundled into the boot of that Volvo. She could imagine Jenny: terrified, alone in the dark, trying to scream through the scarf that secured her mouth. With every breath that she struggled for, more cocaine entered her system – and finally, mixed with the heat and smoke, as the car burned, Jenny's efforts came to naught: she fell unconscious and died.

All that Meera knew, but she did not know who was responsible for Jenny's death. Whoever it was had been careful; the killer had worn gloves, and any DNA they had left was destroyed in the fire. Meera knew the When, the Where and the How: she would have to leave it to Hunter and his team to discover the Who.

***

Meera had a full diary on the day of the funeral, so it was agreed that Dr Aiden Fraser would attend the funeral from the pathology department. The department always made a point of attending the service for the patients they had examined. Aiden arrived with Hunter and Tim to join the small congregation at South Leith Parish Church in Henderson Street.

"I remember coming here as a kid," Hunter said to Aiden. "My dad used to deliver services here when the regular minister was on holiday. The Church was called the Kirk of Our Lady back then."

"Oh, I didn't know your father was a Church of Scotland minister, Hunter," Aiden said.

"Yes, and his first names are Christian Cyril," grinned Tim.

Aiden smiled.

"And you are dead meat, young Myerscough," Hunter growled. "Let's go in."

As he walked in, the only thing Hunter could hear (over the sound of a ghetto blaster playing *Angels* by Robbie Williams) was the sound of Ishbel Kozlowski weeping and sobbing into a handkerchief.

"This is going to be a difficult one," Tim whispered to Aiden. "She was so young."

"I have yet to attend a jolly funeral," Aiden replied.

"I think the boss is planning mine now."

"You got that much right," Hunter said grimly.

The three men sat at the back of the church. They watched carefully as each mourner entered the building. They hoped to see someone unexpected walk in. Sometimes a killer would go to the funeral just for another rush of excitement. Not today.

Just as the doors were closing Jamie and Frankie snuck in and took seats at the back in the row opposite Hunter, Tim and Aiden.

Hunter noticed Jamie's eyes were red. Frankie must be tense too, Hunter thought, because he had been worrying the acne on his face and two spots were raw.

Jamie looked over and caught Tim's eye. He nodded to him and then Jamie blew his nose to hide the fact he had started to cry again.

It was a short service, followed by a miserable eulogy in the graveyard outside. March in Edinburgh usually offered bright, if cold, weather. Today was overcast, wet and windy. It seemed fitting weather for the occasion. Hunter, Tim and Aiden paid their respects to Jenny's mother and went to shake Jamie by the hand before they made their escape.

"The man who took the Bentley for a drive came back in," Jamie said quietly to Tim.

"When?"

"A day or two ago. I meant to phone you, but I forgot. He's

one of the folk you showed us pictures of. The one with light brown hair and the proper beard. You know the one I mean?"

"Yes, I do. I'll get back to you if I need to, Jamie. Are you going to the wake?" Tim said.

"No. Jenny's mam didn't even want us here. Me and Frankie are off home."

***

"Aiden may have escaped to the mortuary, young Myerscough," Hunter said, "but today you and I are in for the double matinee."

"So I understand, Sir. Where is Mrs Pratt being cremated?" Tim asked.

"The small Pentland Chapel up at Mortonhall Crematorium."

"My mum's service was in the main chapel up there. God, that was a fucking awful day."

"I imagine it was. How old were you?"

"Fifteen. Ailsa was only thirteen and Dad was in bits. He's never been the same since. I just didn't notice."

"Of course you didn't; you were a kid!"

"It doesn't stop me from feeling guilty. He did his best for us, but his pronunciation of my French vocabulary was shocking," Tim said, trying to lighten the mood.

"Always difficult to get pronunciation right with a plum in your mouth," Hunter teased him.

"Ha, ha," Tim said. "How is your son getting on?"

"Cameron? That's another thing I hold a grudge about. Fucking Arjun Mansoor introducing him to cocaine. He's still in rehab. The cost is horrendous."

"Are you sure I can't help with that cost, Sir? You know how much family means to me, and I have the trust money from my mother now. I would be only too happy to help."

"You know I believe you, Tim, but no thank you. I'll manage. Still, I appreciate that; it is a generous offer." Hunter looked at Tim. He thought this young man was so different from his father and was a credit to his mother.

176

"I mean it, Sir. No strings, just between us."

"Like my name?"

"Sorry, Sir. Let me know." Tim blushed.

Again, Hunter and Tim sat at the back of the congregation. They sat and watched as the mourners came in and took their places to the sound of Robbie Williams singing *Angels*.

"*Déja entendu*," Tim whispered to Hunter.

Hunter saw Rachael's sister, Sarah, come in and sit near the back too. She must be representing the hospital, he thought. Hunter then noticed Brian Squires walk in with Kasim Saleh. The little man was almost hidden in Squires' shadow. Donald Blair, the lawyer, walked in soon after them with Lucky Buchanan. Lenny The Lizard shuffled along in front of the coffin mopping his eyes. He made his way to the front row of seating.

"Crocodile tears," Hunter said to Tim.

"What is Mansoor's brother-in-law doing here?" Tim whispered.

"Good question," Hunter whispered back. "And Lucky Buchanan and Donald Blair? I didn't expect to see any of them. We shall ask, then we'll get back to the ranch."

Chapter Thirty-Four

Back at the station, Tim was right about his colleagues' reactions to his new powers of delegation.

"So who made you king of the castle?" Bear asked moodily.

"I did, DC Zewedu," Hunter said firmly. "Come into my office if you have any problem with that."

"Not at all, Boss. Excellent idea," Bear replied. "This better involve biscuits, Timmy boy. We could be here all night. I'll make the coffee," he added peevishly.

"Tea for me, please Bear," Nadia said.

"Now we have about fifty years of diaries that Gillian translated and there are five of us. If we take ten years each, we should get through them as quickly as possible. After all, there's only a few lines per day," Tim said defensively.

"Biscuits?" Bear repeated.

"Kit-kats, Blue Riband, Orange Club and Penguins. Oh and I picked up four apples for you, Colin."

"Good man. Shall I take the first ten years? And give the next decade to you, Nadia?" Colin handed papers out.

"Fine. Here's your lot, Mel. And yours, Bear," Tim said. Then he handed a pile of the translated diary entries to Bear with a packet of Kit-kats on top.

Bear grinned. "Okay, you're forgiven."

"Just note down anything that indicates why George was so security conscious," said Tim. "Also anything that suggests who he was afraid of," Mel added. "And why, I suppose."

"Yes, thanks Mel," Tim said.

**

Hunter stopped in to see Mackay before he left the building.

"You slipping off early, again, Hunter?" Mackay asked.

"Hardly, Sir, my shift finished an hour and a half ago. But I did want to speak to you before I leave. There were some interesting mourners at the funeral for The Lizard's mother."

"Nobody unexpected at the girl's funeral?"

"No, Sir,"

"So who was at Mrs Pratt's, then?"

"Well the usual suspects, including Lenny The Lizard and Squires, but also a few less likely contenders – including the new Lord Buchanan and Kasim Saleh."

"Saleh? Mansoor's brother-in-law? Young Lucky Buchanan should be careful about whom he chooses to befriend. And you should have Squires picked up, arrested and held on remand, for the assault on young Jamie Thomson, Hunter. By God! He'll breach his bail conditions good and proper again and be back to Spain, for Heaven's sake, if he gets half a chance."

"Agreed, Sir."

"But I don't see how Lucky Buchanan fits in, or why he would want to. He was always wild, but there was never anything illegal or wicked about his conduct."

"We'll keep an eye on him, Sir. It may be as simple as Blair is his solicitor?"

"Could be."

"Also, I do happen to know that there was only one person to visit Akram Mansoor in jail in the days prior to Sir Peter getting the cocaine, and that person was at the funeral. I want to set up a sting. Sir Peter Myerscough has offered to help."

"Tell me," Mackay said.

"Sir Peter will ask Mansoor for more coke."

"He's not using again, really, is he?"

"No, Sir, he hands it back to a prison officer who gives it to the governor. The governor has undertaken to phone me and give us prior notice of the visit. Then we will know when that request is approved."

"Good. Where do you want the sting to take place?"

"In the prison during a routine search."

"Won't that be a bit strange?"

"No, Sir. I have spoken to Jamie Thomson. He'll also be there, and be searched as if he were going to see his dad. I'll have Tim and Bear going in as if they were visiting Sir Peter; they will be searched too. Then, when the drugs discovery is made, they can make the arrest there and then."

"Good idea, Hunter. Not in a million years will anybody believe that Ian Thomson's lad is assisting us."

"I'm counting on that, Sir. I will have officers covering the entrance and exit gates, and CSIs there at the scene to examine the suspect and their belongings, including their car, immediately."

"Take what you need, Hunter. Just keep me in the loop. You've got detectives scouring the translations of George's diaries too, haven't you?"

"Yes, Sir."

"Fine. Let's have the briefing tomorrow at ten, and gather together all that we know and how to move forward from there."

"Good enough, Sir. We'll do that."

***

Hunter left the station and made his way to The Persevere Bar. He met the rest of the darts team. They had a team meeting once a week. Tonight, Hunter had arrived unusually early. He was early enough for a pie and a pint. That passed for his evening meal.

Chapter Thirty-Five

Tim's seconded group grumbled and complained until he was persuaded to send out for a Chinese take-away. Nadia's Uncle Fred provided the spread from his restaurant.

"Uncle Fred couldn't believe this much food was only for five people," Nadia said as she and Tim set out the dishes and Colin raked about for plates and cutlery.

"Well, it's for three people, plus Bear and Tim. You have no idea how much these guys can eat," Mel joked.

As they all loaded their choices onto their plates, the team began to discuss what they had already discovered. It was good to stop for a meal and take time out. They put their heads together to discuss the information they had learned about George.

"You know, for a man who was in and out of here and an integral part of our investigations, we didn't really know much about George, did we?" Colin said, munching his way through a plate of sweet and sour chicken.

"How much do you really know anybody? We all have our secrets," Tim said through a mouthful of crispy beef and Szechuan noodles.

"That combination looks disgusting," Nadia said.

"Maybe, but it tastes delicious," Tim said.

"It would be a brave man who got between Tim and his crispy beef," Bear smiled.

"It would be a miracle to get between you and your grub, man," Tim retorted. "This is really great, Nadia. Full marks for Uncle Fred. So, what do we know about George that we didn't know when we started?"

"Nothing. Not a single solitary thing," said Mel in a grumpy voice.

"Well, I know where he got his old Stasi gun and why," said Nadia.

"Well, go on," Colin said. "We're not playing *Twenty Questions*."

"I knew he left his village after the Stasi officer's death. But what I didn't know was that, when he bent over the officer and discovered he was dead, he stole the officer's gun and kept it with him as he walked across Europe. He wrote about it when he built a little box safe thingy to keep it in years later."

"That's what Gillian told us at your place." Tim nodded towards Mel and Bear.

"I suppose he was worried about protecting himself," Colin said.

"Well, it didn't work very well," Nadia continued. "When I was at the post-mortem, I saw he had a huge chunk out of the muscle at the top of his left leg. I don't know when that happened, but he should have used his gun then."

"I got that bit of the story," Mel said. "He was chopping wood for an old lady in exchange for a meal and sleeping in her barn, but a pack of dogs set about him and the gun jammed. He tried to get away, but he couldn't, so he whacked the axe at the dogs to get them off him. He killed one of the dogs and the rest ran away, but not without taking a chunk of his leg with them. When he dropped the axe, he hit his leg with it too. Instead of being with the old woman for one meal and a sleep in the barn, she bandaged him up and nursed him back to health. He was there for six weeks. "It was during that time he became aware of the name of the Stasi officer, Hans Merkel, and learned he had a young son, Max. George felt really guilty. He wrote in his diary that he decided then, as a punishment to himself, he would never have children as he had deprived the boy of his father."

"For someone who learned nothing, that was quite a speech!" Bear teased her.

"I mean, I didn't learn anything that helps us."

"It might," Tim said. "Anyone else?"

"He always got copies of the local papers," Mel added. "I don't know how he did, but even in the early days, he kept tabs on his family."

"That would be before the internet," Tim said. "It must have taken a lot of effort to get local papers."

"Yes. He knew his father and brother had been killed in revenge for his act. When he learned his sister had borne a son, nine months after he fled, he guessed the female members of his family had suffered and probably been raped," Mel said quietly.

"Again, more recently he wrote that he had felt so guilty that he punished himself by not only denying himself children, but remaining completely celibate for the rest of his life," Nadia added.

"Wow! George took the weight of the world on his shoulders, didn't he?" Bear commented.

"That's interesting, because George became aware of Max Merkel when he was going to auctions for his books. I wonder if Merkel knew about George too," Tim mused.

"Must have done. All these arty-farty people know each other, don't they? Does anyone want the rest of these spare ribs?" Bear asked.

"You do!" Mel and Tim said together.

The whole group laughed. It eased the tension.

"If Merkel had a client who collected rare books, he may well have come up against George bidding at auctions. I wonder if Merkel recognised the name," Colin mused as he reached for the one of the bananas Uncle Fred had put in the box for him. He handed the banana fritters around to the others.

"We know George knew about his nephew too, I wonder if Heinrich knew about George. He said to us he didn't, but when he was applying for his promotion he told his employers he had family in Scotland." Tim reached for the rest of the Szechuan noodles.

"Do we know when George put in his reinforced doors and bomb-blast curtains?" Bear asked.

"No, not yet," Tim said. "We better get back to the diaries."

By just after two o'clock, Tim felt they had extracted all the information they could from the diaries. Tim let the others go home for a few hours' sleep before they had to be back in for the start of their shift and the briefing. He re-read the information and smiled. Gillian's work had been a big help. There was no doubt in Tim's mind who George was most concerned about when he tried to make his home attack-proof. The postcards that had been sent to him followed one person's travels around Europe.

It was clear to Tim that there were several people who had wanted to kill George and why. But, even with all the security George put in place, with the enemies he had, the poor old man hadn't stood a chance.

***

Before the briefing, Tim went to find Hunter. He wanted to inform his boss of the intricacies of George Reinbold's life that he and his team had unravelled. He found Hunter sitting at his desk staring out of the window.

"Good morning, Boss."

"Well, it is certainly morning, young Myerscough. Do you have any good news for me?"

"Maybe not good news, but useful, perhaps."

"That may be as good as it gets today."

"Why, what's the matter?"

"My fucking idiot son has discharged himself from rehab, and I have no idea where he is."

"Shit, Boss, that's grim. We should prioritise finding him."

"Why? He's an adult and he moved out of accommodation of his own free choice. I am sick of wiping that boy's backside and I will not worry about him."

"With respect, Sir, I don't believe that."

"You're right not to. Where is that incorrigible brat? I just want to know he's safe."

"I understand, Sir. Could he have gone to Shetland early to spend time with your daughter?"

"He's not there. I phoned Alison."

"Shall I instruct our men to be on the lookout for him?"

"Yes, thank you, Tim. You are not a lot like your father."

"Thank you, Boss, I think."

"Now, let's get this briefing started."

***

Mackay was calling the briefing room to order as they arrived.

"Can we get a bit of hush? DC Zewedu, could you at least make an effort to finish your breakfast before a meeting in future?"

Bear smiled. "This isn't breakfast, Sir, it's elevenses. Well, tenses. Breakfast was at seven."

Mackay shook his head.

Gillian was standing quietly beside Mackay. She had been asked to attend the briefing in case there were any problems or issues with the translation of the diaries. As Tim waved over to her and smiled, she made a phone sign with her hand. He gave her the thumbs-up.

"Are you quite finished with your social arrangements, DC Myerscough?"Mackay asked.

"Sorry, Sir." Tim blushed.

"Right. Let's get started, DI Wilson." Mackay deferred to Hunter.

"Elliott Smith, the governor of HMP Edinburgh, has been in touch. The visit we have been waiting for is at two o'clock today. Arrangements have been made for Tim and Bear to be inside the waiting room where the searches are carried out. You are both known to the mark, but that does not matter because you will be discussing going to visit Tim's father. As Bear has been a friend of Tim's since you were both at Merchiston Castle School, that will seem natural."

"Yes, Boss," Tim and Bear muttered.

"When the search reveals the cocaine, you will conduct the arrest. Bear, you will carry the handcuffs. The prison officers will not make any comment about them."

"Yes, Boss," Bear smiled.

"Colin and Nadia will be in one car and Mel and I in the other so that the entrance and exit of the car park are well covered."

"How far in advance do you want us there, Boss?" Tim asked.

"Be there reasonably early, no later than quarter to two."

Tim nodded.

"There is no doubt now that this visitor is the courier, but the one Mansoor calls Bill is the mastermind who arranges the mules and the courier to allow Mansoor to supply the jail." Hunter said.

"What about the supply to the city?" Mackay asked. "Do we know who organises that?"

"We know who used to organise it and how. That was Mansoor," Hunter said. "From what we know, the route is the same as it was before we caught Mansoor. The cocaine is transported in cars being brought into this country."

"Or, as in the case of the blue Volvo, taken from this country and brought back?" Nadia suggested.

"I think that was a rush job, Nadia," Hunter said.

"What do you mean?"

"Arrangements had to be made to pay George's hit-man, so an extra cocaine run had to be made at short notice."

"So they were going to pay the hit-man with cocaine? That's a possibility," Mackay said.

"Or, they were going to sell the extra cocaine in the old Volvo to pay the hit-man," Hunter said.

"It wouldn't sell fast enough, Boss," Colin said.

"It would if you were selling the car load to one person," said Tim.

Hunter nodded. "Yes. And since we told Akram we were going to arrest him for two murders as well as trafficking cocaine, he's been singing like a canary."

"But it was Kasim Saleh who took the Volvo to Thomson's," Tim added." Although The Lizard seemed to think he had a claim in the vehicle."

"Who is Kasim Saleh?" Mackay asked.

"Mansoor's brother-in-law," Hunter replied.

"That numpty, Frankie, identified Merkel as the person who arrived and spoke to Jenny as Frankie was leaving," said Mel.

"I think Frankie is telling the truth," said Hunter.

Tim grinned. "Shit, boss, I've just worked out who 'Bill' is!"

Chapter Thirty-Six

"I don't care who you are, sir," the prison offer declared. "Governor's orders: every visitor to any prisoner is receiving a full body search today."

Tim carried on the pretence by appearing uncomfortable and cross. "In that case, I will leave the visit and not see my father today."

"Sorry, sir. No can do. You are now on prison property and subject to our rules. Got something to hide, Mr Myerscough? Sir Peter asked for something he shouldn't have?" The officer was clearly enjoying this charade.

"You canny force him to visit his father," Jamie contributed.

"I don't need any advice from you, Short-Arse," the officer sneered. "We should just install a revolving door for your lot."

Tim wondered whether it would be the prison officer or Jamie who would win the award for best actor. Tim took off his jacket, stepped forward and allowed himself to be subjected to a thorough search. He opened his mouth and got the all-clear. Then the officer patted down his body above his clothes, but so carefully that anything Tim was trying to hide would have been felt. He crouched on demand easily, but with a poor grace: anything he had hidden up his back passage would have been emitted.

Tim blushed as he realised this was clear to the others in the waiting room. They were all looking very uncomfortable. Tim knew that one of them wasn't acting.

Tim now had his own acting part. He had made a point of leaving his phone in his jacket pocket. As Tim made to put his jacket back on, he grimaced as the prison officer pretended only to notice it then.

"What's this, Mr Myerscough? A mobile phone? I don't

think so. Turn it off and put it in one of the lockers over there."

The prison officer turned to Bear and examined him equally carefully, but without finding anything. It had been arranged earlier that only Tim would be 'caught' before the last frisk was done.

Jamie carried only a few coins in change, allegedly to get coffees and snacks during the visit with his pop. Jamie nodded as the prison officer declared that he was satisfied.

The fourth visitor had waited in silence, watching with increasing horror as the searches took place.

"You're last, sir," the prison officer called him forward.

"I'll have to go back to my car first. I've left something important there," he said.

"Not today, Mr Blair. No visitors leave this room without a full search. Guv'nor's orders."

"But this is ridiculous. I am a solicitor meeting with my client," Blair blustered. "I have special privileges. This is a blatant transgression of my human rights."

"Privileges? Rights? Not here, not now, Mr Blair. Take it up with the police, sir. I'm sure DC Myerscough or the other DC will be happy to take your details. Now, jacket off and open your mouth."

Donald Blair's face was an unhealthy shade of red and he was shaking. Without another word, he removed his jacket and subjected himself to the same undignified search as the other visitors had endured. His squat was far less agile than those performed by Tim and Bear, but he did it. He opened his mouth, then his briefcase, and even permitted the officers to examine his client's file and folder.

The guard glanced at Tim. He gave an imperceptible shrug.

"Thank you, Mr Blair. That all seems to be in order." The prison officer held Donald Blair's jacket up to allow the lawyer to put it on more easily.

"What did you expect, you revolting little jobsworth?" Blair said, just a little too loudly. He moved to snatch his jacket from the officer, just a little too quickly.

"Excuse me, Mr Blair," the officer said.

"God in Heaven! What is it now?"

"Your jacket feels a bit heavier than I would expect."

"It is a very good quality jacket," Blair stated.

Tim watched as, without another word, the prison officer felt first the pockets, and then all around Blair's jacket. He squashed the seams along the bottom of the garment, then turned the seam upside down. Tim could see that it was not sewn, but held together with Velcro.

"Quality isn't that good, actually, Mr Blair."

The prison officer signalled to his colleague who, until now, had simply observed proceedings from the side of the room.

"Do you see what I mean, Paul? Mr Blair should have a word with his tailor. Leaving an important man like this with a shoddy finish to his jacket: well, it's just not good enough. Not the done thing at all." With that, they both pulled the Velcro apart, and little baggies of white powder fell onto the floor. They pulled the seam at the bottom of the jacket all the way around.

"I'll get some gloves and a bag to put these in. We don't want Mr Blair to lose anything," Paul said to his colleague. He managed to do this without a hint of sarcasm.

"I have no idea what that is," Blair bellowed. "It isn't mine."

When Paul re-entered the room wearing gloves, he handed his colleague a pair of latex gloves too. The examining prison officer picked up the little bags and put them carefully into an evidence bag.

"That's not mine," Blair shouted. "I don't know what that is. This is harassment."

"Well I suspect, *I* know what it is," the prison officer said. "It is a white powder, possibly cocaine. Probably heavily cut, and perhaps not the best quality, but I am sure it will be found to be cocaine. Whatever it is, you were trying to bring this into the prison secretly and that is an offence. And, as we found it sewn into your jacket, I think it probably is yours, Mr Blair. Your visit was to Mr Arjun Mansoor, I believe. I will inform Mr Mansoor that you are unable to attend today."

The room was silent, except for Donald Blair's protestations.

190

"I will need you three gentlemen to act as witnesses. And I am sorry to say that your visits today are also cancelled. I know this is a disappointment, but there we are," the prison officer said softly. "DC Myerscough, could you and your colleague do the business for me?"

Tim recited Blair his rights and Bear handcuffed the man. Blair's protestations that the prison officers should have found the handcuffs were ignored as the two big detective constables marched the lawyer outside, to where Hunter was waiting by the car.

"Akram was telling the truth about the drug supply into the prison," Hunter said. "What did you get out of it, Blair? A cut of the profits, or new clients? Whatever it was, I hope it was enough to feed your family until you retire. You certainly won't be practising law again. Now, mind you don't bump your head getting into the car."

"Should Jamie, Bear and I give our statements to the prison officers, and then come over to the station to give statements?" Tim asked. "You can de-brief Bear and me then, I suppose."

Hunter smiled. "That'll work fine, lad. I'll head back to the ranch and the CSIs can do their business. Well done."

"Has Cameron been found, Boss?" Tim asked gently.

Hunter shook his head and drove off.

As Tim and Bear walked back into the prison waiting room, Jamie was finishing his statement to the officer. He turned to Tim.

"Never thought I'd end up helping out fuckin' cops, Blondie. But here we are. You and me on the same side."

Tim smiled. "Don't get carried away, Jamie. You'll need to hang on whilst DC Zewedu and I will give our statements here, and then we'll take you over to the station to give your formal witness statement."

Chapter Thirty-Seven

"Excellent news, Hunter. Myerscough and Zewedu played a blinder," Mackay said.

"They did, Sir. And Jamie Thomson played his part."

"And we have Blair in custody to answer questions now."

"Yes, Sir. I'm just going down to interview him now. I'll take Myerscough with me in case that bastard Blair tries to make up what happened in the prison waiting room."

"Good idea," Mackay said.

"Yes, and I believe this will allow me to establish the case against those who ran Mansoor's cocaine smuggling into the city. I should also be able to prove who killed Jenny Kozlowski."

"And George? Our primary task was to find who killed our friend."

"Yes, Sir. I think I know who did it and why the murder was committed. If I'm right, soon I'll be able to prove it. Small compensation for the loss of a good man, but the best we can do."

***

"Have you any idea how long I have been kept waiting?" Blair demanded.

Hunter shrugged. "Don't know, don't care. Sit down, Mr Blair."

Blair sat down opposite the detectives. He glowered at them with his little piggy eyes. His ruddy cheeks were the result of too much whisky and high blood pressure. His bald head was flaking and raw because of his eczema, and his pudgy hands wound up and down his tie.

"You'll ruin your tie doing that," Hunter said. "A might tense are we, Mr Blair?"

"Furious. Not tense, I assure you."

The soulless interview room was a dark, windowless box of a room painted in faded blue and grey. The vinyl floor was scrubbed every day by cleaners on minimum wage, inured to the smell of dirt, sweat, farts and fear. Even the strongest disinfectants could not vanquish the sour smell of scoundrels.

The furniture consisted of a metal table (bolted to the floor), four chairs (bolted to the floor), and recording equipment (bolted to the table). A camera (bolted high up on the wall in a corner) scanned the whole room and made a visual recording of all that went on.

"Would you like to have a solicitor present, Mr Blair?" Tim asked politely.

"I think you'll find I am a solicitor, sonny," Blair laughed. He tried to sound brave, but he clearly didn't feel it.

"Not for long," Hunter said quietly.

Blair admitted his name and address; his occupation and that he had been at HMP Edinburgh this afternoon to meet with his client, Arjun Mansoor. He volunteered that Mansoor had sought the meeting.

"Is that how he lets you know he needs more gear? By calling you for a privileged appointment?" Hunter asked.

Blair shook his head. "No comment," he said. From then on he answered every question 'No Comment'.

It was then that Hunter tried his trick of shifting blame to elicit a denial and an explanation.

"That's fine, Mr Blair, but Hadi Akram has given evidence that you are the man in charge of this new supply of cocaine flooding that prison. You see, Arjun Mansoor is behind bars, largely as a result of the painstaking work carried out by the late George Reinbold and his team of CSIs. We know Mansoor blamed George for his downfall. He persuaded you, a despicable, greedy lawyer, to take over 'importation' of cocaine – and the poor bloody sod, Akram, was just the mule. Wasn't he?"

"No comment, nothing of the sort," Blair said.

Hunter glanced at Tim. He could tell that the junior detective did not think this mode of questioning would work. And Hunter understood his doubts. After all, Blair was a solicitor and an old hand at police interviews. He must have seen this trick played before. Hunter looked at the lawyer's red, sweaty face and the man's defiance disgusted him. Still, he sat quietly, listening carefully, and pressed on with his line of questions..

"You arranged for Akram to bring in the drugs, and with the money you got, you hired the hit-man who killed George Reinbold. Arjun Mansoor ordered you to do that."

"Nonsense. I have no reason to do that. Anything I instructed Hadi Akram to do for Mr Mansoor was minimal in the grand scheme of things. Oh bugger it – no comment."

A swift smile faded on Hunter's face as he went on. "Mansoor had you over a barrel: you were his cocaine supplier to the prison, and poor little Jenny Kozlowski was just in the wrong place at the wrong time, wasn't she? But you caused her death too."

"No comment. You're making all that up, DI Hunter. You haven't a shred of evidence. There was no woman ever involved. Not at all."

"I beg your pardon. The girl is dead, and for evidence I have twenty-nine baggies of cocaine found concealed in your jacket, your meetings with Lenny The Lizard Pratt and Max Merkel, and the fact that you represent Arjun Mansoor. I think I'm getting there, Mr Blair."

"Honestly, DI Wilson, you are just opening your mouth and flapping your gums. There is no way you are going to make this stick. You must know that. And as for that charade in the prison at Saughton... You are on a hiding to nothing. I wish you good luck."

"Thank you, Mr Blair. I don't need luck. DC Myerscough, charge him: one count of murder, one count of culpable homicide, two of trafficking a Class A drug, and one of being a complete fucking wanker."

"Yes, Sir," said Tim.

"And you, Myerscough. You are probably as corrupt as

your bloody father."

Tim stood up and curled his fist. His big hand looked as if it was clenched around a cricket ball.

"No, young Myerscough, he's not worth it," Hunter said calmly. "I'm going to phone the Law Society of Scotland to start the procedure for getting this piece of shit wiped off their register."

"You really have got it all wrong," Blair said wearily.

"Then give us the right of it all," Hunter said.

The three men sat down again in the stuffy little room. Blair began to tell them his version of the truth.

It was a long statement. After a while, Blair said he required coffee and something to eat. Hunter persuaded Tim to fetch coffee and biscuits to sweeten the deal.

Chapter Thirty-Eight

Hunter left the station at Fettes and walked up to the Cavalry Club where he was meeting Meera for dinner. He wanted to walk to get all that Blair had said clear in his head. The fresh air and exercise would allow him to do that. Hunter felt sad for George now that he knew and understood his fate. It didn't make it right, but the actions of an exuberant youth on his eighteenth birthday had set a chain of actions and feelings in motion which would have led to George's death, one way or another.

The detective strode south towards Comely Bank. The sight of the wide streets with cars neatly parked on both sides was so familiar to him: it made him feel calmer just to be there. The evening was bright and fresh. He passed young parents proudly pushing babies along, couples making their way to the pub for an evening drink, and older folk standing chatting in their gardens, just to be part of the world around them. Hunter did not stop. He was enjoying a perfect spring evening to walk in this beautiful city, but he was bound up in horrible thoughts.

He turned onto the Dean Path that led to the lush nineteenth century Dean Village with its picturesque homes next to the Water of Leith. Hunter thought what a lovely, secret part of the city this was. By the time he reached Belford Road, Hunter noticed he was no longer striding out. He was walking calmly, his breathing was slower, and his brain was slowly considering the complexity of all that had happened. It was becoming clearer in his mind.

He walked past the National Gallery of Modern Art that he and Meera had visited in the morning before Jane and Rachael's celebrations. Hunter preferred the parkland in which the gallery was set to the art it contained, but Meera had seemed to enjoy both during their visit.

When Hunter arrived at The Bruce Hotel, he was tempted to march in and demand to see Heinrich Reinbold and confront the man with what he knew, but that would ruin his plans. These men were clever; Hunter would have to be cleverer.

He walked on, up Douglas Gardens with the fine mature trees on the right-hand side of the road and the handsome nineteenth-century buildings opposite them. He reached the stone bridge over the Water of Leith that led him into the wide sweeping streets of the New Town and past the Gothic towers of St Mary's Episcopal Cathedral and the grounds of St Mary's Music School. Finally, he turned into Coates Crescent and saw Meera getting out of a taxi as he approached. Hunter kissed her chastely on the cheek, but was thinking far less chaste thoughts as he patted her bottom when they entered the restaurant.

***

At the end of the meal, Hunter ordered a large Americano coffee, while Meera preferred Assam tea. He smiled at her and held her hand across the table.

"You've been very quiet this evening," Meera said.

"Sorry."

"It usually means you are cross or brooding, and I don't think you're cross."

"No, you're right, I'm not. I am never cross when I'm with you. I think I learned today exactly how and why George died."

"Poor old soul," Meera said.

"He was an old man, but definitely not poor. That collection of first edition children's books he had was worth over five million pounds. It's no wonder it came to the attention of some unsavoury people. George loved his books for the sake of themselves, but others who knew about them love the wealth they represent."

"George never spoke about his library to me," Meera said. "Did you know about it?"

"No. I don't move in those kinds of circles. But my father collects first edition books. His interests lie in ecclesiastical works and those about the formation and development of the Church of Scotland, its history, that kind of thing. Basically, if I see an old boring book with the word 'church' in the title, I buy it for Dad for his birthday. He's always thrilled," Hunter smiled.

"So did your dad know about George's library?"

"Yes. Yes. He knew of it. Not the extent of it. Apparently George was well-known in antique and antiquarian book circles. He travelled to auctions all over the country to secure books. At least, before the internet, he did. More recently, he would bid online in auctions and get the book mailed to him, as with *Winnie the Pooh* the day he died. I've managed to find out who the previous owner of that *Winnie the Pooh* book was, too."

Meera took another sip of her tea and stared at Hunter thoughtfully with her large, brown eyes. "Surely he wasn't killed because of his books? According to the CSIs there was no sign that the murderer even tried to get into George's home."

"There were people who knew about George's books and wanted to get hold of them, but you're right, he didn't get killed because of them. However, his death did set the tom-toms beating in the world of dusty old books." Hunter called the waiter over and insisted on paying for the meal.

"My turn next time, then," smiled Meera.

As they were getting into the taxi Hunter said, "You're place or mine, Doctor Sharma?"

Chapter Thirty-Nine

The number of people in the briefing was smaller than usual. Jane and Rachael were still on honeymoon, and DCI Mackay had taken Nadia with him to meet June Dormer and Max Merkel at Katz and Roundall's offices in George Street. Nadia was quiet, observant and particular. Her slight frame also provided a surprising physical match for any man. Mackay wanted that combination of skills today.

"Quiet without the girls, Boss. It must be them that makes all the noise, usually," said Bear.

"Aye, right. Sure it is," Mel said sarcastically.

"If we've got the comedy sketch over, let's all settle down," Hunter said. "First thing I am pleased to do today is to congratulate Colin on passing his sergeant's exams."

There was a short burst of applause and whistling.

"Beer, beer!" Bear shouted.

Colin blushed furiously. He nodded his gratitude to Hunter when he quickly brought the noise to an end.

"Thanks everybody. There's a post come up in East Lothian, working out of Haddington, next month. I'm applying for it," Colin said.

"After we become one big happy family in the unified force?" Tim asked.

"Apparently so," Colin nodded.

"Party-time again before you go then, Col?" Bear asked.

Colin grinned. "Of course, and the drinks are on me!"

"At both, celebrations, hooray!" Bear cheered.

"Maybe we can have a chat about that, Colin," Hunter said. "I'd be sorry to lose you."

"Thank you, Boss," Colin said quietly.

"Right, enough, people, enough. Are we all clear what

needs to happen today?" Hunter asked.

"Yes, Boss," Bear and Colin muttered.

"Colin, I need you, Tim and Bear to pick up The Lizard and Heinrich Reinbold from The Bruce Hotel. Check out is eleven o'clock, so you all just get away now."

"Is Squires already locked up on remand, Sir?"

"Yes, Colin, to stop him leaving the country while on bail."

"And we'll be asking The Lizard and Reinbold to help with enquiries, Boss?" Tim asked.

"Yes, unless they resist, then arrest them for perverting the course of justice. Whatever it takes, get them here. The Lizard should have luggage. I'll get a team of uniformed officers and CSIs into the hotel so we can search Reinbold's office and living quarters, but you make sure to bring in his personal computer with you."

"Will do, Boss," Colin said. "Bear, you take one car. Tim, you and I will go in the other. We'll need both to get the men and their luggage and computer back."

The three men left quickly.

Hunter turned to Mel. "You and I are off to Arjun Mansoor's flat to see Mr Kasim Saleh, or Bill, as he is otherwise known."

"Why did Mansoor call him Bill, boss?"

"Well, it wasn't so much *Bill* as *bil*. A code name so simple and effective it had us all fooled, and nobody knew who Mansoor was talking about. It was Tim who worked it out."

"Clever, but what was he talking about?" Mel said. "I'm really not sure how that helped, Boss."

"His *b-i-l:* his brother-in-law."

"OMG! That is so simple!"

"Yep. You drive." Hunter threw the keys to Mel so quickly that she had to pick them up off the floor with a grunt.

***

Mackay and Nadia arrived early for their meeting at Katz and Roundall. Nadia's sharp eyes served their first purpose by finding a parking place within walking distance of the office.

200

"Parking in the centre of Edinburgh is getting worse and worse," Mackay grumbled.

"And more and more expensive," Nadia agreed.

"True," Mackay said as he held the door open for her and they went in. He noticed Mr Roundall, the manager, was at the reception desk, waiting for them. He wore a blue pin-striped suit, and his matching shirt, tie and handkerchief looked a bit retro. Mackay thought Roundall looked old enough to remember when such a look was fashionable.

"Mr Merkel is not here yet, DCI Mackay," Roundall said.

"Don't worry, he will be. In the meantime, we will speak to your colleague, June Dormer. Ms Dormer does use her maiden name professionally, doesn't she?"

"Yes, she always has. She asked that I attend the meeting with her."

"I have no problem with that," Mackay said.

"Does she need a lawyer?"

"I don't know. Does she? It is not obligatory; Ms Dormer is not under arrest. Yet."

"Then, let's go through." Roundall waved the way into the boardroom.

***

When Max Merkel arrived at the auctioneer's office, he was surprised to see June Dormer sitting beside Roundall and opposite Mackay and Nadia. He noticed she was cradling a glass of water and didn't look up from that when he came in. He thought she had been crying.

"Please have a seat, Mr Merkel," Mackay said.

Nadia stood up, looking determined, and went to the door. She was going to make sure that nobody was leaving that room without going through her slim frame first

Mackay smiled and nodded at her. Nobody else except him knew she was the leading British female proponent of Sanshou, the Chinese martial art which has its background in Kung Fu and combines elements of kick-boxing and take-downs. This had proved effective for Nadia on many occasions in her chosen career.

"This interview will conclude at the station, but we are presently waiting for another police car to arrive. You and Ms Dormer (as she is known) will travel to the station separately." Mackay said before he informed Mr Merkel of his rights.

"Ms Dormer has given us a statement. Would you like to confirm that you and she have had a business relationship for some years?"

"That is true." Merkel replied in good but accented English. "Ms Dormer is one of many auctioneers I work with to keep informed of items that my clients may be interested in."

"Did all of those auctioneers become your lovers, or just Ms Dormer?" Mackay asked sarcastically.

June Dormer sobbed.

"That is not a fit and proper question," retorted Merkel.

"Is persuading Ms Dormer to give you information about items in the saleroom, and their owners, a fit and proper way to behave?" Mackay asked.

"How dare you!" Merkel stood up.

"I've got a text, Sir," Nadia said. "The car is here."

"Let's go, then. Formal interviews will take place at the station." Mackay stood up.

"I am sure whatever you need to discuss can be dealt with briefly here," Mr Roundall suggested.

"I don't think so. Discussions will certainly not be brief," Mackay said as he brought the meeting in the auctioneers' office to an end.

***

Hunter and Mel arrived at Gillespie Crescent to speak to Kasim Saleh. His sister, Mrs Mansoor, opened the door and the vast number of rings and heavy gold necklaces she wore glinted in the sun. She looked inwards to the apartment and shouted something that was incomprehensible to Hunter and Mel. The only words they understood were 'Kasim' and 'pigs'. The smartly-dressed man walked swiftly along the hall towards the door and waved the detectives in.

"Good morning, detectives," Saleh said brightly.

"Mr Saleh, thank you for seeing us. We appreciate your time." Hunter shook hands with the man.

Saleh led the detectives into the sumptuously-furnished living room. He paused at the door as he asked his sister to bring coffee for his guests. He went to sit down, but looked up as Mrs Mansoor put her head around the door. She said something in their native language: her tone did not lead Hunter or Mel to believe coffee would be forthcoming.

As Mel sat down she considered the amount of jewellery Mrs Mansoor was wearing and the lasciviousness of the contents in the room. Arjun Mansoor seemed to have provided well for his wife.

"We have spoken to Donald Blair, Mr Saleh," Hunter said.

"Arjun's lawyer, yes, I know him."

"How long have you known him?"

"Not long."

"Perhaps you should let me inform you of your rights immediately, Mr Saleh," Hunter recited the necessary phrases.

"I hear you, but it is not necessary," Saleh said.

"Oh, but it is. Because I believe you have known Mr Blair quite long enough to allow you and Arjun to find Blair's weaknesses and have him work as Arjun's courier to supply cocaine to the prison."

"Nonsense! Blair would never say that."

"It must be a nice little side business to make sure all Arjun's needs in prison are met."

"You talk through a hole in your head," Saleh said.

"Did you take over Arjun Mansoor's drug trafficking as soon as he landed in jail, or was there a break in time? I see you and your wife bought a new, bigger home in Edinburgh about a month after he was sentenced," Hunter said.

"You have made this up."

"No, I didn't need to. The date of your purchase is well documented, and coincides with dates your wife took off from her work. But you needed to blackmail Blair when he resisted taking cocaine into the prison for your brother-in-law during their privileged meetings, didn't you? What did you have on him? Is he a user? Does he fiddle his accounts to the Legal Aid Board? Or perhaps it's child porn?"

"I say no more. You liar." Saleh stood up. He walked uneasily around the room and stood in front of the marble fireplace with his feet apart and his hands behind his back.

"Kasim Saleh, you are under arrest for drug trafficking, blackmail and murder," Hunter said firmly. "Cuff him, Mel."

"Murder! Are you fucking joking me? I don't think so."

"I know so," said Hunter.

"How do you make that out, then, detective?" Saleh asked contemptuously. Then, as Mel approached him he glared at her. "I don't think so, lady."

With one sweeping motion he bent down and lifted the heavy brass poker from the tiles behind him. He swung it and slammed Mel over the head.

Mel fell to the ground with blood gushing from the wound.

Saleh jumped over the coffee table between himself and Hunter, ran out of the flat and jumped into Mansoor's Land Rover.

"Stop! Police!" Hunter shouted. He followed Saleh to the door and watched him leave. But Hunter knew he would not be giving chase. He knew Mel was his first priority. He phoned for an ambulance and then he called the station to put out an alert on the car and Saleh himself. Hunter hoped it was not Bear who found Saleh. He did not want the DC to do anything stupid.

Hunter tried to reach Colin after the paramedics took Mel away to hospital, but there was no reply to his mobile. He and the big men were fully occupied.

***

Saleh wanted to get to the airport and out of the country before the police could stop him. He patted his pocket to check for his passport and credit cards. Then he drove at speed, but decided against the most obvious route to the airport. He decided to drive via Queensferry Road. No way would the police think of that.

As Bear, Colin and Tim arrived at the car park of The Bruce Hotel, Lenny The Lizard was at the front desk settling his account with Heinrich Reinbold.

"It is always good to see you at *Gemuetliche Erholung* hotels, Mr Pratt. I am sorry that you did not recover your car," Reinbold said.

"Yes. That did not go well. Thank you for all your help, anyway, and congratulations on your promotion, Heinrich. This general manager's job is a big step up from Barcelona."

Tim positioned himself on one side of The Lizard, Bear on the other. Colin stood behind them and spoke softly.

"Mr Reinbold, may we all move into your office? We require to speak with you and this guest."

The Lizard turned and tried to make a run for it. Bear stuck out his foot and the man fell heavily to the floor.

Colin shook his head and as Bear and Tim lifted him off the floor and dragged him into Reinbold's office. They flung The Lizard on to a chair while Reinbold stood staring at the detectives.

"What on earth is going on?" Reinbold asked.

"Sit down, Mr Reinbold," Tim said.

Colin informed the men that they were to be interviewed under caution at the station and that their personal belongings would be examined.

"Uniformed officers are going to search your office and your accommodation, Mr Reinbold."

"Do you have a warrant?" The Lizard asked.

"We do." Colin pulled the document out of his pocket.

"We will take your personal computer with us now, Mr Reinbold. Let's get the cuffs on you and go." Tim stood up and lifted the laptop off Reinbold's desk. "The station cells will be busy tonight," he remarked, as The Lizard and Heinrich Reinbold were led away out of the hotel and through the car park in handcuffs. Heinrich got into the car with Bear and watched in sullen silence as Tim put his computer on the back seat.

Colin bundled The Lizard into the back seat of the other car and took up his position in the driver's seat. Tim climbed into the passenger seat beside him.

"Ian Thomson told me you were just a gun for hire, Lizard. Did you do the business on George Reinbold for Mansoor?" Tim asked.

The Lizard stared furiously at Tim from the back seat, but said nothing.

As they were stopped at the lights, Colin noticed his phone and the missed call.

"Can you check that for me, Tim?" he asked.

Tim picked up the phone and listened to the message. His face went white, first with fear and then with rage.

"What's the matter?" Colin asked.

"It's the boss. That piece of shite, Saleh, has attacked Mel with a metal bar or something. He knocked her out and she's on her way to hospital."

"Oh God, no! Where is Saleh now? Does the boss need a hand bringing him in?"

"No. The turd has made off in Mansoor's Land Rover. There's an alert out for both him and the car."

"We'll get this pair dropped off at the station and join the hunt. I just hope for Saleh's sake Bear doesn't get to him first."

Colin looked back through his rear-view mirror and nodded at Bear in the car behind them. Then he drew up at the crossroads on Queensferry Road, he looked to his right. Colin had spent hours watching CCTV footage of Kasim Saleh. He saw the man in his sleep. Then he did a double-take.

"Tim! That's the bastard in the car beside us!"

Tim glanced over. He saw Saleh out of the corner of his eye. The traffic was too heavy. Neither car could move. Reflex overtook thought, and Tim jumped out of the car and stood in front of Saleh. The man made to accelerate, but Tim did not flinch.

"Come on, Saleh, pick on someone your own size!"

Colin was engrossed in the conflict between Tim and Saleh when he noticed Lizard out of the corner of his eye. He watched as Lizard had a flash of idiocy and managed to open the rear door of the car. He tried to make a run for it, but evidently had not given any thought to how poor his balance would be with his hands fixed behind his back. He fell over. Colin looked over at him and laughed because he was quite unable to get up again. Lizard looked furious.

Colin ignored Lizard; he wasn't going anywhere. He took a moment to look at Bear in his rear view mirror. He saw Bear leaned out of his window looking puzzled: it was clear that he could not work out what Tim was trying to accomplish. Colin saw Bear frown and his lips move. Colin got out of his car to speak to him.

"What the hell is Tim doing?" Bear asked Colin.

"If he's not very careful, I think he is going to get killed," Colin muttered.

"Not on my fucking watch, he's not!" With a primeval roar Bear launched himself out of the car, with the keys in his hand. He looked back and flicked the doors locked. Did he see Heinrich Reinbold wink at him?

Bear reached the driver's side of Saleh's car in four strides and hauled the terrified little man onto the pavement.

"Don't even think about running over my friend!" he shouted in Saleh's face. "He's worth ten of you. Probably more since you got your mum's trust fund, right, Tim?"

"Possibly. Thanks Bear. What took you so long?" Tim grinned.

"I couldn't work out what you were doing or why. Then I saw The Lizard make a break from Colin. What's going on? Shouldn't the boss and Mel be dealing with Mr Saleh right now?"

Colin came round to join Tim and Bear. He had dragged The Lizard up off the pavement by the scruff of the neck.

"We'll tell you all about it at the station, Bear. Meantime, can you get Mr Saleh's car off to the side of the road and make sure Mr Reinbold makes it safely to the station? Tim, you and I will drive with Mr Saleh and Lenny The Lizard. I'm afraid you'll be in the back of the car with them."

"My great pleasure," Tim said. "Put the childproof locks on, will you, Colin?"

Chapter Forty

Jamie and Frankie went to visit Ian Thomson together. It was Sunday afternoon and it gave Ian a chance to see his little great-nieces. He was very fond of Kylie-Ann and Dannii-Ann, and proud of the way Frankie and Jamie were coping with them together.

Jamie strolled in and sat down, while Frankie manoeuvred the girls to a table. When Frankie sat down, with a daughter on each knee, he bounced them up and down and smiled proudly at his uncle.

Jamie went to get three coffees from the machine and set them on the table. He liked seeing his pop. Visiting him in prison wasn't perfect, but at least Pop was never late.

"You're all looking good, and those darling wee girls are growing fast," Ian said.

"Aye, we're okay." Jamie replied.

"And I hear you're on the side of truth and justice now, working with Sir Peter's lad?"

"Not really, Pop. Just to get that old bastard Blair taken down a peg or two. He was due that after the rotten job he did for you when you got banged up." Jamie had never forgiven Donald Blair for failing to keep his father out of jail for a bank robbery almost three years earlier.

"Yeh, he wasn't great for me, but I think he deserved his comeuppance more for bowing to Mansoor's demands and bringing coke in here. That's a dirty business."

"I suppose. Did you hear they worked out who Bill was?"

"Aye. Smart bastard. Too clever for his own good, Mansoor. They'll throw away the key this time. I believe his courier, Akram, and Mansoor's brother-in-law, Saleh, are coming here on remand. A real family gathering we'll have here. I just hope they all get the message and stop using my fucking showroom as part of their drug route. It was such a shame about wee Jenny. Have they told you how she died?"

"Aye. She suffocated in the boot of the car and got so much cocaine dust into her lungs that she went unconscious and never woke up. I just don't know who or why."

"That's probably just as well. I don't want you on any vigilante effort for that poor lassie. She was a bright girl, Jenny."

"I liked her. I'll miss her," Jamie said.

"I know, son. I still miss yer mam, even if she is doing the dirty with The Lizard in Spain. He'll be on his way back to her now his own mam is buried."

"Doubt it. Cops took him in with some European guy. Haven't seen him since."

"You know The Lizard, he'll be in it up to his neck and still come out of it all smelling of roses," Ian Thomson winked at his son.

"I don't think so this time," Jamie said. He decided to change the subject. "Any word about your parole, Pop?"

"Not yet, but I should be due a hearing in the next month or so. Fingers crossed it goes well."

"I think we'll need a new house if you're coming back, Uncle Ian," Frankie said. "We'll need another bedroom."

Ian grinned. "You and Jamie can share. It'll be fine."

Luckily Jamie and Frankie's response was drowned out by a loud bell sounding the end of the visit. They left the visiting room bickering, the way they had ever since they were kids.

***

Jamie and Frankie decided to go home via the pub. They were pleased the girls were both asleep in their buggy, and it seemed a good idea to take some time out for themselves. As they entered the bar, Frankie took a seat in the family area while Jamie went to the bar to order their pints and risk getting them back to their table, despite the stooky on his arm.

Frankie heard a toff at the other end of the bar speaking to a pretty lady.

"I've got a new guy starting in the business, Cameron his name is. I think he'll be useful. I've put him up in the Frederick Street flat as he has nowhere to stay."

People always commented on Frankie and his twins, so he wasn't surprised when the toff went on.

"Look, Sophie, those little babies are almost as pretty as the kids we would have."

"That's a lot of pressure," the lady replied. "We've only been dating a few weeks, Lucky."

"Almost as pretty?" Jamie said, as he turned from the bar with the pints carefully cradled in his arms. "There's nae weans in the world bonnier than they babies, so watch your tongue, man, or you'll find it sliced and in a sandwich."

"Don't you speak to me like that, my man. Don't you know who I am?"

"I don't know: I don't care," Jamie said.

"He's Lord Lucky Buchanan," the pretty lady said.

"I said, I don't care. Do I look like I do?" Jamie demanded gruffly He put the beers gently down on the toff's table.

"Jamie, no!" Frankie called firmly.

Jamie's demeanour changed. "No hard feelings." He smiled, took the toff's hand in both of his and shook it quickly, then he seemed to slap the man's side and touch the man's left arm lightly in camaraderie before he picked up the drinks and wandered back to Frankie and the girls. Jamie smiled as the toff sat down and began to chat up his bird again. Jamie was amused. The posh boy obviously hadn't noticed that Jamie had lifted his expensive watch and wallet full of cash and cards. He was glad to see that he hadn't lost the touch.

On their way out of the bar, Jamie tossed the valuables on to the toff's table. The look of horror on the man's face was priceless.

"You don't know who I am either, chum. You should be more careful." Jamie winked at the shocked couple as he held the door open for Frankie and the girls.

"Why did you even do that, Jamie?" Frankie asked.

"Just for a laugh. There's not enough laughter, especially at the expense of folks like that self-satisfied arse."

Frankie nodded and they wandered the rest of the way home in silence.

Chapter Forty-One

Hunter sat on a table in the incident room with a large mug of freshly-brewed coffee in his hand. He knew he would get more information from the suspects if they were anxious, so keeping them waiting was in his favour. They had all asked to have a lawyer present, so he couldn't do anything until the duty lawyer got there. Hunter was glad it was the tall, silver-haired, polite Andrew Barley, not one of the young guns still trying to cut their teeth and get a reputation. Barley and Hunter were well known to each other.

The lawyer had been in his profession for over forty years, and always made things easier with his good nature and self-effacing wit. Although Hunter never forgot the lawyer's sharp intellect. Nobody knew why Barley left his name on the roll of duty lawyers, but he would be busy because of that today.

"Boss, would you mind if I got myself over to the hospital?" Bear asked "I have to see Mel for myself."

"Of course, Bear. Off you go. Take all the time you need."

"Thanks, Boss. I don't suppose I can have five minutes alone with Saleh before I leave?"

"Correct. You can't. Now go and see to your lady."

Hunter watched Bear leave and was then pulled back into the present by Tim. "What order do you want us to see them in, Boss?" the DC asked.

"We've got Squires out of the way on remand. He broke Jamie's arm and threatened him and Frankie, but that's all we've got on him. We can't bang him up for being a big, fat, ugly lump."

"Thank God for that," Tim joked.

"You're not fat," Hunter smiled.

"Thanks very much, I think. Who next, Boss?"

"Probably Saleh," Hunter said.

The phone rang and Hunter picked it up.

"We're on, Barley's here," he said. "Colin, you and Nadia write up the formal charges on Squires. I can't see him getting bail as he's a flight risk and likely to bugger off back to Spain. I'll get Saleh brought up from the cells. Tim, you're with me."

***

"Mr Saleh, you have had time to confer with your legal representative and are aware that this interview will be recorded both aurally and visually," Hunter said, after he had introduced those in the room for the benefit of the recording devices.

"Mr Saleh, you are Arjun Mansoor's brother-in-law. I believe his wife is your sister?" Hunter said.

"Correct," Saleh agreed.

"Today you assaulted a police woman in the line of her duty, and fled from the scene of the crime. I witnessed that incident, and you are charged separately with that."

"My client tells me that was an accident and he would like to apologise," Barley said softly.

"It was no accident, Mr Barley, and his apology is not accepted. But today we are here to take your client's statement about other matters. Mr Saleh, you arranged to collect an old blue Volvo car from Edinburgh Airport for Mr Mansoor and take it to the garage area at Thomson's Top Cars."

"Correct."

"Why did you choose Thomson's Top Cars?

"Everybody knew where it is. No other secret reason." Saleh looked like a sulky child as he spoke.

"Everybody?" Hunter asked.

"My client means it is a well-known establishment," Barley interrupted.

"Sure he does. Can he tell me himself what he means please, Mr Barley?" Hunter turned back to Saleh. "What reason did you give to the mechanic at Thomson's for leaving it there?"

"He was told it needed a service before it was to be sold."

"Was that true?"

"It probably did need a service. The car was about nine or ten years old."

"Can you tell me why the car was really there?"

"It was to be collected by a contact of Arjun's who was doing a little piece of business for him. The car was payment for that job."

"So it was never to be sold. It must have been one hell of a job," Hunter exclaimed. "The car had been reported as stolen from Folkestone, and there were ten kilos of cocaine in the boot."

"I have no knowledge of that. I only know the car was to be his reward."

"Don't take me for a fool, man! A ten-year-old car wouldn't be much of a reward for anybody! Of course you knew about the drugs. The car was left at Edinburgh Airport by Hadi Akram. You had to check Akram had delivered the full amount of cocaine before the poor, sad mule went back to Paris to get another load of coke for Donald Blair that Mansoor could sell in the prison."

"My client says he knew nothing about the content of the boot. He had been told the car was to be exchanged for the work," Barley said.

"What was the piece of work, Mr Saleh?"

"I do not know. I was never told."

"Who was the contact, then?"

"I had no need to know that. I just had to move the car from the airport to its collection point."

Hunter lowered his voice but not his gaze. "But you do know who the contact was, don't you? You are the boss now Arjun is off the streets."

"I say the truth."

"You wouldn't know the truth if it bit you on the bum, Saleh," Hunter sneered. "You're asking me to believe that you did not know the job was to murder George Reinbold? Give me a break."

"DI Hunter, my client is co-operating. Kindly remain

courteous," Barley insisted.

"Mr Saleh, we have evidence that you are running the business for your brother-in-law, Arjun Mansoor. You are Hadi Akram's handler. You required him to steal a car and take it to Calais to collect his first supply of cocaine. You told him to take it to Thomson's Top Cars, but he got another job for Mansoor, direct from Donald Blair this time, didn't he? That was why you had to change your plans. Akram dropped the car at Edinburgh Airport and picked up the plane ticket to Amsterdam that Blair gave him."

"No. Blair has no authority to instruct such actions. That would not happen. And I did no murder."

"And yet Blair did instruct such actions. I have a hospital report on Mr Akram. From this, I know that when the man came back to Edinburgh, by air this time, he was full of pellets of cocaine. So full, in fact, that he nearly died. Was that for Blair to take to Arjun and supply the jail? Akram said it was." Hunter paused and glared at Saleh.

"You know, Mr Saleh, when I spoke to Mr Akram, I met him on his hospital bed. He made it very clear that he doesn't want to be charged with a murder he didn't commit, and so he told me a great deal about your business. How close am I to the truth, Mr Saleh?" Hunter smiled.

"And that is your evidence? The word of Akram, a hopeless junkie who was stuck in The Jungle of Calais for years and is desperate to get into Britain, by any means? That is what you've got? You are a disgrace for a detective, man."

"Who was meant to collect the car from Thomson's, Mr Saleh?"

"Mansoor's man. I don't know the name."

"I think you do. Would you recognise a picture of him?" Hunter spread pictures of Lenny The Lizard, Squires, Heinrich Reinbold and Max Merkel on the table.

Saleh did not speak, but he looked at one of the photos for much longer than the others.

Gotcha! Hunter thought.

"Who did collect the Volvo from Thomson's, Mr Saleh?"

"I was not there, I could not know."

215

"But you have learned who went for a test drive with the young receptionist? She was not meant to die, was she? She was never part of the deal. She died while the car was on fire, breathing in the cocaine in the boot of that car. Your cocaine. That must make you very angry."

"I did no murder."

"Who took the car from Thomson's, Mr Saleh?"

Saleh stared at another photo. Then he looked at Hunter.

"Thank you," Hunter said picking up the four photos.

"I said nothing," Kasim Saleh said.

"Book him, Tim."

**

While Andrew Barley was talking to Heinrich Reinbold, Hunter and Tim took a chance to go up to the incident room. They met Nadia as she went in carrying biscuits.

"Your turn to fetch the biscuits again, Nadia?" Tim teased as he took one from her hand.

Nadia just smiled.

"Boss, I'm going to step outside to try and call Bear," Tim said.

Hunter nodded and walked away to get a coffee from his own office.

**

"Any joy?" Colin asked as Tim walked back into the incident room.

"No. His phone's switched off. I left a message saying we were all thinking of Mel."

"That's good, Tim. I've just heard from Cameron," Hunter said.

"Great! And is he in Shetland with your daughter, Alison?"

"No. He met a fellow in rehab. He's been offered a job with place to stay, in Frederick Street no less: that's why he checked out early. He sounds so happy. Says it was too good an opportunity to pass up. Job comes with a flat and a car. But somehow I don't like it. I can't put my finger on it; I just don't like it."

"Is the job with someone on your radar, boss?"

"No. Goes by the name of Lucky,"

"Lucky Buchanan?"

"I think that's what he said. You know him?"

"Yes, and you know of him too, boss. Lucky Lord Lachlan Buchanan. I've known him since our school days, I was at Merchiston Castle School, while he was at Fettes College. We had debates against each other, rugby, saw each other at parties. I've really not seen him much since school days. But he's dating Sophie Dalmore."

"Your Sophie?" Colin asked.

"Not any more, she's not," Tim frowned. "Lucky inherited the family fortune and title when his father died suddenly a couple of years ago. "

"Yes, come to think of it I read about it in the papers at the time. You like him?" Hunter asked.

"No. I don't trust him either. I certainly wouldn't accept a favour from him, far less a job."

"Great, that's all I bloody need. I just hope Lucky has changed since he came into his inheritance and keeps Cameron out of trouble."

"I hope so too, Boss."

"I do want it to work out for my boy. Just this once."

Tim didn't comment. As he looked up, he noticed Colin and Nadia were huddled over a computer screen.

"Did you know Heinrich Reinbold was a competition marksman, sir?" Nadia asked Hunter.

"No, how do you know this?"

"Well, Colin had a bout of curiosity, brought on by lack of biscuits. He looked him up on Google while you and Tim were downstairs and I went for supplies. Here he is."

Hunter leaned over the screen. "Interesting. So he was a member of the German Olympic Men's Shooting Team, and competed in the 25-metre pistol shooting competition?"

"And he keeps a rifle here," Colin added. "Fully registered and quite legally, of course. He uses it for competitions and target practice."

"Now this is getting interesting," Hunter replied.

"And look at TripAdvisor, Boss." Nadia pointed at the computer screen.

"I really don't have time for that, Nadia."

"No, Boss, look here. The Lizard has praised Reinbold by name on three separate occasions when he was working at different hotels in the *Gemuetliche Erholung* chain. That is important, because The Lizard is a platinum card holder with the group. His comments are influential with Heinrich's bosses." Nadia said.

"Really? Good work," Hunter smiled.

"And we know Heinrich lied about not knowing George was here. Ian Thomson told us that The Lizard would accept any well-paying job, but that he wasn't a good shot," Tim said. "Could he have sub-contracted George's murder?"

"Heinrich certainly had a grudge against George," Colin said.

"The postcards sent to George coincide with Heinrich's moves to different branches in the hotel chain," Nadia added.

"Very interesting. Yes. Colin, see if you can find any more on Heinrich. Nadia, let me know if you find any more about what Merkel was doing in London before Mrs Pratt's funeral. And see if you can find the copy of Ms Dormer's marriage certificate. Tim, you're with me."

Hunter left the room, with Tim in tow.

Chapter Forty-Two

Bear got to the hospital much faster than the speed limits should have allowed. He had phoned Mel's parents in Aberdeen and told them about the incident. He was anxious that they should not hear about it first on the television news.

"No, Mr Grant, I don't know exactly what happened. I wasn't there. She was with DI Wilson. I understand that they were arresting a suspect when he attacked her."

Bear could hear the panic in the other man's voice.

"Yes, I promise I will keep you and Mrs Grant informed. I have just spoken to the doctor. She has had an x-ray and is just about to be taken for a scan of her head and neck now. No, they don't know if she will need surgery. I will call you as soon as I hear more."

Bear could tell that Mel's dad covered the mouthpiece of the phone and spoke to his wife. He heard the woman sobbing. Her dad said they were leaving now and would be in Edinburgh in three to four hours, traffic permitting.

"Of course, Mr. Grant. If you are driving, do you want me to phone your wife's mobile number with any news I get?"

Mr Grant repeated the question to his wife and agreed that would be best.

"I'll do that. I see them coming with her now to take her for the scan. I'll ring off and follow behind. I don't want her to wake up with none of us here. I'll see you soon. Yes, I promise faithfully to call with any news at all, good or bad."

***

Tim entered the interview room with Hunter, and noticed that Andrew Barley abruptly stopped talking. He shut the door behind them. Tim found the interview room stuffy and claustrophobic. Whatever the cleaners used made no impact on the airless quality of the dismal little room. He stood at the door, feet apart, hands behind his back, stared at the floor and listened to Hunter.

Hunter took a deep breath. Tim knew he would regret doing that, because he would immediately discover that the room smelled unpleasantly of rotten eggs. He believed this was, in part, due to the nervous demeanour displayed by the suspect opposite them. Tim leant against the wall and watched Hunter glance at Andrew Barley. He noticed Barley look up from his papers and sigh.

"Mr Reinbold, thank you for agreeing to help us today. I know you are a busy man," Hunter said quietly.

Reinbold nodded and glanced at Andrew Barley, who smiled at him.

"You have not been entirely honest with us, have you, Mr Reinbold? You claimed that you had had no contact with your Uncle George and did not know he lived in Edinburgh before we told you. But that was not true. You told your company that you had family in Edinburgh. So you were well aware that George lived here, weren't you?"

"That is true. I'm sorry."

"Your computer shows that you followed your uncle's career closely over the past five years."

"Since my mother died. I was alone in the world. It is not a nice feeling."

"You are an adult. It isn't as if you were a tiny child being left as an orphan."

"I know, but I travel a lot in my job. I cannot put down good roots or keep close friends. I often felt very alone."

"But you loathed your uncle, and hated what he had done to your family."

"He was all I had left. I decided to try to get to know him."

"Did you really? How did you do that?" Hunter asked scathingly.

"I wrote to him."

"Like this?" Hunter pushed the plastic bag containing the

220

postcard from behind the clock towards Heinrich and Barley.

"What is this?" Barley asked.

"This is one of the postcards your client sent to his uncle every time he moved jobs or visited a different place. Isn't that so, Heinrich?"

"It is."

"But in German it reads only '*Beware your sins will find you out.*' No signature, no address, no identification of any sort. These were not true attempts to get to know your uncle, were they?"

"No, not really."

"Not really? Not at all!" Hunter shouted. "You'd sent him postcards from all over the world. Unsigned postcards. Cryptic postcards. That was unnerving for George. Indeed, the menacing cards terrified him. He increased the security within his home each time he received one. Did you think about that?"

"Yes. No. I don't know. I thought I wanted to get to know him, but more I wanted to punish him for all the suffering he gave to me and my mother. Do you know, no you cannot know, what it was like, growing up in East Germany as the bastard child of the Stasi? The Stasi despised my mother and me, the townsfolk spurned her. It was bloody awful. All the while he was here, doing fine. Getting rich with a fine home, good job and fancy books like a western fat-cat."

"When did you learn about your uncle's collection of first edition books?"

"Not long ago, a few days ago, probably even after he was dead. I overheard a guest in the hotel talk about *Winnie the Pooh* and the new owner Reinbold. Then I read a bit in a paper. We get newspapers to the hotel for guests. I knew it had to be him."

"Yes, yes. But for the first time? When did you find out for the first time, Heinrich?" Hunter asked tetchily.

Heinrich Reinbold smiled. He looked at Hunter.

"Are you a detective who is only asking questions to which he knows the answer?"

Hunter pierced him with his keen eyes. "What do you

think?"

"You are a man with short brown unfashionably styled hair: you are not so tall as to be noticed, but it is clear you are a detective of worth. You do not skip on preparation for this interview. So I suppose that I might as well tell you truly what I know."

"That will certainly allow us all to get out of here a great deal quicker. Feel free to go ahead, Mr Reinbold."

"Years ago. Every household had a family Bible when I was growing up. I asked my mother for ours. She brought out a small book with a few notes in the front. It was not a proper family Bible. Those are big books. Expensive. They have all the history of the family."

"I can imagine," Hunter nodded.

"I asked my mother where our proper family Bible was, and she burst into tears. She cried a lot when I was young. She told me about Uncle Georg having to run away, and how the only things of value in the house were the family Bible and an old book written by an acquaintance of my great-grandfather. The old book was a signed first edition; very rare, hugely valuable. Both books were given to Georg so he could sell them when he needed money."

"But he never did sell them."

"I searched. I became a member of as many libraries and book collectors clubs as I could. The family Bible was nowhere, so I knew he must still have it. And that first edition book was so valuable and so rare it would have been auctioned if it were ever offered for sale. But there was no trace of it. Maybe now, I will get it back at last?"

"Above my pay grade, Mr Reinbold. When did you meet Max Merkel?"

"He was a guest in the hotel in Edinburgh here."

"Oh, for God's sake. Let's not go through all that again. When did you *really* first meet Max Merkel?"

"It's true. I had not seen him before."

"But you knew of him: who he was?"

"Since I was a little boy, I knew who he was. Then he went away. To Berlin. To study antiques. Much later, I heard his

222

name as an expert antique dealer. But I kept my distance. I knew better than to get too close to Max Merkel. He hated me. He hated my family. He hated my uncle as much as I did. I understand that. I have always understood. I am probably the only person who did truly understand. Because it was his father that Georg killed. Like me, he grew up fatherless. It cannot have been easy in his household either." Heinrich Reinbold stared at Hunter.

"And did you hate Merkel, Mr Reinbold?" Hunter asked.

"No. I did not hate him. But I had no wish to be his friend. His father was a ruthless, dangerous man. I believed he might be dangerous too."

"I think we should take a break now," Andrew Barley said.

"Just a couple of additional questions, please, Mr Barley," Hunter said. "Where do you keep your rifle, Mr Reinbold?"

"At my gun club. I joined it almost as soon as I arrived here. I enter many competitions. It is my hobby. But I only use it in competitions."

"Have you used the pistol since you arrived in Scotland?"

"No, your guns laws are very strict. I was not permitted to bring a pistol into this country. I only have my rifle."

"Have you used the rifle, even at the gun club since you arrived here?"

"No. I've been too busy with the hotels opening."

"How long have you known Lenny The Lizard Pratt?" Hunter asked.

"Mr Pratt? I do not know him well, but I have known him for some years. He is a valued platinum card member of our chain of hotels. When he books into any of our establishments, his favoured status is flagged up. He always gives very generous tips, Mr Pratt. That way, everybody wants to assist him, to serve him. Everybody on the staff likes him. He talks to all of us like we are people. If we do a good service, he names us in his reviews. The directors see that and it helps us get bonuses and promotions. Platinum card members are important guests to us."

"And did you help him by asking to test drive a car from Thomson's Top Cars the evening before your uncle was murdered?"

"Yes, anything for Mr Pratt. But I knew nothing about a murder, of course."

"Of course. And were you instructed to ask to drive the beautiful Bentley or the old Volvo?"

"Period car. We do not say old. It is a period car. I like cars, but when would I ever have another chance to drive a Bentley, detective? There was no contest."

Hunter got up and walked out. He thought he now knew how it was done.

Chapter Forty-Three

Colin walked into the incident room with Nadia. He was carrying a tray with coffee for himself and a tea for her. She held the door open with her foot, as her hands were full with a bag of cheese and onion crisps, biscuits and a bag of Twiglets.

"Which is my tea?" Nadia asked.

"The brown cup, that says tea. Mine is red and says coffee."

"Sorry, I didn't hear the cups properly!"

"Ha, ha! Very funny just remember to give me the Twiglets then there will be no problem. They're mine!" Colin snatched the bag from the table.

"I won't be fighting you for them. How can you eat those things? They're disgusting!" Nadia wrinkled her nose.

"And that from the girl who likes moon cake!" Colin smiled.

"What's all the hilarity? Too much happiness isn't good for you. Quieten down, you pair," Hunter said crossly as he entered the room.

"Have you heard from Bear, Boss?"

"Yes. Mel's had x-rays and she's just back from a CAT scan. They're waiting for the results of that before deciding whether she needs an operation."

"Oh, God!" Tim said quietly.

"Why oh why didn't I cuff that nasty little bully myself?" Hunter muttered.

"Don't torture yourself with that, Boss," Tim said. "Her parents are driving down from Aberdeen. They should be at the hospital any time now."

"Facing them will be a little slice of Heaven."

Hunter looked around the room. Each tired face in front of him remained committed to solving this case. He smiled at

225

them. His team had certainly put in the hours. He knew they would do that for any murder victim, but for George they had gone that extra mile and put in their emotion too. No wonder they were exhausted.

Hunter liked and respected George. He just wished George had felt able to trust him enough to explain his fears. Then, maybe, Hunter thought, he could have protected his friend.

"Oh George, why wouldn't you let me in? Would've, could've, should've," Hunter muttered.

"Sorry, Boss, I didn't catch that," Colin said.

"I'm just muttering, Colin," Hunter tried to smile, but it came out more like a grimace. "All Tim and I need to do is to interview Ms Dormer and Mr Merkel, and then I think we can all go home. Colin, have you and Nadia got me a copy of Ms Dormer's marriage certificate?"

"It's on its way, being faxed from Register House. We're lucky they got married in Scotland."

"And, did you manage to check Merkel's movements in London?" Hunter asked.

"Yes indeed, Boss. Your hunch was right; he wasn't just there for the art show he talked about. Your London contact had him followed and he took time out to visit Country and Hound."

"And? What is Country and Hound when it's at home?"

"It's a shop in Mayfair, Boss. It's been there for ever, and deals in new and used guns. They normally only deal in rifles and shotguns, but you were right, the manager confirmed to our colleagues down South that Merkel took a handgun in to them. It was disassembled and all in pieces. A Smith & Wesson .38. The manager was very uncomfortable about talking to the police about it, because it is completely illegal to have such a weapon here."

"I bet he was!"

"His argument was that as the gun arrived in pieces, the parts were cleaned and returned to the customer in pieces, they were just bits of metal, not a pistol," Colin said.

"I doubt our colleagues will agree with him! I certainly don't. Why did. Just like he return the bloody gun to Merkel?"

"He is a long term and respected customer. He assured the man it wasn't his, but for a European client."

"I can't see that being accepted by the Police in London. Anyway, was it the same calibre as the one used to shoot George?"

"The very same. With instructions that it should be taken apart, thoroughly cleaned, and left in pieces. HeMerkel collected it the following morning."

"Do we know if it's the same gun? Did we find it in his case, Colin?"

"No. And it's not in with his things now, Sir. Although his own pistol is there, in bits, all spotlessly cleaned."

"I suppose he'd returned the other one to its rightful owner," Hunter said.

"Perhaps we could get the ballistic expert to test both pistols?" Colin asked.

Tim entered the room, backside first, carrying mugs of coffee for himself and Hunter.

"Ooh, teacher's pet. Getting the boss's coffee, Tim," Nadia teased him.

"I grabbed a mug when I was getting yours, Boss, I hope that's okay?"

"No problem. Why would Merkel need a pistol, though? And how dare he bring it into our country surreptitiously," Hunter mused.

"Well, if I had clients like Mansoor and I were dealing with such valuable artifacts, I might want one too," Colin said.

"You wouldn't stay on our thin blue line for long, if you did!" Hunter said.

"I saw PCs McKenzie and Larkin too. The search of Reinbold's office and accommodation is completed. They found a few things they didn't expect," Tim said.

Hunter sipped his coffee. "I bet they did. And anything on the computer?"

"Nothing on that back yet, Sir."

"Let's grab a sandwich from the machine and then go and speak to Ms Dormer, shall we, Tim? Colin, interrupt us when that copy marriage certificate comes through."

***

Bear met Ross and Ginny Grant as they entered the hospital. Both parents looked exhausted and emotionally drained.

"They've put her into an induced coma," Bear said.

"Oh God, Ross!" Ginny sobbed. "Our baby is going to die!"

"No, not at all, Mrs Grant," Bear said quickly. "I am told it is quite normal to do this for a head injury, until the results of the CAT scan are evaluated and the doctors decide what to do for the best."

"Of course, thank you, Bear. But you can't know that," she said.

"Shall we go and sit in the cafeteria? I'll get us some sandwiches and coffee. I think we could be here a while." Bear directed the worried parents and found them an empty table. He didn't bother to ask them what they wanted. He was quite sure they wouldn't taste a thing when they were so worried. But he did think they should eat. He bought three large coffees, plus a selection of sandwiches and slices of cake, and took the food to the table. Then he sat down to tell Mel's parents again, face to face, everything that he knew.

Chapter Forty-Four

Andrew Barley was sitting beside June Dormer as Hunter and Tim walked in.

"You are having a busy day today, Detective Inspector Wilson," he said.

"As are you, Mr Barley. Have you managed to get something to eat?"

"I had a bite in your eminently forgettable canteen, but I think my client and I would appreciate a cup of tea."

Hunter nodded to Tim and asked him to fetch two teas and two coffees for the four of them. He watched Tim leave the room quietly without a fuss. That man was so unlike his father.

***

"Ms Dormer, you were born and brought up in Edinburgh?" Hunter asked.

The woman nodded.

"For the benefit of the tape, please?"

"Yes. I went to The Royal High School."

"What did you do after school?"

"My grandfather had a second-hand book store. I worked in there."

"And that is when you became acquainted with George Reinbold?"

"That's right. He liked to come in and rummage amongst any collections my grandfather got in. We got a lot of collections due to house clearances after people died. Mr Reinbold was very knowledgeable about books, especially German and Russian books. He only collected children's books, though. First editions."

"Why was that?" Hunter prompted.

"He said he didn't have any family of his own, so his books were his children."

"How long did you work in the book store with your grandfather?"

"Until he died. Just over five years. But I was only twenty-one and I couldn't keep the place going, so it had to be sold."

"What happened to the stock?"

"It was auctioned off at Katz and Roundall. They must have seen that I knew a bit about books, so they offered me a job. I've been there ever since."

"But not always in the Edinburgh Office?" Hunter asked.

"No, I was sent down to London for two years to learn about paintings, antiques and classical art. They wanted me to know about more than just books."

"And when did you meet Mr Merkel?"

"Max? I first met him in London. He would attend auctions on behalf of his clients."

"How did you and Mr Merkel get on?"

June Dormer blushed. She lowered her eyes and began to cry.

"I think maybe we should take a break, DI Wilson," Andrew Barley said.

"No, I'm all right," the woman said quietly. "It's just that I've been such a fool. When Max and I first met, I was very young. He was so knowledgeable, exciting and fun. I didn't know many people, and London is a big city."

Tim nodded. "It can be very lonely."

"It was lonely. He was kind. He would take me to dinner, to the theatre, sometimes we would just walk. He was company. Apart from the people I worked with, he was all the company I had."

"You could have joined a gym, or a church, or a knitting group. You didn't have to become the lover of one of your company's clients," Hunter grumbled.

Tim looked sharply at Hunter. The young man was confused. He had not made this deductive leap. He was surprised when June Dormer went on speaking, calmly.

"I know that now. I'm older. But we were both single. Looking back, I was naïve, but I didn't see it that way. It was romantic. I thought it was love."

"Carry on," Hunter said shortly.

"At first, he would ask me little favours. Perhaps about details of what was coming up before the advertising announcements, so that he could give his clients the heads-up, look good to them, you know? I wanted to please him. Then, later, he wanted more than information. He would suggest ways his clients could secure items cheaply. I thought he was my friend. I was stupid and I went along with it."

"When did you and Max Merkel become lovers?"

"Quite quickly, I suppose. But it didn't last long, because I when was sent back to Edinburgh and Max wasn't there so often. I wasn't useful to him anymore, I suppose."

"Was it back in Edinburgh that you met up with George Reinbold again?"

"Yes, I saw him at a preview of an auction for children's books. He was very excited by some of the lots. He even remembered me. He was a lovely man, quite the gentleman."

"Did you tell Max?"

"Yes. He seemed interested in Mr Reinbold. I didn't know why. I was surprised. Mr Reinbold was just a little old man, not a major dealer. When I asked Max why he was interested, he just said that he had known George years ago and didn't realise he was still around the antiques markets."

"What about your husband? Did you tell him you liked George Reinbold and had dealings with him?"

"Yes, I did. It made him so angry. I had never seen him so furious. He said the man had brought nothing but trouble to his family, and deserved everything he had coming to him."

"Really? Did he say what George had coming to him?"

"Yno, but he was livid, and said I must have nothing more to do with George Reinbold and never to mention that name in his presence. I was afraid of him that day."

There was a knock on the door. Colin handed the marriage certificate to Hunter.

"You have never used your married name, Ms Dormer?"

"No," she said defensively. "I don't have to."

"No, you do not. How long have you been married?"

"Married? Coming up four years."

"How did you meet?" Hunter asked.

"Does that matter, DI Wilson?" Andrew Barley asked.

"I suppose not. But you have always lived in the UK, Ms Dormer?"

"Yes. Always in Edinburgh, except for my two years in London."

"But your husband hasn't, has he?"

"No, and he still travels a lot with business. He is now in charge of the family business."

"I'll bet, Ms Dormer. What kind of business is that?" Hunter asked.

"Not very exciting: import, export."

"Import export of what?"

"Herbs, spices, things you can't get here. I don't have anything to do with that."

"Well, would it surprise you to know the herbs and spices were a cover for cocaine smuggling?"

"Good Lord, no!"

"Oh yes. And I think that, if your husband became angry because you liked George Reinbold, he would have been even less understanding when you met Mr Merkel recently in Edinburgh and resumed your relationship with him."

"True. But how do you know that?" She looked at the table.

"Why else would you give Max Merkel information about George Reinbold's book collection after my colleague brought the *Winnie the Pooh* book to be valued? Your husband would not have been very understanding of any of this, would he?"

"Not at all."

"Did Mr Merkel know you were married?"

"Yes. I wear my wedding ring. He didn't care. He said he was just happy to have me back, even if it was just a part of me. Max never married. He has always been a player."

"But your husband would have cared that you were having an affair behind his back?"

"Very much."

"When did Merkel discover your husband's identity?"

"Just before that poor wee girl died. I feel so guilty. I was told she wasn't meant to be there. But she couldn't be allowed to give it all away."

June burst into tears. Tim took a packet of tissues out of his pocket and handed them to her.

"You gave Merkel information about George Reinbold's books and his address?"

"He knew the address. I just confirmed it. When I told him George loved his books like his children, he smiled and said something strange. He said 'That's how to get him, then'. Next thing I know, Max is selling his prized, signed, first edition of *Winnie the Pooh* on the internet and ensures that George is the purchaser. The rest you know."

"Just one more thing, Ms Dormer. How did your husband, Kasim Saleh, plan to supply payment to Lenny the Lizard Pratt for the hit on George Reinbold?"

***

"One more to go, Tim. It's Andrew Barley I feel sorry for. He's getting a bit long in the tooth for a series of interviews like this."

"Don't you believe it, Hunter," Barley said as he walked up behind them. "When did you discover June Dormer was married to Kasim Saleh? She didn't tell me. I haven't had this much fun in ages."

"Then you should be getting out more," Hunter smiled.

"You're probably right." Barley laughed as he went in to meet with Lenny The Lizard Pratt.

***

Tim decided to take a walk outside in the car park while Barley did his initial interview with The Lizard. He had been inside for too long today and needed some fresh air. He walked to the far side of the station car-park, stared back at the building and shivered. He should have put a jacket on.

He couldn't stop thinking about George. He had been a quiet, studious, solitary little man, but he had collected almost as many enemies as books. Tim sighed. Poor old George: all that security, but he never stood a chance.

He took his phone out of his pocket and phoned Bear. This time his friend answered the call.

"Bear! What news?" Tim asked quietly.

"I'm with Mel's parents just now. She's in an induced coma until they decide what to do, so I'm taking the chance to tell Mr and Mrs Grant all I know. We're having a bite to eat too, because when Mel wakes up we all want to be there and I have no idea when that will be."

"Are Mel's brothers there?" Tim asked.

"No, they're on a stag do in Prague. Mr and Mrs Grant have decided not to worry them at this point. I'll keep you posted Bro. Bye Tim."

Tim ended the call, went back into the station and leapt up the stairs two at a time to find Hunter.

"Mel's in an induced coma."

"God's sake! Her parents must hate me."

"I doubt you've crossed their radar, Sir. They are far too worried about Mel."

"You're probably right, for the moment. But I will if this goes any more wrong. Now, are you ready for this, young Myerscough?" Hunter asked.

"Yes, Boss. Let's get it done!"

***

Tim opened the door to the interview room for his boss and Hunter walked in. Tim closed the door behind them.

"Lenny, what a mess you've got yourself into this time. Ian Thomson told us you are a gun for hire, but a rotten shot. Bad combination. Is he right? How is the lovely Janice, by the way?" Hunter asked as he and Tim sat down.

"She is lovely, but my Gawd! That woman can spend money. Nine grand for a designer handbag. No wonder Ian Thomson was out robbing banks when he had to fund her lifestyle."

"And how do you fund it?" Hunter asked.

Andrew Barley nudged his client and advised him not to speak except in answer to questions, as they had discussed.

Hunter began the formal interview.

"Lenny, how long have you known Arjun Mansoor and Kasim Saleh?"

"Arjun, about two or three years. He was minding Ian's place, Thomson's Top Cars, while Ian was in the big house. He ran the business there. Janice took up with me and we moved to Spain. It's lovely there."

"No doubt. Now, it wasn't just the car business Mansoor was interested in, was it? He made far more money importing cocaine. Did his brother-in-law help him?"

"Yes, he did a bit of importing business too, but from the other end, I understand. I don't know if Kasim was involved back then. I met Kasim after Arjun was put away. He took over the whole business while Arjun was inside. Arjun was furious about getting caught. Blamed George Reinbold and his CSI team, mainly. Said you lot couldn't get pissed in a brewery."

"And Arjun Mansoor wanted to get his own back on George Reinbold. So he asked you to sort him out."

"I never said that, DI Wilson, I was in Edinburgh to tend to my poor sick mother. She sadly died. You know that. You respectfully attended her funeral. Thank you for that. Wonderful woman, my mother."

"Shut up, Lizard. You're making me sick. You were here to do Arjun's bidding and kill George. You needed the payment to keep the lovely Janice in the style to which she insisted on being accustomed. Finding your mother ill was just a useful bonus."

"But I didn't kill anybody, did I? So payment for what? My poor mother died in hospital. Her heart it was."

"Indeed? How interesting. We were told it was an aneurysm."

"Interesting and true."

"What payment?" Tim sat straight in surprise and stared at

The Lizard. He realised what Hunter was trying to get at.

"Okay, let's pretend I accept that. How long have you known Heinrich Reinbold?" Hunter asked.

"I don't really know him that well. But he works for the chain of hotels I use most often. I have a platinum card, so I always get treated like royalty."

"Very nice for you," Hunter said sourly.

"I have witnessed Heinrich Reinbold climb the company's promotion ladder. He's a very accommodating fellow. When I found him in the Edinburgh hotel, it jogged my memory. It was the same last name Arjun Mansoor had mentioned, and I asked if Heinrich was any relation to George Reinbold. He said George was his estranged uncle. He had no time for him."

"Moving on. How long have you known Max Merkel?"

"We met at the hotel. We were guests there and occasionally would have a drink together. Often there was nobody else in the bar."

"But sometimes there was: you were seen in the bar with Max Merkel and Donald Blair."

"There was something going on. A wedding or the like. The three of us were about the only ones not invited. We felt a bit like gooseberries. Still, someone put money behind the bar and we managed to get a free dram or two."

A low growl came from Tim. "Coincidence you and Merkel being in the same hotel. There are so many hotels to choose from in Edinburgh."

"But it was a coincidence. I always stay in that chain when I can. It gets me points. Merkel is something to do with art and wanted to be near the Gallery of Modern Art. It's just down the road."

"Indeed. Well, where did you keep your gun, Lizard? Was it in your mother's house? Perhaps that's why you went over to see her so promptly."

"I beg your pardon?" Andrew Barley asked.

"What nonsense is this?" The Lizard demanded.

"Oh come on, man!" Tim sounded exasperated. "We found a .38 pistol when we went through your luggage today. It was in pieces, but it is the same type of gun that shot George and it has been professionally cleaned, but soon I will know if it is the same gun."

"Why were you so anxious to get your hands on that old Volvo?" Hunter asked.

"I was not!"

"I think you were." Tim said. "In fact, you told Jamie Thomson that it was *your* car."

"Yes," Hunter added. "You wanted it so badly that you got Squires to break Jamie Thomson's arm to try to get him to tell you where the car was. But it was gone because Merkel had taken it, and Jenny, from Thomson's Top Cars."

"This is rubbish!" The Lizard squealed.

"Sorry, Lizard, it's the truth," Hunter said. You were to get the cocaine out of the boot. Weren't you? That was your payment for shooting George, wasn't it? How did Jenny end up dead too? Why did you need Merkel to collect the Volvo anyway?"

"Heinrich Reinbold was already set up to cause a diversion for you. He asked to test-drive the Bentley from the showroom," Tim added.

"And how did Merkel get the gun to arrange to have it cleaned, if you didn't give it to him? I need answers, Lenny. Or you are going down for the lot," Hunter growled.

Lenny looked at Andrew Barley.

"I think my client and I may need a few minutes of privacy, DI Wilson. Give us half an hour. And a cup of tea?"

Hunter suspended the interview. He and Tim went back up to the incident room, to find Colin and Nadia tucking into a takeaway delivered by Nadia's uncle Fred.

Colin nudged containers over to Hunter and Tim. "Dive in," he said.

"I will." Tim smiled at Nadia. "Uncle Fred doesn't know the meaning of *nouvelle cuisine*. He's my kind of man."

***

When Hunter and Tim reconvened the interview, Andrew Barley had stopped smiling. They noticed he was suddenly looking his age and rather drawn.

"My client has asked me to read a statement. It confirms all he knows about the unfortunate deaths."

"Murders, and drug trafficking," interjected Hunter.

"He was not involved with any drug trafficking. Indeed, if he had any intention of illegality with cocaine, that intention was thwarted. You cannot charge him with hoping to commit a crime, DI Wilson. Anyway, Mr Pratt would like to request that, in light of his co-operation, he might receive leniency in any charges made against him."

"Let me see what he's got," Hunter said. "Then, if I believe him, I'll think about it."

I, Leonard Pratt, residing in Malaga, Spain, was contacted by Kasim Saleh on behalf of Arjun Mansoor, with a view to terminating the life of George Reinbold. I arrived in Edinburgh and went to my mother's home where I still kept some personal items, including an unregistered .38 pistol for my personal security. I found my mother seriously ill and had to take her to hospital. She later died in the Western General Hospital. I did not want to stay in my mother's home so I booked into The Bruce Hotel. I always stay in Gemuetliche Erholung hotels when I can.

I discovered the general manager of The Bruce Hotel was a member of staff whom I knew from previous visits to Gemuetliche Erholung hotels in Europe. His name was Heinrich Reinbold. I asked if he was any relation to a George Reinbold living in Edinburgh. It transpired that he was my target's nephew, but they were estranged.

The nephew agreed to assist me by making a distraction so that the blue Volvo car which had my payment in the boot could be taken from the garage area of Thomson's Top Cars to a place where I could retrieve it. To do this, he agreed to take an expensive car for a test drive at the same time as the Volvo was removed from Thomson's Top Cars, as this would distract the staff. He chose to drive a Bentley.

Heinrich deduced my business might have something to do with his uncle, because of the questions I had asked him. But he did not ask what my interest in his uncle was.

238

Max Merkel and I got on well when I met him in the bar of my hotel. I discovered he is an art dealer, and knew of George Reinbold because of his interest in collecting antiquarian books. Mr Merkel did not disguise his dislike of George Reinbold. He did not tell me why he felt so strongly about him, just that he had known him many years ago in Germany.

Arjun Mansoor's lawyer, Donald Blair, had telephoned me at Arjun's request. Blair advised me to have the Volvo collected by a third party, as I would be recognised by Jamie Thomson because of my relationship with his mother. I thought this was a good idea so I asked Mr Merkel for his help.

It transpired that Mr Merkel and I are mutually acquainted with Arjun Mansoor. Both Arjun and Mr Merkel blamed George Reinbold for suffering in their lives. Mr Merkel agreed to do me a favour when he learned I had a car to collect in payment for a piece of business I had been asked to take care of for Arjun, relating to George Reinbold. I told him to get the Volvo that had been left for me at Thomson's Top Cars, perhaps by asking to test drive it, as if he were going to buy it. He agreed and was going to leave it for me at a place we arranged in Comely Bank, so that I could retrieve it.

The girl from the garage messed everything up. She insisted on going for the test drive with him. Merkel could not let her see where he was leaving the car. She could not witness anything. So he decided to bundle her up into the boot. That was when he found the cocaine. He tried to cut me out. He did not leave the car where we arranged, but it was found near the airport and had been set alight.

I put out word that I wanted that car. But when I was told where it was, that the car was burned out with a corpse in the boot, I was furious and went to Thomson's to get what I was owed. There was not any chance of that, so Squires punished the boy.

I am innocent of all crimes. I intended to commit a crime, but was denied the opportunity to do so.

Hunter looked at Tim and smiled.

"I don't think keeping an illegal pistol, inciting Squires to injure Jamie Thomson, and conspiracy to receive a Class A drug leaves you, as you put it, 'innocent of all crimes'. Do you, Lizard? And neat as your story is, it doesn't explain why Merkel had your gun cleaned for you when he was in London. I doubt this story is complete. Do you have anything you want to add?"

"I have advised my client to make no further comment," Andrew Barley said.

Hunter got up and left the room with Tim.

"I am not convinced that The Lizard is giving us the whole truth, Tim. His story just doesn't make sense. Let's go and have a last quick chat with Heinrich and Max, young Myerscough. I think that will allow us to put the rest of the pieces together. Then we can call it a day.

"That sounds the way forward to me."

Chapter Forty-Five

Hunter sat down in front of Max Merkel and Andrew Barley and sighed.

"Mr Merkel, tell me the truth. Start at the beginning."

"DI Wilson, I have hated George Reinbold and his family all my life. I was robbed of my father as a child. I like the ladies. I have had many women. June Dormer is just one. I like beautiful women, fabulous cars and expensive art, but I am not a criminal. When The Lizard told me of his problem, I agreed to collect the Volvo for him. I did that under the pretext of going for a test drive. I led the girl at the garage to believe that I had made an arrangement to buy the car. That is not a crime, but the young woman in the showroom said she had to come with me. That was a complication. I also arranged to have The Lizard's gun cleaned by my gunsmith, so that he could not be wrongly implicated in George Reinbold's death. That is all."

"That was extremely unwise, Mr Merkel."

"Yes, but not illegal."

"Yes, illegal. You have no licence to carry that gun. And neither does The Lizard."

"I never carried it as a gun. I carried it as several bits of metal."

"You also had your own .38 pistol with you, which you did not have permission to bring into this country at any time. It is strictly illegal for you to own that at all here. And let's not forget that you tampered with evidence, and you were the last person known to have seen Jenny Kozlowski alive. I have enough to put to the Crown."

"Perhaps you do," Merkel said, "but don't be too hasty, Inspector. I can help you."

"You think so? You agreed to remove the old Volvo from

Thomson's Top Cars as an accommodation to The Lizard, but the young assistant said she had to come with you?"

"Yes."

"You killed her."

"No. I did not. I put her in the boot of the car. I tied her up, but I did not kill her."

"When you opened the boot, what did you find?"

"Packages. Lots of packages that looked all the same."

"How many?"

"Ten, but I could only get at nine. A spare tyre was fixed over the tenth one."

"What was in the packages? What did you do with them?"

"I did not know, at first, but I knew they must be important, valuable. So I took them and hid them in my room. Later, I dispersed them throughout my luggage."

"Would you be surprised to know we have found them?"

"No." The man wore an angry expression. He looked steadily down at the table.

"Do you know now what was in the packages?"

"Yes. I opened one and it was white powder inside. I rubbed it on my gums and found out it was cocaine."

"But you didn't think to phone the police?" Tim commented.

Merkel shot him a furious glance. "No."

Tim shrugged. "What did you do with the car?"

"I hid it. I agreed with The Lizard that I would hide it in Comely Bank. There are so many cars there, nobody will notice one more."

"But you didn't put it in the agreed place in Comely Bank?"

"No, that is true. Not at the agreed place," Merkel blushed.

"And the girl?"

"I left her in the boot of the car."

"You left her there to die."

"She was still alive the next morning. I gave her some water and I was going to give her chocolate, but she bit me, so I bound her back up and shut the boot."

"Then what did you do?"

"I drove over to George's house. I had my gun with me. I

meant to kill him."

"What were you wearing?"

"My suit; one of the ones I wear for business. My grey suit. White shirt. Blue tie."

"What then?"

"What do you mean, what then? He was dead already, so I turned around, got back into the car and left. I left the car at Edinburgh Airport and came back on the tram."

"And Jenny?"

"She was alive when I opened the boot. So I when took the car to the airport and dumped it, I didn't set it on fire. I learned later it had been set alight. I don't know who set it on fire. Honestly."

"Honestly? That's rich! Did The Lizard not realise you had taken his cocaine?" Hunter asked.

"No, I told him that the car must have been stolen, and when it turned up burnt out, he believed it. That's why I agreed to take his gun to be cleaned in London, so he would think I was still on his side. He was pleased with the job. I put a lot of business with Country and Hound for my clients."

"And why order the flowers for George?"

"My way of saying 'Good riddance', I suppose. I would have got June to help me buy those books at knock-down prices, you know. But they never came to the saleroom. You don't know where they are, by chance?"

***

"Thank you for allowing us to continue your interview, Mr Reinbold," Hunter said.

"I don't have any choice in the matter."

"You went to Thomson's Top Cars because Lenny The Lizard Pratt asked you to help him."

"Yes."

"You took the Bentley for a test drive."

"Yes, Mr Pratt asked me to do that to help him out. It is not illegal."

"I am so sick of being told what is illegal. Book him, Tim.

Book each of them with something, anything. I'm going home to bed."

Chapter Forty-Six

DCI Mackay looked very pleased with himself, and beamed beatifically across the team at the briefing.

"I understand you have been busy, and we have results."

"Yes, Sir." Everybody nodded.

Bear grinned. "Most importantly, Mel didn't need surgery. She is pretty sore because her wound needed staples, but she should be out of hospital later today."

"I am delighted, DC Zewedu," Mackay said. "Send flowers from us all, will you, Hunter?"

"Done, Sir. They will be waiting for her when she gets home," Tim said.

"Bear, I would like an opportunity to see Mel and speak to her parents," Hunter said.

"Of course, Sir. You are welcome anytime. But I have to warn you, we only have instant coffee."

Nadia walked around collecting the cartons from the Chinese takeaway of the previous night. The room smelled of fried food and garlic. She opened a window just as Mackay called for attention.

"DI Wilson, can you bring me up to speed?"

Hunter stood up. "We have charged Brian Squires with assault on Jamie Thomson. But it's a first offence, so I wouldn't hold out for a long sentence."

"We can't have everything, I suppose," Mackay said.

"June Dormer, otherwise known as Mrs Saleh, will be reprimanded by her professional body, and also, I suspect, by her husband. But she has committed no crime."

"I still wouldn't like to be in her shoes," Tim volunteered.

"Hadi Akram and Kasim Saleh have both been charged with drug smuggling and trafficking," Hunter said. "Saleh has also been charged with assault on a police officer in course of their duty."

"What about Reinbold?" Mackay asked.

Hunter sighed. "Nothing, really. He did send George postcards, which frightened him. He also agreed to facilitate Lenny's intended crime by causing a diversion, but apart from that, and hating George, he's off the hook. He's been charged with conspiracy and on bail at the moment, but I can't see the Crown taking this one forward. There are bigger fish to fry."

"What will happen to George's books?" Tim asked.

"I don't know for sure, but if George hadn't made a will, Heinrich will inherit them by default," Hunter said.

"That's galling, isn't it?" Tim sighed.

"Hunter, what I want to know is who killed George and who did in that poor wee girl. Do we know?" Mackay asked.

"Yes, we do, Sir. Well, I do."

"Go on, Hunter, my patience is wearing thin."

"Merkel and The Lizard were both economical with the truth. They were honest up to the point when they both told us that The Lizard got Merkel to pick up the Volvo for him because Jamie would recognise him."

"That makes sense," Mackay said.

"Merkel is going to face drug charges because we found him in possession of such a huge quantity of cocaine. We have charged him with Jenny's murder."

"But she died after the car was set on fire, didn't she, Boss?" Nadia asked.

"Yes; Doctor Sharma found evidence of burning in her lungs. That proves she was breathing during the fire, although we don't know if she was conscious."

"God, I hope she wasn't, poor kid. What a horrible way to die," Colin said.

"The positioning of the car means we are unable to see who started the fire, but my guess is it was Merkel," Hunter added.

"Guesses don't provide us with evidence to convict, Hunter," Mackay said.

"Even if Merkel didn't set the car alight, surely, as he left her bound and gagged in the boot, we can charge him with murder – or at least culpable homicide?" Tim asked.

"Yes," Hunter said. "We can and we have. I will be glad if we can get justice for the girl, but I'm still not looking forward to telling Mrs Kozlowski."

"Can I tell Jamie, Boss?" Tim asked.

Hunter nodded.

Mackay banged the desk. "What I really want to know is: who killed George?"

"That was Merkel too. He went to check out the house, didn't he, Boss?" Colin asked.

"He did check out the house, and he intended to kill George," Hunter said. "But no, it wasn't him. He told the truth when he said that he went to George's house intending to kill him, but George was already dead when he got there."

"Really? The Lizard said it wasn't him." Tim looked confused.

"He did say that, Tim, but he lied," Hunter said. "I couldn't understand why The Lizard needed both Heinrich Reinbold and Max Merkel to use cars from Thomson's at the same time. Then it clicked. The Lizard was in this up to his neck. He needed money to finance the lifestyle demanded by the lovely Janice, and came over here precisely to do the job for Mansoor, receive the cocaine hidden in the Volvo as payment, and sell it to keep Janice. It was just his bad luck – or maybe good luck – that he was delayed by his mother's illness. That delay meant he never collected the cocaine, even though he'd kept his side of the bargain. That's why he was so bloody furious."

"Of course; that's why he thought of the car, and its contents, as being his," Tim said.

"Do you remember when we saw him at breakfast in the hotel, Tim?"

"Oh, yes, the waiter made a comment about how smart The Lizard looked that day in his suit rather than his tracksuit, and asked whether he hadn't gone for a run. It was around the time that I hurt myself whilst I was running," Tim agreed.

"That's right. The morning George was killed, The Lizard went early to do the deed and claimed he had been for a jog.

We had no witnesses to this earlier visit to George's home, only the later one when Merkel tried to kill a dead man, just before the *Winnie the Pooh* book was delivered."

Tim nodded. "Now it all makes sense, Boss. That's why The Lizard was so angry when he found he had been cheated out of the cocaine, his payment. Why did he send Squires round to collect the car when he had made an arrangement with Merkel to pick it up from Comely Bank?"

"Because Merkel didn't leave the car in the agreed place, so The Lizard couldn't find it. He supposed, wrongly, that Merkel had returned the Volvo to Thomson's Top Cars by mistake, and Lizard sent his muscle, Squires, to Thomson's to get the car."

"Why not just get it himself?" Tim asked.

"Because The Lizard knew Jamie would recognise him. And he also needed time to get rid of his bloody tracksuit. Our uniform guys found it in the hotel bins. "

"Ugh! That must have been a dirty job," Nadia said.

"It was. If they get hold of The Lizard after that job, we may have another murder on our hands."

"I don't blame them. Nasty!" Tim said.

"So how do we know Lenny killed George, and that Max Merkel and Heinrich Reinbold are telling the truth about that, Hunter?" Mackay asked.

"Jane's witness saw the blue car and the man in the grey suit. Heinrich wears a grey suit to work. Surely Heinrich killed his Uncle?" Nadia asked.

"No, Nadia. Heinrich was certainly angry enough to kill George, but he didn't do it. He terrified George with the menacing postcards, but he didn't murder him."

"So what happened, DI Wilson?" Mackay asked.

"Merkel saw Heinrich take the Bentley for its test drive, and that was when he forged his plan. He knew this distraction bought him time that evening. He also knew the book George had purchased from him was being delivered the following morning, because he tracked it. It was an opportunistic plan. He went to shoot George about an hour before the book was due to arrive."

"I can see that," Tim said.

"But Merkel's plot was foiled because The Lizard had already killed George before he arrived. Merkel was telling the truth about that. He felt cheated about evening the score with George as he had killed his father, so he ordered the meaningful wreath as a final 'Fuck you' to George.

"The Lizard felt cheated because he did the job for Mansoor but didn't get paid," Mackay said.

"Ian Thomson told us early on that The Lizard was a gun for hire. We should have listened," Hunter said.

"You're right, Boss, we should," Tim said.

"So it was Merkel that Mrs Roberts saw?" Bear asked.

"Yes, Bear. Jane's witness saw Merkel in his grey suit and blue Volvo pull up outside George's home, but neither she, nor any of the other witnesses, heard a shot, because Merkel didn't fire one. George was dead when he got there. Merkel simply drove the Volvo out to the airport and got a tram back to the hotel, where he had breakfast, as if nothing had happened. It was early. Nobody thought about it because he was there for breakfast as usual."

"So the car the witness saw was the one Merkel was in," Tim said.

"Yes. The witness confirmed Merkel's version of events. The blue car pulled up, the man got out, walked up the path, paused at the door and walked back. We saw the Volvo on the CCTV, but couldn't identify the driver. We weren't looking for another earlier car." Hunter paused.

Nadia and Colin looked disappointed.

"Nadia and Colin, you did good work," Hunter continued, "but The Lizard slipped through the net. Merkel did take The Lizard's gun away and got it professionally cleaned. He must have cleaned his finger prints off his own gun himself, to avoid having to explain two revolvers to the gunsmith."

"With German precision, Boss," Colin said. "There's not a mark on it."

"Unlike my poor Mel," Bear sighed. "She's all bruised, and they had to shave the back of her head to put in the staples. I can't wait to get her home."

"Then go, Bear," Hunter said quietly, "and do just that."

Epilogue

George's funeral took place shortly after Jane and Rachael got back from their honeymoon. The whole team turned out, along with every CSI in Lothian & Borders and any others who could get the day off. The Main Chapel at Mortonhall Crematorium was full; standing room only.

Mel wasn't back at work, but she was well enough to attend the service. Jane stood to make sure she got a seat.

Heinrich Reinbold was there. Now he was the only surviving member of his family.

Superintendent Graham Miller, MBE, volunteered to give the eulogy. He spoke for thirty minutes, without notes, remembering George and his contribution to fighting crime in his adopted country. It was a fitting tribute.

"Thanks for delaying the service, Boss," Jane said to Hunter. "It means a lot to Rache and me to be here."

"Of course, I understand, Jane," Hunter smiled.

"And me, Boss."

"Mel, are your parents ever going to forgive me?"

"You, yes. Saleh, not this side of Hell," Mel laughed.

"George will be buried here, so we can visit him, if we need his guidance," Meera said.

"At least I know the old bastard is dead and gone. May he rot in hell," Heinrich said.

"George didn't deserve that," Meera said to Hunter.

"No. But Merkel, Saleh, Squires and The Lizard deserve absolutely everything that's coming to them."

"And the single Scottish Police Force comes into being next month. Exciting times." Meera smiled.

Hunter sighed. "Yes it does. I'm not sure I'm ready for that much excitement."

Hunter's Force will follow soon.

Fantastic Books
Great Authors

CROOKED
CAT

Meet our authors and discover
our exciting range:

- Gripping Thrillers
- Cosy Mysteries
- Romantic Chick-Lit
- Fascinating Historicals
- Exciting Fantasy
- Young Adult and Children's
  Adventures
- Non-Fiction

Made in the USA
Columbia, SC
20 July 2018